Skeletons in the Attic

More Tales from a Mortician

By

Thanks for Reading...

Michael Gore

DARK INK

www.DarkInkBooks.com

ISBN: 978-1-943201-14-3

Library of Congress Control Number: 2018934085

First Published by *Dark Ink Books*, 6/13/2018

www.AMInkPublishing.com

Dark Ink Books is a division of *AM Ink Publishing*. *Dark Ink* and *AM Ink* and its logos are trademarked by *AM Ink Publishing*.

Printed in the United States of America

Also by Michael Gore

* * *

Tales from a Mortician

TABLE OF CONTENTS

For *Her*--
I never knew you in life, but in death,
I knew you so well that you became my muse.

PARALYZED

Every day was a fucking nightmare. Seth wanted to die
and thought about death incessantly. He was constantly a
rude asshole to everyone in the hopes that someone
would put him out of his misery or forget to give him a
necessary medication, allowing him to slip into sweet
darkness. Three separate times he tried to kill himself,
but the attempts ended up looking like a joke from a
slapstick movie. There wasn't much you could do as a
quadriplegic. His first attempt at killing himself-- by
blowing into his straw to move the chair towards a
staircase-- ended with one wheel stuck on the first step,
his shoulder crammed against the wall and the back
wheels of his ten-thousand-dollar chair spinning
peacefully in the air. His caretaker, a large Jamaican
woman named Alvita who did not put up with his shit,
simply righted the chair and fixed him in his seat and
didn't mention it again. The second time he did it, he had
better aim at the staircase, but he got stuck on the second
step. After that, she moved a few items to block his
access to the sole staircase that could kill him.

His third attempt at suicide was a bit more
thought-out: he stopped taking the medication necessary
to keep his organs functioning properly. He didn't know
what half the shit he was forced to take was, but he took
them dutifully until he hatched his plan. After Alvita

slipped the pills in his mouth and gave him a sip of water, he slid the pills to the side of his cheek, swallowed the water, and then held them in his mouth until he could roll away and spit them out. It would have been a good plan, but his spitting skills were on par with someone who didn't have lips. With diminished lung power and weak neck muscles, the pills didn't reach the floor; if he were lucky, most of them ended up on his lap. The attempt lasted exactly one day, as the pills sitting on his lap were a dead giveaway of what he was trying to do. After that, Alvita inspected the inside of his mouth with a small flashlight after every single pill. While he wanted to die, he somehow feared Alvita's wrath as she had an authority in her thick accent that sent quivers down his spine, even though he couldn't feel it.

After the pill spitting, he gave up trying to do it himself and instead tried to talk anyone he saw into killing him, even strangers. On the rare chance he was taken outside to go somewhere, he would ask anyone who got close to him to push him off a cliff, slit his throat, let him drink some Drano: he'd pay them! Some thought it was a funny joke; others were disturbed and walked away. If Alvita was in earshot, she would jump in and apologize and make excuses for Seth before slapping him across the back of the head. On the rare chance his mother, the only family member who still visited, was around, she would be mortified when he asked her to kill him, start to cry, and beg him to *please stop talking that way*. It didn't deter him, though; in his mind, he had died three years ago when his spinal cord was severed.

It was fall, Seth's favorite season, as he was obsessed with Halloween and horror movies. He was in his third year of film school in New York City, was twenty-three, and had a life that was smooth sailing: it consisted of wealthy parents who paid for a sweet midtown apartment that made all of his friends jealous, plenty of girls to choose from, and an award-winning short film he did in his sophomore year. Everyone thought he was going to be the next Steven Spielberg, but with more edge. He was in shape, ran four miles every day, and had no medical issues besides a bad case of genital warts his freshman year. Girls said he was easy on the eyes, sweet and confident, yet not cocky. Life was perfect and was only going to get better and better, and then it happened.

It was a little after midnight when he walked out of the theater on the east side. His four "film nerd" friends from school discussed the movie they had just seen, *Hatchet 3*. While the others did not like horror as much as Seth, since it was a week before Halloween, they had all agreed to go to the showing. As they talked about Kane Hodder, the legendary actor who played the lead role of Victor Crowley, Seth noticed a man standing by the alley watching them. At first, he ignored the guy, assuming it was another person who had just left the film and probably was waiting for someone, but there was something about how the man had his face covered in a scarf that bothered Seth: it wasn't that cold. Two of the friends decided they wanted to go for drinks, but Seth and the fourth friend turned down the offer as they had the Advanced Cinematography class at nine in the morning and with the subway commute, that meant

getting up before seven. After a series of quick bro hugs, the group dispersed and went their separate ways.

Seth pulled his coat closer and started a brisk walk towards the R train, which was a good seven blocks away. It would take him almost twenty minutes to get to the subway. Then he'd probably have to wait another twenty, hell, maybe even thirty minutes for the train. Then it was another fifteen minutes back to his apartment and another ten-minute walk. He loved the city, called it his home, but at night, when he was tired and just wanted his bed, it could be exhausting. The thought of getting a cab crossed his mind, but he always felt a bit snobby taking a taxi: hell, even the mayor took the train in the morning, so he trudged on.

Thinking about the movie and the bodies he saw torn apart, he could sense someone was behind him, but it was the city: there was always someone around. You could go out at four in the morning and there would be people around; the classic *city that never sleeps* line popped into his head as he tried to brush off the uneasy feeling. Finally at the subway, he went down the stairs, slid his metro card through the slot, and walked through the turnstile. The warm, yet pungent air was welcoming. As if on autopilot, Seth went down the hall, down another set of stairs onto the platform, and then right to the same yellow I-beam post he always leaned against. Pulling a book out of his pocket-- he had learned how vital it was to have a book at all times in the city after getting stuck in a subway tunnel for an hour and a half the first week he lived there-- he flipped it to the marked page. It was by his favorite horror author, Richard Laymon, whose books dripped

with boobs and blood. Finding his spot, he started to read, ignoring the world around him.

While the sense of someone being too close to him was still there, he ignored it and disappeared into a sick, demented world. Looking back, he would always analyze the moment and wonder why he didn't trust his gut feeling that something just wasn't right that night. Why didn't he just look up from the book, turn around, and pay attention? If he had, his life would still be on the gifted path he was going down. Instead, he had kept his nose in the book and let the man attack him.

The knife had almost penetrated his neck before the gloved hand slipped around his mouth. It was a quick and skilled movement, started and finished in less than three seconds. Many a night Seth woke screaming, unable to move, as he thought of that hand around his mouth. It wasn't until three months after the accident that he realized the hand wasn't there to silence him, it was there to steady his head so the knife could find the exact path it needed. As for the pain of the knife, it hardly hurt; it felt hot and sharp, almost like a flu shot. It was the sensation of everything being shut off in his body, like a light switch being flipped, that haunted his memory. There was the hand, a quick shot of pain, and then he was falling, unable to put his arms out to break his fall. It was an abysmal feeling, to have no clue what was happening and not be able to stop himself from slamming into the ground. When he hit, he blacked out. Some doctors said it was from the impact, but most agreed it was shock that knocked him out.

That was it, that was the entire incident. Seth never saw the man, never knew anything about him, and never did anything wrong. While he spent years wracking his brain, there were no answers: he was purely a random choice. While he told the detectives he felt like he was being followed after the movie, none of the camera footage from the countless streets, shops, and ATMs that caught him walking saw the man. In fact, the subway footage showed the real perpetrator simply walk down the stairs two minutes after Seth's arrival. The man didn't hesitate-- didn't even look anywhere else-- he simply walked right up to Seth, his face covered in a black scarf, winter hat, and sunglasses, reached up, and did the quick thrust. Before Seth even hit the ground, the man was walking away, back up the stairs and out of the subway station. They lost footage of him in a crowd that was watching a television show being filmed a few blocks away.

Seth's story was on the cover of countless newspapers and websites the next night. *Man Stabbed in Random Act on Subway. City in Fear of Attacker. Second Victim Paralyzed.* There were countless stories. Come to find out, Seth was the second victim, but not the last. Over three months, all of which he spent in the hospital, the attacker paralyzed six more people and killed three others. They assumed the three died because they moved and the knife hit an artery. The eight surviving victims all had their spinal cords cut between the C5 and C4 or the C4 and C3 vertebra. It was surgical, precise, and pundits on talk shows argued that the man had to have had a great knowledge of the body and had practiced his technique

many other times; otherwise, how could he have done it so perfectly and not messed up?

Two months after the last attack, the stories stopped and subway passengers started to put their noses back into books and onto their phones rather than looking around them constantly. A year later, only a few journalists cared about it. Two years later, it became an urban legend that teens shared on long subway rides that was filled with more fiction that truth. Before the first anniversary, Seth was approached by countless news outlets to do interviews, but he refused them all. One time, he even got a call from a movie producer asking if he'd like to participate in the film version, which was going to be a horror movie, "but tastefully done." Seth didn't even respond to the man on the other line, he simply rolled away, letting Alvita apologize for his rudeness. The concept that *he* would never make a film and yet someone was going to make one about *his* pain was what set off the deepest of his depression.

As the third anniversary of the attack approached and the Halloween season began, Seth's mother tried a new tactic to cheer him up: decorate the entire house for Halloween. She knew he once deeply loved the holiday and that his only enjoyment now was watching horror movies, so she turned their house into a virtual Halloween wonderland. Every room had pumpkins, ghouls, and ghosts hanging from the ceiling, sitting on shelves, and adorning any inch of open space. There were leaf garlands throughout and signs with stupid quotes like *Stay Calm and Be Scary* decorating every door. Deep down,

Seth actually liked it, but he still wanted to fucking die and fast, so he kept up his miserable attitude with everyone, despite the change of scenery.

On the anniversary, his mother acted normal and did not mention what the day was as she left for work. It was such bad acting, Seth just rolled his eyes as she kissed his head goodbye. When Alvita walked into the room, she looked at him, straightened her shirt, which was a nervous habit of hers, and said, "Boy, it's just another damn day. Don't go and act like more of a dick than normal. Today means nothing more than the fact that God blessed you with another year on this earth."

Seth clenched his teeth. He wanted to go on one of his screaming rants where he called her names he would always apologize for after. The rants usually consisted of saying, "If God existed, then he can suck my cock for doing this to me because he is an asshole." The first time he said that, Alvita actually slapped him and then quit. But she came back an hour later with wet eyes and told him, "I understand you have pain, but I will not let your pain ruin me. I will pray for you and take care of you like my own, no matter how much you try to hurt me." It was the only time Seth ever cried real tears. From that day forth, they fought and called each other names, but they had a relationship stronger than any he had ever had.

At ten o'clock of that day, Alvita pushed Seth in front of the large television to take her break. While she was only fifty, the first three hours of the day always exhausted her. Having to bathe, shave, and dress Seth was hard. But then she also had to stretch and feed him. The three hours of constant physical labor, let alone the

8

mental torture of listening to a bitter asshole, was beyond tiring. In front of the television alone, Seth would try to melt his mind away into whatever mind-numbing show was on. Using voice commands, he would change the channels. Some days, he sat and watched *The Price is Right* and *Let's Make a Deal* and hoped each contestant failed horribly. Other days, he watched horror movies with the TV turned up so loud, Alvita would come in screaming at him. Occasionally, he just shut the television off and stared at the blank screen and imagined the films he wanted to make playing on the smooth black surface. That particular morning, the anniversary had him in such a mood that he stared at the blackness, but instead of a movie, he thought of that fateful night over and over again.

A mere ten minutes after Alvita left him, he saw a dark figure in the glass of the television behind him.

"Just can't take being away from me, Al? I understand: I *am* fucking charming," Seth said, staring forward. There was no answer, which was not like her. Seth squinted and looked into the television harder, and when he realized the image was a lot smaller than Alvita's large frame, his heart sank a bit. Licking his lips, he leaned his head forward and bit the straw, blew, and pushed it to the right to swivel around and see who his visitor was.

The man standing behind him, who Seth did not recognize, was dressed as if he were going for a jog. Black sweat pants with a gray stripe down each pant leg, a smooth, dark gray zip-up hoodie, and black gloves. Studying the man's face before he spoke, Seth figured the

man to be in his early forties. He was decent looking--there was nothing particularly distinguishable about him, just a typical white male, though he did have a small, deep scar above his left temple. Seth instantly knew it would be the only defining feature anyone would use to describe this man. Seth took the deepest breath he could without the help of his breathing machine and nodded slightly. While he had never seen the face, he knew exactly who the person was.

"I always thought you'd come one day," Seth said with no expression or tone at all. Part of him was relieved, hopeful that the man would finish the job and kill him. His only concern was for Alvita, who would have noticed the man coming in. The man took a step into the room and looked around.

"Nice to finally meet you, Seth. I've kept a close eye on you for the past three years, along with all of my other children." Seth busted out a laugh at the man's statement. The man's face scrunched up, clearly offended by the laugh.

"Holy shit. Who do you think you are, Dracula? Your children? What a delusional asshole." Seth burst out laughing again, but he was quickly cut off as the man rushed over and slapped him across the face hard. It hurt, hurt bad: in fact, it was the only real pain Seth had felt in a long time.

"Don't speak to me that way. You are alive because I let you live." Seth listened to the man, wiggled his cheek to stop the tingling, then spoke.

"I'm not alive. This is much, much worse than death and I have a feeling that you know that." The man slowly

nodded and then grabbed the heavy sitting chair, dragged it in front of Seth, and took a seat. "Before you go on your evil villain soliloquy, can you tell me what you did to Alvita?"

The man smiled largely and looked over his shoulder as if someone might come in and interrupt them. "She… she won't be interrupting us." The man said with relish in his voice.

"Dickhead, stop with the movie-like dialogue. Is she alive or not?" The man again looked furious as if Seth was ruining this for him.

"She has about thirty minutes before she bleeds out. Give me ten minutes of you not acting like a wiseass and I'll call an ambulance when I leave. Maybe she will make it and live to wipe your ass another day." Seth swallowed hard as the rage he held in for the past three years suddenly bubbled up inside of him. This, this was the man who did this to him, who ended everything good and put him in a permanent hell. And he couldn't do a fucking thing; he couldn't even spit far enough to hit his face. It was in that moment that he realized that this moment was what this was all about. This sicko got no pleasure from stabbing people: it was the suffering afterwards that got him off. He wanted to watch what he created, that was why he called him "my children." Seth was part of this man's sick quadriplegic family fantasy.

"So this is what it's about, isn't it? You get off on seeing the misery you caused me all these years. The pain you caused my family."

The man raised his eyebrows and nodded slightly. "You can say that. It's also sort of an experiment. You

11

were not chosen by accident. I expect you figured that out though, right?" It was Seth's turn to nod. He'd always thought it wasn't random, that he was followed that night, but no one believed him.

"All of you, the ones who lived, came from different walks of life and had different paths ahead. You, you were the one with the bright film career ahead of you. I had high hopes for you, Seth, and you disappointed me."

Seth's face scrunched up at the man's comment. "Gee, Dad, maybe if you didn't sever my spinal cord I'd have been able to follow in your footsteps and become a sociopath." The man leaned back in his chair. Seth could tell he really didn't like the snide comments. Part of him wanted to throw a barrage of them at him, but he also knew he had to shut up so that Alvita could live, so he looked down at the floor to show the man he was done with the comments.

"Tragedy affects all of us differently. Have you kept tabs on your siblings... as in your fellow victims? They, too, all followed different paths. You have the money and means to still create. All a man needs is his mind and he can do anything, yet you choose to sit here and wallow in your pity. You still could have directed and made movies. The heroin addict I stabbed, the one with no future, the one who would have died of an overdose if I didn't paralyze him, do you know what he is doing now?" Seth was getting annoyed that this man, the one who took away his *life*, was accusing him of not living.

"Well, I'll tell you. He is now a public speaker. Jackson goes to rehab facilities, schools, and countless other places giving motivational speeches about drug

addiction and turning one's life around. He calls the attack his lifesaver, imagine that! There is a six-figure book and movie deal he is negotiating right now and he just got engaged. And what are you doing? Trying to kill yourself and pissing off your caregiver on a daily basis. What a pity, Seth."

Seth's face was redder than it had ever been, and he leaned forward and bit his straw hard, blowing into it with all his might to run his wheelchair into the man's shins, a movement he knew was pointless as the chair moved at a ridiculously slow speed. The man simply got up and moved before Seth could even come close to hitting him.

"What do you want, for fuck's sake!? Just say or do it, then get Alvita help! She is innocent and doesn't deserve to die because I disappointed you," Seth screamed as tears started to burst out of his eyes.

"Listen to me carefully, Seth. You failed the first test. The second test is going to make the last one seem like it was a slap on the wrist. I really hope you don't disappoint me this time."

Seth could not see the man as he had walked behind him. His mind raced with fear of what the hell he was talking about. As the hand grabbed his forehead from behind, he prayed a knife was going to slit his throat and end it all, but what happened was worse than anything Seth could ever imagine.

The knife was thin, perfectly thin and sharp, a scalpel to be exact. Seth saw it right in front of his eye, the man holding his left eye open and his head steady. Unfortunately, in his state, he had minimal neck muscles

to fight back with. As the blade came closer to his eye, he screamed and screamed. When the cold steel touched his iris, he didn't so much feel anything other than pressure, and then a sudden burst of blackness and stars overcame his vision. His left eye was gone, sliced open. The hot chunky wetness that fell over his cheek made Seth vomit. With his head being held still, the bile simply poured out of his mouth and down his chest. The man then let go of his head and grabbed Seth's jaw. This confused Seth, as he assumed his other eye was next, but he was wrong. It was his tongue.

As the man stuck a metal device between his teeth and cranked them open, Seth gave up and just hoped the new wounds would kill him. The blade was so sharp, it cut his tongue out with a mere three swipes of the blade. The man was kind enough to hold it up and show it to Seth, opening his one good eye to make sure he saw the long piece of raw meat dangling in front of him. Then it was back to his other eye. Seth started to lose consciousness at this point, but the man snapped open a smelling salt and shocked him awake again. As his other eye was sliced open and the world went permanently dark, Seth wanted to cry, but he didn't know if he could anymore without eyes. It was then he thought his torture was over as the hands left his head, but the worse was still to come. After a few seconds, the man's gloved hand grabbed his forehead once more and then he felt something cold as night enter his ear.

Seth's right ear drum split open with a noise that sounded like the world's largest balloon popping underwater. Amazingly, this pain was worse than his two

eyes and tongue put together. After a few moments, which he assumed was the man allowing him to settle, he felt icy lips and warm breath on his left ear.

"You have three more years to impress me, son. Let's see what you can do in your new state. Welcome to phase two... darkness." Seconds later, there was another giant balloon exploding and with that, the world went dark.

The man was right. This new world of not hearing, seeing, or being able to speak was hell beyond all hells. He longed deeply and desperately for being simply a quadriplegic. Lying in what he assumed was a hospital, all he had left was touch on a mere few inches of his face. Seth faded in and out of sanity. Random things poked and prodded, strange hands tried to communicate with him through taps and soft touches on his face; it was frightening. The only solace he had was the touch of Alvita, which he could recognize by its warmth and softness. The fact that she lived was his only consolation.

Seth felt alone in his own world of blackness; his only companion was his imagination. He wasn't even able to *ask* for death. And yet for some reason, he no longer wanted to die. Three years, that is what he had to figure out how to communicate with the world and how to get revenge on the man who did this to him... and he planned on doing just that.

SKELETONS IN THE ATTIC

Alex was the oldest; Tony, the second youngest. A solid ten-year age difference. They were still close, but in a family obligation way, not an open, emotional one. Tony blamed this emotional distance on Alex's constant insistence to act like a third parent rather than a sibling. Regardless, they never really fought, but they also never hung out unless it was a family function.

Looking around the living room, memories flashed behind each of their eyes, fifty years' worth. The moment was still, long, and filled with deep sighs by both. While Christmas mornings, Easter Egg hunts, and birthday parties, hot summer days wrestling on the floor and cold winter nights by the fire watching movies with Dad and Mom snapped through their minds like an old-fashioned slide show, the two did everything to avoid each other's eyes. They were not the most macho of men, but they were not going to cry in front of each other: they had done enough of that at their parents' funerals.

"We should take one last walk through, make sure we didn't forget anything," Alex mumbled, holding back his emotions. Tony nodded, not able to speak. They took their time in each room, even though a quick glance would have done. As they walked into the empty rooms devoid of anything but walls, they looked around, clearly

seeing the house how it had appeared in their youth. They paced the floorboards, opened the closets, and looked up at the ceilings as if something might be there. In their parents' bedroom, they both allowed each other a few hard sniffs. Alex even patted Tony's shoulder once: lightly, but sharply. Upstairs in their old bedrooms, they did the same thing, looking for something that just wasn't there. Looking out his old window, Tony spoke.

"I can't imagine other people living here. It's just, it seems... it makes me sick." Alex wanted to put a hand on his shoulder but opted to fight the urge. He didn't want to think about this anymore.

"Let's get out of here." The two started for the stairs when Tony paused for a second, not sure if he was delaying or if he really was thinking about something.

"The attic is clear, right?" The two looked at the tiny hole in the ceiling. Though they could tell from the layer of dust on it that it hadn't been touched in years, they both shrugged.

"I thought you checked it out? Or maybe one of the girls did." Alex let out a frustrated sigh, happy at the aspect of getting to spend more time in the house yet annoyed at the possibility of having to remove more junk.

"Can't be much up there, if anything. I don't remember Mom and Dad ever using it. Hell, Dad could have never fit through that hole, could he?" Alex thought of this and agreed that he too could not remember anyone ever going up there.

"Well, we still have to check it. You never know: maybe Dad stashed some money up there, or vintage porn!" Alex said to lighten the mood before reaching up.

The panel was a few inches from his fingertips; they needed a ladder.

Twenty minutes later, after clearing the last two boxes and running down the street to Tony's house to get a step stool, they were back under the square hole. Tony opened up the small, four-foot ladder and took a step back, expecting his big brother to take the lead and go up and look. Realizing he had to go, Alex took a step up and thrust his hands toward the cover. He pushed it up lightly and it popped it out of place, sending a burst of dust flying towards his face. After a few spits and blinks, he was ready to take another step up and look. As his head crossed the hole, he had a strange feeling: he was seeing a place that had been right above his head for decades, but one he never seen and really never even thought about.

"What do you see?" Tony asked, as if they were searching for hidden Christmas presents.

"I need a damn flashlight. Looks like nothing, though." With that, Tony handed him the light that Alex had forced him to take earlier that day. Alex had trouble putting his arm and shoulder through at the same time; it was a tiny entrance and probably the chief reason their parents never used the attic. Once his head was up there, his chest being crushed on all four sides, Alex turned on the light and started searching the cramped space. On the side he was looking at, he saw nothing but the ancient white insulation, which looked like globs of rotting maple cotton candy. He mumbled to himself about it being asbestos and did his best to take shallow breaths. To see

the other side he had to pull himself back out, climb off the step stool, reposition it and start the process over again. It was on that other side, the deep side that led to the front of the house, that he saw the only object that remained in the house...

Seeing the object, Alex instantly kicked his legs with panic. The stool shot out from under him. Alex's legs kicked comically into the air for a solid two seconds until gravity pulled his body down. If his chest hadn't been crammed so tightly, he would have fallen instantly; regardless, he hit the floor hard, sending the air out of his chest like a rocket. Tony took a few steps back in panic rather than rushing to his aid. Alex sat up and pushed himself against the wall, trying to catch his breath as the pain overtook him. What was worse? The sight he saw or the searing pain in his lower back? His back would be sore for weeks, but what he saw could have ramifications for a lifetime.

Tony, trembling, approached his brother like a scared cat, and made an off-color comment about how lucky he was that he didn't fall a few inches to the right or he would have gone down the stairs.

"Thanks for the help, asshole. You could have caught me or broken my fall," Alex said with spite as he got up by himself, avoiding talking about what he saw. Rubbing his back, he paced back and forth as Tony righted the ladder and watched him. Looking back at the hole, Alex sighed heavily and blurted it out.

"There's a fucking body up there."

Tony laughed heartily. Alex shot back a look that told him to shut up. For a while, Alex paced the empty rooms trying to calm down, rubbing his back while his brother stared at the attic hole as if the body might come out on its own.

"How could there be a body up there, Alex? I mean, we could hardly fit through there. How could Dad or Mom get up there, let alone pull a body up there? I mean, Dad was too big: he's bigger than us. Mom might fit up there, but she could hardly carry laundry. Wouldn't it stink? Who would it be?" Tony rambled, never once looking away from the hole.

"I have no fucking clue," Alex said. "I think we need to relax first. I need to get a better look at it before we go jumping the gun. It might not even be a body."

With that, Tony looked away from the dark square for the first time. "You mean, it could just be something else? What does it look like? Is it wrapped up or something? Why do you even think it's a body?"

"Stop asking questions and take a look for yourself." Alex barked with pure anger. Tony looked back at the hole, took a step back from it, and bumped into his brother. Alex pushed him forward a bit, straightened the ladder, and nudged his brother forward. Alex had to keep his hands on his brother's back to get him up the stairs; he was always weak when it came to confrontation or emotional issues. Even when Mom was in the hospital those last few weeks, Tony could hardly go to see her.

It was like a child taking his first steps: slow and unsteady, but Tony finally got his footing on the step stool and pushed his head up through the hole. Alex told

him where to look, then watched as his brother froze. After a full minute, he stepped back down, pale, sweating, and looking like he was going to vomit. He hurried over to the window, opened it up, and stuck his head outside to suck in fresh air. Alex watched him for a minute, then climbed up the ladder to get another look. He was sure now... it was a body. It looked to be about five feet or so long, wrapped in a green tarp. Two ratty, old, white shoes stuck out from under the green plastic covering. They were filthy and looked like the kind nurses used to wear in the fifties. Stick-like bones, covered in what looked like dusty old beef jerky peeked out from the shoes and disappeared under the tarp. He didn't see any pants; the person either had on shorts or a skirt. Alex stared at the shoes for a while, trying to figure out if he had ever seen them before. They tickled some faded memory but he couldn't retrieve it.

A few moments later, they sat on separate sides of Tony's old room, the windows open, both of them with their backs to the wall and their knees up. It was more than uncomfortable sitting that way, especially now that they were middle-aged, but it seemed fitting. The breeze cut through the room, in one window and out the other, but it hardly touched them as they crammed themselves hard against the wall.

"Well, Alex, you have always been the adult one. What do we do?" Alex looked down at the floor. Everyone always got pissed at him for acting like a father, but being the oldest, married at twenty years old before his brother and sisters were freshman in high school, he

didn't have much of a choice. In this moment, it was the last thing he wanted to do, make another adult decision. He already had to do all the funeral plans, be the executive of the will, and handle all the damn paperwork and sale of the house; it would be too much, adding… whatever this was. It was going to break him.

"You're almost fifty yourself, asshole." Alex said defensively. Tony nodded up and down as if the insult was a comment.

"Well, if we report it, call the cops, the house becomes a crime scene. It will hold up the sale. Hell, it might even ruin it. After it gets in the papers, who is going to want the house that had the dead body in the attic?" Tony said this out loud as if thinking more than to Alex, who was actually listening and not interrupting for one of the first times in their lives. Tony licked his lips, squinted his eyes in thought, and continued.

"If we don't report it, we *cannot* leave it: the new owners will find it and we'll open ourselves to lawsuits. Also, if we did report it, it would ruin Mom and Dad's image in the town, in the rest of our family's eyes too. They were good goddamn people… at least, I thought they were." Alex's eyes popped open at this.

"They were. Don't you go saying shit like that. For all we know, someone else put the body up there. Hell, you had your issues back in the day. All that drug shit. How do I know you didn't stuff someone up there?" Tony shot up, took three fast steps at Alex, balled his fist, then turned around and punched the wall, leaving a fist-sized dent in the old plaster board.

"For fuck's sake! Now we have to fix that!" Alex yelled, getting up slowly.

"Why do you have to bring up that shit all the time? I was a kid. I've been clean for twenty years now," Tony said, putting his palms on the windowsill, looking out to avoid contact with Alex.

"You were a piece of shit back them. Makes more sense that *you* did something. Hell, your room is right by the damn hole. Dad and Mom were amazing damn people, you know that. They never even spanked us, and you think they are capable of killing? Fuck no. You, you on the other hand have been to jail four times and even stabbed a fucking guy," Alex said with anger, getting closer to Tony with each line. Tony kept still, his fingers digging into the window frame.

"Cut it the fuck out. You think *I* would have said to look up in the attic if I put a damn body up there? I would have made you avoid the fucking thing and then gotten rid of it when no one was around. I might have been an addict but I'm not *that* stupid." Tony finally let go of the window and turned to Alex to see his brother's face was red and he was a bit sweaty.

"Can we please think this out and not fight?" Tony asked, using everything he could from what he learned in years of therapy to not snap. Tony watched Alex sniff hard a few times, then blink. Thoughts of Alex having a heart attack flashed in his mind, but he pushed them aside, figuring it was just a panic attack at the situation. Tony calmed himself as Alex leaned against the wall and took a few deep breaths.

"Listen… you want me to be the adult, then I'll be the…" Alex paused to catch his breath, reached up towards his chest but he caught himself and put his arm down.

"Fucking adult. We get up there, take the body out and get rid of it and never talk about it again. We are not ruining the sale for the family." Alex took another few deep breaths.

"We all need the money. And we are not ruining our parents' image." Alex looked relieved that he got out his statement. Tony paced a bit. He seemed to be arguing with himself in the head.

"But, the person. They had a family too, they probably never had closure. Getting rid of it would be wrong, Alex." Tony watched Alex grit his teeth and his hands clench. Tony put up his hands in a calming gesture.

"How about we get the body down, see if there is an ID or something, then make a decision." Tony pleaded in as calming a tone as he could muster. Alex's fist was still clenched, his teeth gritted tight. He simply nodded up and down, then muttered.

"Fine, but you go up there. You are smaller." The two of them walked out of the room into the small landing above the stairs where the ladder waited for them to climb into the hole once again. Alex nodded to the ladder with a *hurry up and do it* look. Tony sighed, put a fake smile on, and took a few steps up. Before taking the third step, he hesitated.

"Why do *you* not want to report this so badly? You are the one with anger issues. Mom always said it would

get you in trouble one day. For all I know, you did this," Tony said with a tone that was sly and snotty as if he had finally thought of a witty comeback. Tony watched as Alex's face got even redder. It was now the shade of beet juice: deep, almost purple.

"You little fucking shit!" Alex said, darting his short stubby hands at Tony's throat, which was just out of reach. Tony pushed himself back to avoid the meaty hands that were gripping with such anger. The last time Alex attacked him, he got a broken rib that ached for six months, and that was the last thing he wanted. Avoiding those hateful hands was a good idea, if he hadn't been on a ladder on top of the stairs.

At first, the sensation of flying through the air was confusing for Tony. As he saw the small hole grow even smaller, he realized he was falling far and fast. His first instinct was to try and turn and put his hands out to break his fall, but the second he tried to spin his body around, he heard a sickening crack, like a watermelon slamming into a pile of small twigs. There was no pain, just instant, permanent, and indefinite blackness.

Alex stood helpless, and more so, in shock. The small dark hole in the ceiling seemed to be laughing at him as he stared at his brother's body, crumpled like a piece of trash at the bottom of the stairs. His instincts told him to run downstairs, call for an ambulance, and make sure Tony was alright, but he knew, *without a doubt*, that his brother had died instantly. And it was *his* fault. Alex had no clue a neck could snap so violently, so completely, or so quickly. Tony's head sat sideways on

his body. A bone bulged out of his neck like the world's largest Adam's apple, only in the wrong place. The sight made Alex's stomach do a few flips.

The realization that he had murdered his brother had not really set in, but panic had. *What to do, what to do?* There were three options that came to mind. Call the police now, tell them about the body upstairs, and say Tony fell, or, get rid of *both* bodies and make up a lie how they both left the house but he had suspected Tony of being on drugs again, giving plenty of reason for him to disappear. The third option was to get the body out of the attic, stash it in his car, and then call the cops and say Tony fell, and get rid of the old body later. Yes, that was the best option. Keep his parents' names clean and get away with Tony's death as an accident.

Taking a big breath, Alex shook his head, frustrated he couldn't get all the air he really wanted into his lungs. He had never felt like this before. When the cops came, he was going to have to have them check him out. It was probably just stress, but the way his heart was dancing like an ecstasy user at a rave was making him nervous. Regardless, he had no choice but to cram himself into the attic and get that fucking body down. Fixing the ladder, he took two steps up, paused, and looked down at his brother. The thought of falling himself made him feel a bit weak, so he grabbed onto the edge of the hole and looked away from Tony's staring eyes that now looked cloudy and creepy. For the first time in his life, he was conscious of the blood flowing through his body. He could feel each and every vein and artery as the blood slid

through and around the miles of minuscule tubes. It did not feel right.

Ignoring the warning signs his body was screaming at him, Alex stuck one arm up in the air, then the other, and took an awkward step onto the top of the ladder. His head and arms were now through the hole. Blinking a few times from the dust, but more from the whooshing of the blood in his head, he grabbed the edge of the entrance and started to pull himself up. Instantly, his chest was crushed against the sides. He could almost hear his wife nagging at him, *I told you to eat better! You never listen to me! Now look: you are going to get stuck because you are too fat!* Suddenly, whether it was the odd sensation of the blood or that fabled "adrenaline" he had always heard of, he pushed himself with all his might right up into the attic. With a quick turn like a gymnast, he was sitting on the edge, his feet dangling down in the hole. It wasn't until he looked at his shirt that he realized it was ripped in a dozen places and blood was quickly filling the spaces where the cloth was missing. *Fucking slivers.* That would be hard to explain to the cops. Now he was going to have to change his shirt and bandage his wounds first, and he was going to have to hurry, because if all the crime shows he watched were true, they could always pinpoint the time of death. If he left Tony too long, they would be suspicious.

Remembering his mission, Alex rolled over, found the wood frames and started to crawl across them, being careful not to slip off. The heat was almost unbearable and it did nothing for the constant swelling rhythm of the blood pulsing throughout him. He wanted to keep his

head up to watch where he was going to see how far it would be until he got to the body, but when he tried to lift it, the thumping of his pulse made him dizzy and his left eye go blurry, so he kept it down and shuffled. After what he felt like was the length of the football field, his hand slid into the desiccated old tarp. It made a dry leaf crunching sound as he grasped it in his trembling hand. Looking at his hand is when he started to get nervous and realized he was not in good shape at all. The skin, which was normally pink and puffy with an extra layer of fat, was unrecognizably white, covered in a slime of sweat, and shook like a wet, cold Chihuahua. He told himself that he had to just grab the body and shuffle back, and then he could get out, get air, and get help for himself.

While that thought was all well and good, it was too late. As the heart attack took over his body, Alex started to faint. With his last gasp of effort, he scooped his arm around the body and pulled it close to him. Just as he blacked out, he thought about how odd the body felt. His tremendous bulk falling as dead weight, even though from a kneeling position, was too much for the old plaster ceiling to handle. His body cracked through instantly but stuck between the rafters for a solid twenty seconds before the blood from his cuts lubricated the few sticking points. As Alex slipped through and started to fall through the air, he awoke just in time to see his dead brother's eyes looking up at him as if in shock at the sight he was seeing.

Had the heart attack not been working hard to kill him, Tony's body would have broken Alex's fall enough to save his life; however, the attack was angry and intense.

Groggy, with seconds to live, Alex propped himself up on his elbow enough to see that his brother's head had been cracked open under his bulk. The mixture of bone, blood, and brain matter that seeped out made him think of the time his dog threw up a hairless mole he had eaten. Giving up on everything, Alex then noticed that the body that was in the tarp had come unraveled and was lying next to him.

He was dizzy and fading fast, but Alex forced himself to roll over enough to see the corpse. He had to know who it was-- who it was that had gotten their revenge all these years later by killing their murderer's sons. When he saw the bony, plastic face lying next to his, Alex let out a hard, whooping laugh that quickly turned into a cough.

As if opening a time capsule he had forgotten about, the face he saw next to him brought back a memory so clear, he was shocked that he had forgotten all about it. He was five, maybe six years old, when his father purchased a skeleton from the Five and Dime for Halloween. His dad was so proud of it, he had sat it on the front steps, dressed in his mother's old clothing. Alex had been terrified of it, so much so that one day, his father got so pissed, he wrapped it up in a tarp so that his son couldn't see it, and when Alex continued to cry about it, his dad had stormed off into the house, saying he would hide it where no one would see it again.

Alex set his head down, closed his eyes, and felt his heart squeeze and thump, squeeze and thump, and he wondered if the sale of the house would go through, now that there was going to be three, well, two, dead bodies found in their parents' home.

WAITING

It took twenty-seven days before anyone found my body. When they did find it, it was because of a goddamn cliché. Stupid dog chewed off my hand and brought it back to his owner's house: your stereotypical opening of a movie or an episode of *Law and Order*. Of course, that started a search and they found me hours later. I would have been happier with a hiker finding me, but a freaking dog? As I watched him run away with my hand, I knew I would be found pretty quickly, but as relieved that I was, I was pissed. Couldn't I at least have a decent story to tell in my death?

When I first died, I was shocked to say the least. No one expects to die at a young age. I'm only twenty-three for crying out loud… and I died alone, in the woods. What was more shocking than my death was the fact that I was still… around. Standing next to my own body, looking down at it, was hard to take, especially with my being an atheist. After several hours of screaming and trying to shake my body back to life, I came to the terms with the fact that I was dead. Why my "spirit" or whatever you want to call it hadn't left was beside me, both figuratively and literally. I had seen enough movies to expect a bright light to come down or some smiling relative to show up and offer me passage to the beyond,

yet nothing happened. It was just as if I was alive, only...
I couldn't walk more than twenty feet from my own
body. Every time I tried, it was like hitting a wall. No
matter how I tried, I couldn't move any further away.

By the second day, when I realized it wasn't a dream
or that I wasn't in a coma, I figured out that while I could
touch things and sit down on a stump, I couldn't
physically move anything. I could smell stuff, feel it on
my skin, but I couldn't affect anything physically. I didn't
get hungry or even thirsty... I could cry though, and I'm
not afraid to admit I did a lot of that.

The third day, I started to get insanely bored. I had
nothing to do but watch my body start to rot and bloat.
It was horrible. There were ants and bugs all over,
crawling in and out of my nose, mouth, and ears, finding
new homes. It was a nightmare watching them crawl all
over and not being able to brush them off. I screamed at
them, tried to flick and blow them, and nothing
happened. They just went about their business of
exploring every orifice. My stomach grew to three times
its normal size as the gasses caused by my rotting
expanded it. It was disgusting.

That night, I realized I hadn't slept... and that I
couldn't. I no longer had a body, which is why I didn't
need to eat, so if I didn't need the other things a human
would, why would I need to sleep? This became a
torture. Though I was never tired, I wanted nothing
more than to kill the hours by dozing. Instead, I was
stuck to stare at falling leaves, the occasional bird, and
squirrel, and if I was lucky, I could watch a slug cross my
path and count how long it took him to do it. Anything

to keep my mind off of my rotting body. Of course, I couldn't help but look at it now and then-- hell, I couldn't get far enough away from it to *not* see it. Saying this was torture is an understatement.

The days went on and on, and as they did, I slowly went crazy. I wanted nothing more than to kill myself, which was fucking impossible being that I was already dead. Somehow, as my mind started go, as it thought of ways to escape this hell, I was able to keep track of the days. Ten, then fifteen slipped by. They started to blur into each other and fade into one giant nightmare. On the eighteenth day, I spent, what I assumed was, five hours backing up, getting a running start, and slamming into the invisible wall the kept me bound to my body. As much as I knew I couldn't break through, I tried over and over again, like an insane person.

Around the twentieth day, I started to think about religion and God. You'd think that would have been the first thing I thought about, the moment I died, waiting for the big white light to show up, but not believing in that shit, I refused to believe that I was stuck in some sort of purgatory. Yet on that day, I came to the conclusion that that was what was happening: I was stuck in my own purgatory, doomed to be bored, invisibly chained to my body for eternity. I thought about how, when I was found, I would sit and watch my parents, family, and the few friends I had stroll into the wake and cry over my body. I'd want to go home with them, but I wouldn't be able to. I'd be stuck in the dark freezer with my body until they buried it. Then I would be forced to stay in a graveyard forever and ever.

I started to wonder why I was stuck in purgatory. Yeah, maybe I had killed myself, but it really was an accident… or at least I wanted people to think that. I guess if there were a God, he'd be able to know my thoughts and the fact that I fell out of the hunter's nest on purpose. Of course, to make sure I didn't just get hurt, I fell off the side where there were jagged rocks to land on, and they sure did the trick. Was my life that bad? Yeah, yeah it was, but it was nothing compared to this. I'd take it back in a second, go on living what I thought was hell with a smile on my face after I knew what this was like. Shit, I'd become a minister, start praising the Lord, and be a teen counselor as I went down the road to Enlightenment. It was too late now, though.

By the twenty-fifth day I didn't care about God, or purgatory, or anything for that matter. My mind was numb, I had almost no thoughts, I didn't care about the slugs crossing my path anymore, and looking at my body didn't gross me out. Watching it was my only form of entertainment. Hour after hour, I sat and watched my corpse slowly but surely fall apart. The bloating had stopped and my stomach had once again collapsed; my face was nothing more than puddle of very unnatural browns and greens. There were large chunks taken out of the meat of my arms, legs, and neck. Foxes, crows, a coyote, and even a small mountain lion all had their share of me (in fact, watching myself get eaten was the highlight of my days as it was at least interesting). While the bugs were the first to feast, the maggots were now the last to find my body interesting. Thousands upon thousands burrowed their way through every orifice, both the ones I

had in life and the ones created in death. The way they wiggled and squirmed fascinated me. It didn't turn my stomach or even make me angry; I ended up finding their progression from slimy bug to fly a beautiful thing.

The day the dog showed up, it took me off guard, snapping me out of my daze. When I heard his low growl as he approached my body, I moved for the first time in days. I looked around me in shock as the leaves were starting to change ever so slightly to brilliant oranges and yellows. Then I looked back to the dog that walked towards my body, sniffing nervously. When he felt it was safe, he went in and bit at my hand. Watching him, I stood up and walked over. I wanted nothing more than to feel his orange fur against my face, to rub his belly and give him a big hug. I hovered my hand above his back as he gnawed at the already loosened and slimy flesh of my index finger. With only two tugs he yanked it off and went running away with it, proud to show his owner.

About three minutes later I heard the scream, and an hour after that, a row of police came marching through the forest until they found me. Some gagged, one threw up, and another laughed as if he didn't know how to handle what he saw. I laughed with him, as I was getting ready to leave this place and seeing another human (if I was one anymore?) was such a sweet sight. In a way, I felt as if I'd won the lottery; that is, until they had my body in the bag. Being alone in this whole situation, not being able to talk to someone or to get answers was the worst part, because none of it made sense. The second they zipped up the bag, I was suddenly in the bag as well, crammed in with my body. I couldn't feel or see

anything, and I couldn't get out. Why I could wander around my body before but could not get out of the bag was beyond my comprehension, but I didn't dwell on the *whys* as I had given up on them a long time ago.

A day later, I was able to stand as some medical examiner poked, prodded, and dissected by body. But again, the second they put my body in the cooler, I went with it, stuck inside until I was pulled out again. Then it was another body bag and off to the funeral home. Again, I got to watch the fascinating magic the man did to my body, making it look somewhat whole again, so my parents and my parents alone could sob over it for a mere thirty seconds: that was all my mother could take. Thankfully, they didn't have to ID my body earlier as I had a record and they matched my fingerprints from the one finger that had them left. From there it was a closed casket service. I could hear the familiar voices all around me, but I all I could see was blackness as I was locked in with my damn body.

When I heard the cement sarcophagus close around the coffin, I was suddenly able to move. I could stand up. It was fascinating; I was standing, under the ground, yet inside of it. All I could see was dirt and rocks rubbing against my eyeballs but it did not hurt nor did it scare me. I tested my boundaries and found I could only walk the length and width of my coffin. I could, however, step up onto of my coffin and then on top of the cement box around it. When I was jumping as high as I could, my eyes would break the surface ever so slightly and I'd get a quick glimpse of the grass, then the beautiful sunlight and blue sky. After a few jumps, I recognized the cemetery as

the one down the street from my parents' house. Sadly, I could only see the outside world for a flash with each jump. There was no way to ever get high enough to just stand and look out.

After seeing the grass die, the leaves fall, and then the snow come down in tiny glimpses from my daily thousand jumps, I realized a year went by… after that, I stopped counting. Now, I assume it's been five, maybe ten years that I have been down here. I don't jump up that much anymore, so I don't get have a grasp on days. It's more of seasons. The few times I jump up I catch glimpses of snow or heat waves rising off the graves. As the years slip by, I become more and more like my body, sedate and rotting from the inside out. Once every two years or so, I have a screaming fit that lasts what I think is days, followed by weeks of sobbing, and then I'm back to my months and years of numbness. I can go years without thinking or even moving. Only once in a great while do I wonder if this will all end, if I will suddenly see a light and I'll get to go towards it, or if I will be forever waiting for the world to end.

TIME IS EVERYTHING

It all started with an innocent mistake.

Michael's flight was late, meaning *he* was late for his big meeting in New York City. This was the exact reason he asked his boss to fly him in the night before, but that would have required a hotel and food costs, which were "not in the budget," so he ended up on a five A.M. flight, a flight that should have gotten him to his meeting four hours early. At four in the morning, staring at the board with the red blinking sign reading "Delayed," Michael opened a bottle of Tums, something that always sat in his suit coat pocket, and popped four tropical-berry-smoothie-flavored tablets into his mouth. By the time his flight landed-- three hours late-- he had eaten the entire bottle. Knowing he would only have a matter of minutes to get his luggage, hail a taxi, and make it to mid-town from JFK, a tough ride as it is, Michael constantly fidgeted and felt nauseous. He wished he had more Tums, but he did not have time to stop at the airport store. If he was lucky, really lucky, he might be a few minutes late but would still be able to give the presentation.

Cursing himself for checking his bag, Michael anxiously waited by the slow-moving belt, hoping and praying that the next bag would be his. After almost forty

frustrating bags, his finally made it up the peak, slid down the shiny metal slide, and slammed onto the belt. Once he had grabbed it, he raced to the door, jumped into a taxi, and offered the driver an extra twenty bucks if he could get him to mid-town *fast*. Since it was late morning, the man just rolled his eyes and hit the gas. Amazingly, the un-identifiably foreign driver, who did not speak a word the entire time, got him to the black high-rise building three minutes before Michael's meeting was scheduled.

In the lobby, Michael ducked into the bathroom, freshened himself up, and tried to dry the sweat pouring down his face before he made a run for the front desk. He was two minutes late, but that was not bad, not bad at all with the delay he had. After checking in and slapping a guest badge onto a breast pocket, Michael started to relax as the elevator took him up seventy floors. When the doors opened, he was instantly greeted by three hands to shake, all of whom said they were more than excited for his presentation. Within a minute, he was left alone inside a massive boardroom to set up. He was told he had ten minutes before the committee would arrive and he should help himself to any refreshments.

Michael had prepared for this meeting obsessively. He was going to nail it out of the park, secure the deal his boss didn't believe was possible, and then be on his way to a raise, bonus, and new title in the company. The nausea was settling down and was being replaced with a little bubble of excitement. He couldn't help but smile as he took off his jacket and tossed his suitcase on the table to open. With a quick zip and flip, he had the flap open,

but seeing the contents sent off a series of explosions in his head. Severe confusion, anger, and frustration instantly poured over him like someone had dumped a bucket of ice cold water right on top of his head. *It wasn't his bag.* There were no charts, no folders that cost almost a hundred bucks to print, no displays, and no banner. Instead, there was clothing, a toiletry bag, and lots and lots of black socks. *How could he have been so stupid… He shouldn't have checked a bag. He should have taken two that he could carry on, like everyone told him.* He always laughed at the stupid signs that warned, "Pay Attention! Many bags look similar, please check the tags for your name!" How could someone be so stupid as to grab the wrong bag? And now *he* was he idiot who had done exactly that… on the one day it *really* mattered.

After sitting down, catching his breath, and trying not to cry, he reached for his Tums, forgetting the bottle was empty. Gathering himself, he prepared to give the proposal without any materials, which was basically just him talking. It was no use though: it would be about as successful as a magician doing a magic show with no tricks.

As the board arrived and took their seats, he did his best to shake their hands and smile as the sweat formed on his forehead and the acid rose in his throat. *God, he needed some Tums.* Michael tried to explain the situation, but the board didn't seem to care that he had grabbed the wrong bag. In fact, they seemed annoyed that he was wasting their time each time he tried to explain what he *would* have shown them. As they rose from their seats bored and annoyed, he asked for another chance to give

his pitch to them when he had his materials, but the grumpy old man at the head of the table barked a loud *NO* and left the room. Everyone followed.

When he pleaded with one of the straggling minions, the man replied curtly, "You get one chance with the big man; time is everything to him. You waste his time, you'll never get more of it. Sorry, man: 'better luck at the next company." Five minutes later, Michael found himself outside with another man's luggage: defeated, miserable, and needing an antacid more than ever.

With his return flight not scheduled until ten that night (he had planned on having a celebratory dinner after he sealed the deal), he had time to kill and wallow in his mistake. Noticing a park nearby, he decided to sit there a while to collect himself; maybe he'd calm down enough to talk himself out of jumping into traffic. It was a beautiful park on a glorious day. The sun was shining, people were having picnics, kids were playing, and businessmen ate dripping sandwiches at tiny green tables while pigeons fought over crumbs. Life was wonderful-- for them, at least. Frustrated at seeing all of this happiness and not wanting to think about his failure, Michael focused on the bag and finding out who it belonged to. Of course, he could just bring it to the airport and drop it off and grab his without ever looking inside, but for some reason, he felt compelled to find out whose bag it was. Maybe he blamed the guy a bit, maybe it was just curiosity, or a need to distract himself from the debacle, but whatever made him look in the bag changed the course of his life.

The bag was identical to his suitcase: same brand, model, and color, only it was filled for what looked to be an extensive trip. Clothing, mostly men's trim, size medium shirts and thirty-inch-waist pants. *So it belongs to a small man*, thought Michael, mentally comparing his own XXX-Large shirt and forty-five-inch waist size. Something about this man being slim annoyed Michael. As he rummaged around, he hoped to find some Tums, but small men usually didn't need them. As he dug around, the sheer number of socks seemed odd. There were eight outfits, yet about forty or so pairs of socks all tucked into the mesh pouch on the bag's flap. The oddest part was that there were no shoes. Dozens of socks, but no extra shoes? It was suspicious, to say the least. Unzipping the mesh pouch, he grabbed a pair and instantly realized that this suitcase was not what it seemed. There was something heavy and solid in the socks he grabbed… and in every pair, for that matter.

Looking around the park, he made sure no one was watching him; then, he pulled apart a pair. As his fingers touched the object within the black cotton, he knew it wasn't drugs. It felt too hard, too metal-like; really, it felt like a watch. This excited Michael a bit. Someone wouldn't hide watches in pairs of socks unless they were expensive. With a quiet prayer, he pulled the timepiece out and stifled a scream of joy. *It was a Rolex.* The next five were as well. In total, he found forty-seven watches, mostly Rolex, but several Montblancs and a few Patek Phillippes (which he heard could cost upwards of a million a piece). Thoughts of returning the bag left his mind. They were obviously stolen or "hot," as he heard

41

people say. Why return stolen items to a thief? Why not profit from this mistake? They had to be worth something, especially if they were real. Maybe he could make some money back on this disastrous day. Normally he was a law-abiding citizen, but profiting off of a criminal did not bother him a bit. The thought of them finding out did, but he lived thousands of miles away and would be gone in a matter of hours, so why not?

Four hours later, Michael indulged in his celebratory dinner at Toa, the place he'd seen on TV many times before, though this dinner was not to celebrate a deal. It was to commemorate the fact that he had gotten four hundred and twenty thousand dollars for the watches he sold. It was a fraction of the face value of them, but by selling them to a pawn dealer in the jewelry district, he knew he could only get so much. Besides, the amount he got was more than six times his salary. After a bit of calculating, he estimated that if he had gotten a raise from the deal like he was hoping, he would have made less than ten percent of this amount over the next ten years. This was *much* better. There was more than enough reason to celebrate. *Funny how things turn out,* Michael thought, not once thinking about the Tums he had yet to replace.

With his stomach full and his head a bit light from the thousand-dollar wine he had drunk, Michael checked his new watch, a new Rolex with blue crystals, to find it was almost nine at night. Normally it was his bed time, but he did not want to stop celebrating and he definitely did not want to be alone. Patting his pocket, he felt the ten grand in hundreds folded up nicely. It made him happy to have

so much in his pocket at one time-- something he had never had before-- and he planned on spending it all that night while the rest was safely tucked away in a new bank account his wife didn't know about. While he had never paid for sex in his life or done a drug harder than pot, he had always wanted to. Now, here in the Big Apple, alone, where no one knew him and with more cash to burn than he would ever have at once, he was going to do just that. Hookers and drugs. He hoped for at least three women at once and to do coke off all of their asses, just like he had seen in *The Wolf of Wall Street*. It was against everything he was, which is exactly why he wanted to do it, just this one time.

An old co-worker of Michael's once told him that when traveling, if you ever wanted to "indulge" in anything of excess, to talk to a busboy at a high-end restaurant. He followed this advice and within ten minutes, he was on the phone with a very business-like woman who went over a few quick terms before telling him that three women, one blonde, one brunette, and one redhead, along with enough coke for a "good party for a first timer" would be at his hotel in midtown within one hour. Hanging up the phone, he couldn't believe how easy it was. He had more trouble ordering a pizza than that. A brief flash and desire to have more money, to have this power and ability on a daily basis, ran through his mind, but he kept telling himself, just this once, as he tipped the busboy two hundred dollars and rushed back to the hotel he had booked last minute. His flight was in two hours, but he no longer cared. He would text his wife that he missed it and catch one in the morning.

Within ten minutes, the private black cab (no need for a yellow when you have money) took him to the W Hotel in Times Square. Within seconds of checking in, he was whisked to the upper floors to a room unlike any he had ever seen. As he wandered around the recessed living room, past the one of three bathrooms and the built-in bar, he couldn't imagine what the "expensive" rooms above him that cost twenty grand a night must look like; this one alone was costing him five grand. When he thought of the number and how much money it really was, he reached for the Tums and remembered he still had not replaced them. That kind of money was a week's vacation with the wife. He could pay off some debt. No. Shaking his head, he pushed all of those thoughts out and told himself that this was free money and that he still had almost half a million extra to do all the other stuff. Looking at his beautiful new watch, he jumped. The ladies would be there any minute. He had to shower the day's sweat off of himself first.

In the shower, Michael looked down at his belly, how round and hairy it was. He hadn't seen his dick without a mirror in over a decade. His typical self-pity and pep talk about getting into shape and taking care of himself automatically started in his head. Instantly, he turned the heat up. The rain shower spray, which was something he had never experienced before, turned almost scalding hot. *They will treat me like I look like a god because I have money... don't worry about what you look like.* Michael started to breathe heavy and felt the acid coming up in his throat; he needed those Tums. Sitting down on the warm, exotic tile seat (which, to be honest, he got a brief thrill out of:

he'd never been in a shower with a seat before), he felt a wave of doubt and worry wash over him along with the water. *What was he doing? What if he got caught cheating, selling stolen goods, doing drugs, paying for prostitutes?!?!* His mind swirled over and over with various thoughts between how excited he was to fuck three women and how the hell he could be doing all of this. His wet hand fell into his lap, and when the back of his hand felt the warm, round head of his penis become hard and excited, he instantly knew he would go through with the night's festivities.

A mere eight minutes later, Michael was dry, still hard, and in the hotel's luxurious bathrobe, which felt softer than anything he had ever felt in his life. The doorbell rang-- another thing he had never experienced in a hotel before—and his heart jack-hammered, sending a sting of bile up the back of his throat. When he heard a young man say it was room service, he swallowed hard and answered the door; the five-hundred-dollar-a-bottle champagne he had ordered was there. He rushed to the door and opened it to see a man who had the stature of a small teenager but a face that was impossible to tell the age of. Michael would have believed you whether you said the man was seventeen or fifty-four. He marveled at the man's, the boy's, face as he ushered him in and told him to place the cart by the bed. Reaching into the robe's pocket, he pulled out two twenties and smiled to himself at the idea of tipping the guy so much. It made him feel... cool. When the man (boy?) turned around and flashed a big smile on his smooth face, Michael realized that the man was not in a uniform but wearing what

seemed like a smoking jacket from the twenties with black velvet trim and black pants. It was as if he was some sort of playboy from another decade. Michael thought this was curious, but he figured he must be some sort of special valet for the wealthier guests.

"Will there be anything else, Sir?" The youngish, oldish man asked Michael, who was now holding out the two twenties with a sly grin on his face.

"No, that will be all. Here you go." The man's face contorted into an expression of concern as he looked at Michael's hand holding the money but did not reach for it. Michael couldn't understand, then quickly felt stupid: it was probably way too little. The rich bastards that spend five grand on a hotel and two thousand on a few bottles of champagne probably tipped a few hundred bucks, not forty. Fumbling, he reached into the pocket and pulled out the wad, grabbed five more twenties and held them out. The man's face did not change, nor did he reach for the money.

"That's still not enough?" Michael asked with amazement and slight curiosity.

"The watch," the boy... or man said. "Where did you get it?" Michael felt his stomach drop. The acid shot up his throat like a volcano erupting; the need for Tums had never been worse. Foolishly, he placed his hands over the watch as if obscuring it from view would make the conversation disappear.

"Uh, I bought it today. At a pawn shop downtown," Michael said with an incredibly unconvincing tone. The man's face contorted into a greedy smile. This, again, made Michael's stomach do a few somersaults.

"I think you should go now. I have company coming," Michael found himself saying, shocked that he stood up for himself. The man didn't move; he just looked down at Michael's hand that was still covering the watch.

"Your *company* won't be here any *time* soon," the man said, pointing a long, pale finger at Michael's wrist.

Confusion set into Michael's mind. *What did this man know? What the hell did he mean? Why won't he just freaking leave?* Annoyed, he let go of his watch, stood up straight, and pointed to the door himself. "Leave or I'll call security."

The man smiled at this comment as well. "Let's cut the games, my friend. You have some things of mine and I want them back." Michael suddenly felt the overwhelming need to sit down. He felt faint, and fear that was almost painful washed over him; he could not stand any longer and found himself falling into a chair that was in the entryway. Sitting down, he didn't even notice that his now flaccid penis was sticking out from the robe.

"Michael, I have a bad feeling that you... got rid of my watches. Regardless of what you did with them, I *must* have them back by midnight." Michael listened to the man's cool voice as he stared at the tile floor, taking slow deep breaths to relax. This had just gone from what was to be the best night of his life to the worst in a mere second. With his lungs filled with some air and the acid still licking at the back of his throat, he spoke up.

"The money, it's, it's in the bedroom in my bag. Take it, take this watch, and I'll write you a check for rest and

for what I already spent. I, I have never done anything like this. I'm sorry." He felt like an elementary school child apologizing for sticking gum in a girl's hair. He felt his cheeks flush hot with embarrassment and his hands trembled with fear of what the man might do. The entire time, he kept his eyes on the tile floor, which he noticed had tiny hairline cracks buried deep in the dark tan tile.

"I don't think you are understanding me. I could give a shit about the money. The time on the watches is the only thing that matters to me. If I don't get them back, your time will run out as well."

Michael's brain hurt. The rush of adrenaline caused by the fear was making it hard to think. He had no clue what the man was talking about or what the hell he meant. "The pawn shop I sold them to is probably closed, I'm sure we can go back in the morning, try to get them back. Though he will probably want more money that he gave me, of course. I can give you the address. You can take the money and go down there yourself," Michael said, and finally noticing his dick was sticking out of the robe, he quickly covered it up. Looking up at the man, he was once again taken aback by the inability to pinpoint his age: he just couldn't figure it out. The man sighed heavily as Michael watched him, then reached up and rubbed his eyes.

"Michael, you are not understanding. You have until midnight to get *all* the watches back to me, or your time will run out." The man started to walk towards the door.

Michael didn't know what to do, so he just sat there. Finally, he realized the least he could do was give back the one watch he was wearing. Eagerly, he unclasped it, slid

it off, jumped up, and held it out to the man whose hand was on the door handle. "Here, here is one. I'll go to the shop and try to get the others."

The man, his back to Michael, sighed heavily, then turned around. Michael almost jumped back as the man looked to have aged thirty years in a mere second.

"I don't think you understand, Michael. That watch is now *yours*, it holds all of your time. At midnight, if you are not back in this room with all of the watches, that one," the man pointed a long, suddenly wrinkled finger at the watch, "will stop ticking... and so will you. There are no other choices, no running away, no buying more time. We all only have a set amount, all of us. Time can easily be taken away, but to add time, that requires time from others and that can be messy." The man stopped speaking, moved his eyes around the room as if thinking of something more to say, then looked back at Michael. Somehow, his face looked even older. When he first arrived, Michael thought he could have been a mere seventeen years old, at most fifty, but now he looked like he was seventy and not a day younger.

When the odd man's eyes locked on Michael's, he felt a wave of cold anxiety rush through him, and acid shot up in the back of his throat again and spilled into his mouth. A hot, acidic juice washed through his teeth and over his tongue. He wanted to lurch forward and spit it out, throw up, but he couldn't move; he held the unappealing liquid in his mouth and stared at the man's eyes. Michael felt like he was going insane, but he could almost see a second-hand ticking in the back of the man's dark black irises. As he looked at the faint seconds ticking away,

Michael suddenly realized he *had* to get the watches back. He had no choice.

Six minutes later, Michael was dressed and in the elevator, sweating profusely. Looking at the watch he had put back on his wrist, which suddenly felt like a major part of him, almost like it was an organ, he saw that he had two and a half hours until midnight. It was horrifically little time, considering he had to get downtown to the pawn shop and back to the hotel, which would lose him an hour alone. He just prayed the man had not sold any of the watches yet. There was some sort of law that made shops hold items for a certain amount of time in case they were stolen, but Michael had a feeling that the store he had chosen did not follow the rules. As the elevator doors opened, three stunningly gorgeous women, dressed a bit too sultry for this fancy hotel, were there in front of him, giggling to each other. Michael's heart sank and he felt his dick instantly swell as he knew they were the hookers *he* was supposed to be screwing all night long. Part of him wanted to say screw it, to stay on the elevator, ride up with them and enjoy the last few hours of his life, but as this thought came over him, he felt a sharp pain around his wrist, as if the watch knew what he was thinking and was slapping him to get moving, so he did. He politely smiled and rushed past the three stunning women without a word.

Twenty-seven minutes later, a yellow cab let him out at the pawn shop, *Paul's Pawn*. To his utter shock, the lights were on and the store was still open. Part of him laughed as he thought, *New York, the city that never sleeps!*

Bursting inside, he saw a few people standing at the counter; to him, they all looked like drug fiends trying to hawk whatever they had just stolen. Ignoring them, he rushed to the back counter where he saw an old Hasidic Jewish man sitting on a stool, doing the crossword puzzle of the *New York Times*. With sweat pouring down his face, Michael put his hands on the counter and said *Excuse me*, trying to keep the panic out of his voice. The man did not look up, but merely lifted his pencil and pointed at the other counter. Michael turned and looked at the line of crack addicts.

"You don't understand, I'm not here to sell. I sold something earlier and I need it back, immediately."

The man sighed heavily and looked up from his puzzle annoyed; his *peyot*, curly and dark brown, swung forward like a grandfather clock's arm when his head moved. "Wait in line." Again, he pointed, then looked back at his paper. Michael couldn't help but stare at the swinging hair, gently moving back and forth against the man's cheek.

"NO. I will die if I don't get back these items within the next few minutes." The man looked bored and annoyed as if he heard this nightly. Again, he pointed to the line again and repeated one word.

"Line."

Before the man could look back down to his puzzle, Michael lunged forward and grabbed both of the man's curly ringlets, pulled him forward and screamed into his face. "I need my fucking watches back!"

Michael had never attacked anyone in his life. Besides a fight in the third grade over a grilled cheese which lead

to a tiny scratch on his friend's forearm, he had never been physically violent, ever, and it scared him. His heart was pounding as he looked into the man's face, which oddly did not look frightened or even annoyed; it just looked blank and bored. Michael pulled outward on the *peyots*, trying to push across his point. The man reached up, put his hands on Michael's, and gently pulled them away.

"Leave now," the man said, checking his curls with both hands.

Michael looked around the room, saw some of the watches in a case, and ran to them. Time was short. If he had to break some laws to save his life, then so be it.

When he turned around again, he saw a golf bag with some clubs; he raced over to it, pulled out a nine iron, and ran to the case. Without thinking, he raised the club over his head and brought it down on the glass. To his amazement, it did not smash into a million pieces like it did in the movies; it only spider webbed an intricate pattern of cracks. Two, three, four more swings and it finally cracked open, sending shards into the display and onto the floor. As he reached into the case, he saw three men-- big men-- suddenly surrounding him. He was old, fat-- really fat-- and beyond out of shape: he couldn't win a fight with a six-year-old, let alone three beefy men, yet with adrenaline suddenly pumping through his veins, he turned and swung the golf club at the closest one. The man, sporting a shaved head and a good foot taller than Michael, put up his forearm to block the swing. Normally, he would have gagged at the sight of the man's forearm snapping and his hand bending over to touch his

elbow in an incredibly unnatural way, but he didn't have time to stop. As the first man fell to the ground screaming, Michael swung at the other who ducked the swipe, though it ended up working in Michael's favor as the third man, the fairest of the bunch, didn't expect this and the club caught him right in the eye. The crunching bone could be felt all the way up the handle of the club, and Michael watched in awe as the eye bulged out and then dropped down his face like it was trying to escape his head.

While the adrenaline was still pumping, Michael stopped to watch the man fall to the ground, his mouth opening and closing like a fish trying to get air. Just as the man hit the ground, the other one who ducked lunged at Michael and sent him into the case. His back instantly screamed with pain as the metal bar dug into his skin and shards of glass bit at him like angry dogs. The man hadn't planned his attack too well though, as his head, which was at Michael's side, went right into the case, glass cutting the sides of his face. Michael, being the one on top, was able to hold him down, pushing him against the glass. As the man reached back, Michael picked up a shard of glass and without thinking even for a split second, slammed it down on the back of the man's neck. The shard slid in with ease, and the man's arms dropped as he, too, fell to the floor.

Backing up, Michael looked around, in shock and a bit excited that he had just taken down three men who were trained security guards. Trying not to waste time, he reached into the case and grabbed the four watches he recognized. Stepping back, he noticed the man he had

just stabbed was no longer moving; his chest went up and down ever so slowly, then stopped. A mere fraction of a second later, the watch on his arm suddenly stung him. It was like the watch came out of a fire-hot oven and slapped around his wrist. Michael screamed and lifted his arm to look at the watch. It glowed orange ever so lightly and the hands suddenly spun rapidly backwards. Then it instantly cooled and started to tick normally.

Michael didn't have to think about this: somehow, he knew what had just happened. By killing the man, he had stolen the man's "time." He let out a loud laugh, then looked at the man who was lying on the ground, his hand over his drooping eye. The guy's mouth was still opening and closing. Stepping on glass with soft crunches, Michael took two steps closer to fish mouth, steadied himself, raised one foot, then stomped down on the man's head. The feeling of skull was odd under his foot. It was solid yet had squishy elements. The second stomp felt the same, but the third one was different: there was some give to it. The fourth one cracked through the man's skull like a cantaloupe being crushed. Instantly, his watch glowed and the time spun backwards again. Michael laughed, then looked to the man cowering against the case behind him, holding his floppy arm. Michael reached into the glass case, picked out a nice, long shard of glass and went over to him. The guy mumbled and shook his head "no" frantically, but Michael put a finger to his mouth to shush him.

"I need to know where the rest of these watches are, I need to know now or else I'll have to take away your time."

The man's eyes were wide. "Ask Akiva, ask Akiva: he is in charge. I only do security. I'm just part-time man. Please, please: I already have broken arm. Just let me go," the man begged with genuine fear.

Michael found the man's terror exhilarating. Having this power of knowing he could make someone live or die: he had never felt such a rush before. Michael put his hand on the top of the man's head, like a priest blessing someone. As he was about to get up, he changed his mind and quickly plunged the shard behind the man's left ear. It didn't go in as far as he liked and it snapped off when he tried to pull it back up, so Michael reached down, grabbed the man around the neck and started to choke him. The way the man's throat felt under his fingers and palm was nauseating. Thick, stringy veins and tendons undulated and popped under his fingers. Thick cord-like muscles strained and he could even feel the man's Adam's apple snap and push into his throat with a gurgling sound. After what seemed like an eternity and twenty different shades of color washing over the man's face, Michael's watch glowed hot again and the man dropped to the ground. *This is what POWER feels like,* Michael thought as he got up and confidently strode toward the back room where the man he had grabbed earlier fled to hide.

Before he could walk behind the counter, the loudest sound he had ever heard rang in his years and a fiery hot poker of pain burst through his shoulder. A bullet had ripped right through him from the back, came out the front, and lodged itself in the wall ten paces away. Looking down at the gaping wound, he saw the skin

slowly start to crawl together, like some sort of sci-fi movie. As the wound closed, his watch turned icy and started to glow, this time a pale blue as the hands spun backwards. *I'm fucking invincible!* he thought incredulously. Michael turned, giving his best demonic, tough guy look and saw a small man nervously looking at him, holding a gun. When the man saw the wound was gone, he dropped the gun, made the sign of the cross on his body, turned, and ran. Michael laughed out loud, then headed for the back room.

To his dismay, there was no one there; the man had left out the back door. Quickly, Michael searched through every box and drawer trying to find his watches, but he surmised they had to be in the giant safe built into the wall unless they were already sold. As he heard sirens, he raced to the safe and gave it one quick test. Locked, of course. Running out the back door, he decided he didn't need the watches: he had all the power he ever needed with the one on his wrist. He could simply *take* all the time he ever wanted. Hell, he could live for centuries. There was just the matter of dealing with whoever the guy was back at the hotel.

Michael debated just getting the hell out of the city. The chances of the man following him seemed astronomical... but he did know where to find him. He had seen enough movies to know loose ends always come back to bite you in the ass. He'd confront the man, ask him some questions about the watch and the powers it held, and if it didn't go well, he'd take the man's time away from him. Part of him didn't believe he had no qualms about taking a life, not even the slightest

hesitation, but he was a new man now. No longer was he the weak nobody who meant nothing to anyone and would die with only his wife crying at his funeral. History would not remember that man anyway. The new Michael: *he* could do and become whatever he wanted: people would remember him, but first, he had to take care of that dead end.

By the time he started up the elevator, he noticed that there was a mere ten minutes left on his so-called "deadline," and he laughed at this thought. As the door opened, he felt in his pocket to make sure the small knife he just bought at a hardware store on Eight Avenue was still there and ready to pull out at a moment's notice. He liked how hard it felt in his pocket; more so, he liked the idea of having a weapon on him, as he had never carried one before. Originally, he was going to take the gun the man dropped, but a shot in a swanky hotel would cause a SWAT team to arrive before he could ever get down to the lobby. As he patted it, a small part of him knew that he was not going to let the man live, regardless of what happened.

He pulled out his key, stuck it in the slot, turned the handle, and entered the room with a confidence he had never felt before; it was as if he owned the damn place and nothing could ever touch him. He was a bit surprised to see the man was already there, sitting on chair in the room's entrance area, the same chair he felt so weak and exposed in just a few hours before. The man looked... old, though like a gentleman you'd see in old time England: cleanly dressed, hands folded on his lap, legs

pressed together. Part of Michael wanted to run right to him and stab that oddly changing face fifty times, but he pushed down the urge and shut the door. Reaching into his pocket, he pulled out the four watches and threw them on the seat next to the man, who casually looked down at them.

"That is all?" The question was light, not abrasive in any manner, as if he were asking if that was all of the cucumber sandwiches left at the tea party. Michael nodded his head and licked his teeth in an odd sucking manner, another first for him. It was in that moment he realized: he had not a drop of indigestion. He hadn't even thought of Tums in the past two hours, the longest stretch in his memory. Again, he chuckled to himself. He liked this new life.

"What a shame." The man got up, brushed his jacket off, looked at his own watch and sighed. Michael reached into his pocket, grasped the knife and started to breathe heavily, not from fear, but excitement.

"Two minutes left, my friend. Any last requests?" The man said, again looking at his watch as if watching the second hand and waiting for the two minutes to expire.

"I could ask the same thing," Michael said, pulling out the knife. The man looked up curious, but then quickly rolled his eyes at the sight of Michael presenting the small, three-inch work knife. As the man looked at his watch again, Michael pointed the knife at him and readied his feet as if about to lunge.

"I figured out how this thing works. I already got three people's time... don't mind getting some more either."

Hearing Michael's comments, the man's face finally showed a bit of concern. "Did you now? Well, I guess you are a fast learner." Again, the man brushed his smoking jacket, trying to get off invisible lint.

"Why did you have so many watches, can we use more than one? Do you have them in case one breaks? Are you a... time dealer or something?" The curiosity spilled from Michael's mouth uncontrolled.

The man took a step to the side, a tougher look on his face now. "Fine, you win. There is no point in me staying. You will live a long, long time, just like me. Let me tell you, though, with this power comes a lot of complications. Time and power can be addicting; don't let the ideas overtake the reality. Let me show you a few things, so you don't kill yourself or others with the watch. Take it off."

Michael hesitated, but part of him believed the man and he wanted to know all of the secrets. "You try anything and I'll split you ear to ear and suck up whatever time you have left," he warned. The man nodded and gestured for Michael to take the watch off.

Keeping his eyes on the man, he kept the knife in his hand and unclasped the watch. Slipping it off his wrist, Michael felt a strange tingle all over his body, like a million miniature fireworks going off. Instantly, he felt dizzy and stumbled for the seat. Falling into it, he noticed how the cushion was still warm from the man's body. With his left hand shaking, he looked at the skin

on the back of it and realized that it seemed to be undulating. Before he could even flinch, the man snapped the watch out of Michael's hand. The second it moved away from his body, Michael let out a gasp. His skin suddenly puckered and shriveled like a prune. His skin was suddenly becoming old, really old.

"Lesson number one, Michael: never, ever, take off the watch. If you have lost your personal time, the time you were born with-- and I can tell you have by the blood and the smoky hole in your shirt-- you lose *all* time. Not just yours or the time you stole, but all time. Once you have the watch on, it bonds with you. When your time is gone, you are living on borrowed, or more so, *stolen*, time that the watch feeds you. Without it on your body, your own time doesn't exist."

Michael looked at the knife in his hand, tried to get up to stab the man and get his watch back, but his fingers ached: he could hardly squeeze the handle. As he tried to stand, his knees popped with pain. His teeth then started to feel loose and somehow ancient. The room started to blur and skin sagged more and more.

"Wha...why are you doing this to me?" Michael asked in a raspy voice that he did not recognize.

"Because, you stole time from me, time I might never get back, so I need all the time I can get now," the man said, slipping on Michael's watch. When the clasp was hitched, Michael noticed the man suddenly looked young again.

"If... if the watches were so powerful, why on earth did you check the bag?" Michael asked weakly. The now younger man smiled widely.

"There is much you will never know. But I let you take the bag. I sat and watched you. I'm a watchmaker, Michael. I was giving you a chance to... join the ranks of our kind. Instead, you let greed and desire win. It's a shame. The others told me you didn't have what it takes and they were right."

Michael's breathing got harder and harder as he watched the man once again brush the nonexistent lint off of his coat and walk away. The confusion and desire to know more was intense with him, but then he knew his time was up and he would never know more than the fact that there was much more to the world than he ever imagined.

Falling over onto his side, his face pushing against the plush cushion of the opulent chair, he couldn't focus his mind on anything in particular. He thought of his wife briefly and how she would always wonder what happened to him. The body they will find in the hotel room will be that of an old man, so he would just be a missing person forever.

He thought of the life he was going to have with the watch.

He thought of the watchmaker and what the hell it all meant. Then a brief flash of guilt washed over him for the men he killed, but it was replaced with the joy it had brought.

Lastly, he thought of his luggage and how he wished he had just gotten the damn colored nametags his wife had told him to get. If he had, he'd be home right now, lying in bed, with all the time in the world to kill.

DELICIOUS FLESH

Do you like pork rinds? If you do, you'll love this. Even if you don't, I suggest you try it anyway. Oh, how about bacon? Everyone loves bacon! That is really the closest thing to it, I guess. What I am saying is that once you get past the idea that you are eating human flesh, it is rather delicious. Seriously. I mean, really: think about it. Besides those stupid vegetarians, most people eat meat every day: cow, pig, lamb, and countless other animals. So why should humans be off the list of edible creatures? Just because we talk and think? What the hell is a *moo* then? Animals communicate; they think. See? No difference. Now try a bite.

Fine.

But I'll tell you right now, I'm only going to give you one more try before I start to cut pieces off you and cook those. Lose one toe and you'll be greedily gobbling down one of my dishes. You do know I am a chef. These are not some run-of-the mill Hamburger Helper meals I'm trying to feed you. Vichyssoise of eye. Nicholas Wellington. Cream of Tim for dessert. Really: it is good stuff. Trust me. Once you try it, you'll realize I was right, and you'll be begging me for some Sam-ka-bob. You'll be raving to everyone about my food!

Only instead of going to the grocery store to shop, we'll be hunting in the aisles. It really is the best place to find people to eat. I bet you are wondering why. Well, the reason is because you can walk around with a cart, pretend to look at items, but really be watching someone. As long as you are not stupid, no one notices you doing it. Then, while you watch, you can size them up. Will they be too fatty? Do they have too much muscle? The more muscular they are, the tougher the meat. Best of all, you can see what the person eats. That has a lot to do with flavor, you know. Sort of like how poultry changes color by what the chicken eat or how those Kobe cows are feed beer so they taste better. You see, I won't pick anyone that buys Oreos. Someone who buys a lot of vegetables on the other hand? De-Lish!

Say the word *cannibal* and what do you think of? What's the first thing that pops into your mind? I know, you can't say it with the gag in your mouth, but I'd be willing to bet that it is Hannibal Lecter or *The Texas Chainsaw Massacre*. Was I right? I knew it! Anyway, *Texas*? Piece of shit. So stupid and fake. Hannibal, on the other hand: that is more like me. Sophisticated, elegant, and smart. Though with me, this isn't about killing. In fact, I try to follow the strictest of humane killing methods. I do my best to research the meat I hunt to minimize the effects of the kill. The less family, the better. The older, the better, though too old gets sort of funny tasting. Ideally, I go for a single, late-thirties human. Then, when I go after them, I try to kill with one smack to the back of the head. Even if doesn't kill them,

they are at least knocked out and then I can kill them quickly and they feel no pain, so it *is* humane.

The hard part is getting rid of the evidence. Filleting the corpse is no problem: I learned how to do a cow in culinary school; this is not much different. With these, though, you have to dispose of all of the trace elements to make sure you don't get caught: the blood, the hair, the skin, the clothing, and worst of all, the bones. I have gotten my methods down pretty good now. Haven't gotten caught yet, have I? Those secrets I won't tell you though. Once I get rid of that stuff, I'm left with some wonderful meat. From a two-hundred-pound person, I usually glean sixty to eighty pounds of good meat. It looks pretty much like beef, so when it is in the fridge, no one will ask questions. Usually. If they do, well, then I end up with some more meat!

As for the cooking process, I don't really do anything different than I would with regular meat. Maybe I add a bit more tenderizing or marinating on certain pieces, but mostly, I just use my cooking magic to whip up something amazing. I have been telling my customers that they are eating exotic animals from Africa. People have been going nuts for it. It is what brought you here, isn't it? Your review is going to get me a five-star rating. Of course, you had to do research before coming here to eat, nosy bitch. You had to go and find out that no sellers sell African game. You had to look up African elk and find out that they are endangered and can't be sold for their meat. You had to go and confront me in my own kitchen-- in front of my staff, nonetheless. You dare to threaten to expose me in the paper? 'Threaten to have

the Board of Health come in and examine my meat to find its origins and see if it is legal? You have a lot of balls, Miss. A lot of balls.

Thankfully for me, you don't have a doorman at your building. And you haven't submitted your article yet. I guess it is my lucky day. Then again, if it was my lucky day, you would have a better-stocked kitchen. You know, for a food critic, you really have shit for food; not only that, but your utensils and cookware: I mean, really. How can you criticize someone and not even have a proper sauté pan? Hypocrite.

Okay, last chance. Take a bite of my garlic and chipotle crispy flesh appetizer or you'll lose your pinky toe. Not going to open your mouth, huh? Fine, toe it is. Yikes! Hurts like a mother, doesn't it? You know, you'll always walk a bit funny now, though that is nothing compared to the big toe. The big toe totally controls your balance. I'll take that one next if you don't take a bite. I really don't see what the big deal is: hundreds have eaten this stuff and loved it; the only difference is, they didn't know what it was. Oh, oh, you are opening your mouth. Ata girl! Now chew it. Chew. Good, good. Here, take a sip of this wine: it goes perfect with it. Great. Now... what do you think?

Holy... shit, right? I knew it! I knew it! You love it, don't you? I understand: the thought is conflicting. That is just your upbringing speaking to you. Once you get around that, you'll have no problem. You'll be eating better food than you ever have before.

You want to try more, right? Ata girl! Keep eating, make it through all three courses, and I'll untie you, and you will want to hug me, not kill me-- trust me.

Was that not the best meal you ever had? I mean, *ever?*

I'm glad you can admit it. Now here is what you will do with your review. You'll tell the world it was the best meal you ever had. I'll become famous-- rich-- and I'll always feed you like a queen.

Sadly, I'll only be able to get away with this for a short time. If you caught on, someone else will too. What will you do then? It doesn't matter. By that time, thousands will have had human flesh, will have loved it, and when they find out, they will be disgusted, but they will then look at their lovers, their friends, and their bosses a bit differently: they will be wondering what they taste like, because the best meal in their lives was a human.

DRIP

The blood started to coagulate on the table. Thomas always loved this part; it was the calm after the storm. He would sit and dip his finger in the thickening puddle, lift his finger up, and let the blood drip off. When it got thick, making it harder to drip off his fingers, he would smile. The thickness would bring back flashes of the memory. The memory wasn't clear; in fact, he didn't even know what it was really. All he knew was he was young, covered in someone's blood and... happy. Although he only got flashes of the memory, he knew it was the best moment of his life. It was why he now played with blood, for it was the closest he could get to that happiness.

Regardless of how many times he did this ritual, he never got the full memory back. He was always chasing it, though it didn't matter: the moments he had with the blood were his happiest. The ritual always started with the need of fresh blood. He tried bottled pig's blood from the butcher once, but it didn't do anything for him. It was cold and not fresh. From there he went on to small animals and worked his way up to cats, dogs, and even a goat once. Seeing the furry corpses next to him ruined the moment; animals just were not enough. The first time he used human blood, he had a moment of

clarity. When the blood thickened and dropped off of his finger, the world stopped spinning. Nothing mattered; there were no problems: *everything* was perfect.

Victims didn't matter. He had no preference: white, black, Hispanic, male, female. They all had the same red, wonderful blood pumping through them. There was no time wasted finding victims. He didn't stalk prey like a lot of killers; Tom would merely drive around until he found someone alone and vulnerable. Using an excuse-- directions, a lost pet, or even acting as a sales man-- he would get them close enough to grab, knock them out, throw them in the car, and drive off. In his house, he would drag them inside, tie them up to a chair at the kitchen table, and then take a shower to relax and prepare. Clean of the dirty outside world, he would approach the table naked. When he first started this, he had a wooden table, but the wood soaked up the blood. He wanted it all for himself, so he bought a solid marble table, and it worked wonders.

At first, he cut their necks to release their precious liquid, but it squirted all over and made a mess; besides, he lost too much that way. After a few experiments, he devised a method of tying their wrists to the chandelier above the table and cutting a small hole in their armpit to bleed them out. It was easier to control the blood that way. Of course, there was always spill over, but that didn't matter. When he did that, the table was covered in a nice thin layer. Once it was, he would tie off the arm. At first, he killed the victim at this point, but then he realized if he kept them alive, he could repeat this several times before they would die, which was much more

efficient than having to get a new victim each day. Some he could keep for up to a few weeks if he fed them. This was very convenient, as he never enjoyed the hunting.

Disposing of the bodies was not a problem. Owning a pottery studio made things easy. When he started his hobby of bloodletting and killing, he purchased an industrial kiln, as no one would ever be suspicious of a pottery studio buying a kiln. Only, he used his to incinerate his victims. Almost no one realizes that a kiln reaches above what a crematorium does, upwards of 1900 degrees. A body only needs around 1400 to turn to ash. With a few chops, he would get the bodies down to a size that fit in the large oven. After a few hours, nothing would be left but a pile of ash and some bone chunks. After a quick cool down, he would scoop up and pour the ash in the river that ran behind the studio. It was perfect: everything always went well and he never feared getting caught, and every night, he was able to bring himself to heaven.

Late one night after cleaning up after his last victim, disposing of his ashes, and taking a quick nap, Thomas set out to get a fresh source of blood. It was not that he was going to do it again that night; he just wanted to have a fresh source on hand for the next morning. It was a little after twelve at night when he started his usual route, a carefully planned path that steered clear off all security cameras. On his second tour, he saw a young Hispanic-looking man bundled up and scurrying down the sidewalk. Tom pulled up alongside of him and tried the casual routine first.

"It's freezing out, man: you want a ride?" The man jumped a bit, backed away from the car, and stared at Tom like he was the boogeyman. Tom let out a laugh to show him he was kind and put up a hand to indicate he was not a threat.

"Sorry to scare you. I'm just heading home from work, I'm a cook at Lucky's Dinner down the road." The kid looked around as if to make sure no one saw him talking to the car. Tom could see the snot building up around the guy's nose, his cheeks burning red with beautiful blood pumping under the skin.

"Hey, no skin off my back if you don't. I'm not the one freezing, man: have a good night," Tom said, starting to slowly roll up the window and pull away.

"Wait!" It was too easy. Within seconds, the man was in the car and putting his hands up to the heater to warm. Tom didn't even bother to pretend to be nice: as soon as the door was shut and locked, he swung his forearm into the middle of the man's forehead. There was a loud wet smacking noise and the man fell unconscious. Tom's technique almost always worked, hardly needing more than one hit. By strapping a metal pipe to his forearm, then concealing it under his coat sleeve, he was able to knock them out with ease.

Parked in his garage at home, he quickly and efficiently dragged the man out of his car and into the kitchen. It took all of eight minutes to have the man tied to the chair (which was placed in a small plastic Kiddie pool to catch any spilled blood), his arm dangling, eyes covered, and his mouth gagged. The man would wake up any minute, but it didn't matter. They all kicked and

thrashed. Most cried and tons pleaded through the gag, but Tom never humored them by talking or listening. They were not people to him-- they were just like a water bottle that held what he needed: once empty, they were discarded. Only when he fed them, he would remove the gag and let them drink a nutrition shake. They would always scream bloody murder and cry for help, but Tom's house and connecting studio was on three acres of land, isolated from any nearby houses. The screams were never heard.

As Tom slept that night, he heard the screams and thrashes, but they didn't bother him and he knew his restraints would hold, so he slowly fell asleep and dreamed of what the morning held.

After waking up and having a quick breakfast, Tom sat down next to the man to make the first cut and fill his bowl. Almost instantly, the man woke up and started the typical kicking and screaming. Thankfully, the chair was bolted to the floor through the small plastic pool. Tom sighed and stepped back to let the man settle down for a minute. Staring at the blood vessel of a man in front of him, he wished there was another way to get blood without having to kill, for humans were such a pain in the ass. If he could just get the blood warm and fresh from some other method, he would, but there was no other way.

When the man finally stopped thrashing, Tom quietly snuck up from behind and stuck the knife into the left armpit. Of course, there was more kicking and screaming now, but the man couldn't move too much, so it didn't

bother him. There would be some blood spillage, but some was acceptable; humans have a lot of it, after all, and the body will replenish what it loses… to a limit. of course.

Once he filled one bowl, he set it on the table and quickly filled another, setting that on the table as well. Then he took his rubber tie off, which consisted of a bungee cord, a patch of cloth, and some rubber from an exercise band, and tied it around the man's shoulder and armpit to seal off as much of the bleeding as possible. *Waste not, want not!* Already naked, Tom could feel himself getting aroused; this was the part, this was the thing he loved. Hoping up on the table, the cold marble stung his ass, sending a wave of goose bumps over his body. He once thought about having a heated table, but he decided that the sting of the cold made the warmth of the blood even more enjoyable.

Holding the first bowl to his nose, he closed his eyes and took a deep breath of the copper smelling liquid. Tom could feel himself about to cry. Then, with one quick motion, he poured the blood over his face, letting it drip down over his chest and down to his groin. Lying back on the table, the cold nipped at his back, but the front of him was warm and moist. Setting the bowl aside, he started to rub the precious liquid all over his body. Opening his lips, he savored the bitter familiar flavor as gobs of blood spilled into his mouth. He never swallowed it, though; he just tasted it then gently pushed it out of his mouth, letting it drip down his body. Of course, his hands quickly found their way down to his hard penis;

using the blood as a lubricant, he slowly stroked himself, trying to savor each long caress.

As the blood cooled on his skin all too quickly, like always, he picked up the next bowl and slowly poured it over his stomach and groin. He always saved a little bit in the bowl so he could pour more on himself in case he didn't "finish" his routine quick enough. This time, though, he finished stroking himself seconds after the second warm splash covered his penis. The fluid that came out of him-- the white, disgusting stuff-- always bothered him, but it was a necessary evil. He could not have that wonderful feeling without producing that white shit. It was the stuff his mother used to make him swallow if she found him masturbating as a child. He always would purposely point his shot away from his body so that it landed down by his feet, away from the precious blood.

As he went soft, Tom would lay there, letting the blood get cool, slowly playing with it on the table, dipping his fingers one at a time in as it congealed, watching it drop off, waiting for it to thicken. This part was always the most relaxing. The moments leading up to this were intense, but this, this was pure heaven, when nothing was on his mind but the blood and how beautiful it was.

Sometimes it would take an hour, maybe two, before he would get up from the table; other nights it would only be minutes. It was just a matter of mood and the blood. Tonight, it was only an hour or so before he got up to do the clean-up, which he hated. Not only did he hate it because it was work, but it killed him to see the beautiful red stuff washed down the drain. The table cleaned up

with a squeegee, the floor with a mop, and himself in the shower. There were designated "blood" mats throughout his house that he would walk on to and from different parts of the house in order to not get red drops anywhere else. Amazingly, after thirty-three blood donors, he only had to rent a carpet cleaner once: the time he slipped and fell on living room carpet.

In the shower, with the water on scalding hot, Tom did his best to not look down at the drain the first few minutes. If he saw the red turning to pink as it swirled in the drain, he would have a breakdown. It happened many times before: he would see it leaving him, disappearing into nothing, and he would start to cry. A few of the times this happened, he found himself sitting on the shower floor, hugging his knees and sobbing until the shower ran out of hot water. He was very careful to not have this happen, but it still did from time to time. Tonight, he was able to clean up without looking down at that awful drain.

Dried off and in his comfy flannel pajamas, it was time for a light snack and some television before going to bed. The blood donor would stay in the kitchen; most likely, he would thrash and scream through the night, but the sounds never woke Tom up, and in a way, it lulled him. Walking down the hall, he tried to decide if he wanted to be good and have some fruit or if he was going to be bad and eat the leftover ice cream he bought last week. When he rounded the corner to the kitchen, still going back and forth on what to eat, he almost fainted when he saw that the chair was empty. *Impossible...*

This had never happened before. How could it? His knots were perfect; the chain on the man's hand was tight: Houdini himself couldn't get out of his ties. How could... it didn't matter, what mattered was that some lunatic was loose in his house, or maybe even gone, trying to get help that very moment. Tom shook his head, trying to snap himself into the reality of what was happening. *Think, think, think... the man will have a concussion, he will be dizzy. The wound in his pit won't affect him much, though it will bleed. I took about a quart of blood out of him. The human body has six quarts, forty percent blood loss equals death. That means he has about eighteen percent less blood than normal; his heart rate will be picking up, and he will be weaker. That will make him a bit slow as well. He shouldn't be getting too far. Then again, with adrenaline, he might be able to... STOP!* Tom snapped himself out of his thoughts, knowing he had to move and find him, not stand and think.

Racing to the back door, Tom was amazed to find it shut and locked from the inside, which meant he didn't leave that way. A quick sprint to the front door told Tom the man hadn't left that way either. *A window?* Tom thought, as he raced from window to window, finding them all shut and locked. *He is still in the house.* With this knowledge, Tom relaxed a bit. He didn't have to worry about the man bringing back the cops; all he had to do was find him and knock him out again. His house was a decent size, but not that big, so it shouldn't be too hard. He just had to make sure the man didn't jump out and attack him-- he did leave a few knives on the counter after all... and two of them were missing.

Tom searched slowly and carefully, making sure he checked every possible hiding spot in his house. He checked the cabinets, the closets, even the fridge, but he just could not find the guy. Room after room, he was shocked to not find this man, not even a drop of blood. When only one room was left, the office, he was sure the man was in there; if he wasn't, then he had just disappeared. A cursory glance told him that the room was empty. The man *had* to be in the closet then. Creeping towards the door, Tom planned his attack. *Open it quickly and surprise him, or open it slowly, let the man try to jump out, then slam the guy's arm in the door?* Regardless of the decision, his heart was racing. Even when he got his donors, his heart didn't race this much. This was probably because none of them were ever expecting to be attacked, so they were off guard. This guy had a knife-- no, two knives-- on him and was *waiting* for him.

Trying not to tremble, he put his hand on the handle, readied the knife in his hand, and took a deep breath. He would open it a few inches, keep his foot at the base, and as soon as the man jumped, he'd slam the door on his arm, then swing it back open and attack him. *One, two... three.* Tom inched the door open, waited for the attack... and nothing. A few more inches open, nothing. When he swung the door all the way open to see no one was there, he felt faint. *What the fuck was going on?* Frantically, he raced through the entire house again. There was nothing, not even a sign of the man. No clues, no blood drops, nothing out of place. It was as if the man was never there.

Back in the kitchen, he put his hands on the cold marble, the marble he had been on, covered in the man's blood, only an hour before. *What the fuck?* Tom did his best to think. Was he going nuts? Losing his mind? It couldn't be: he had done this dozens of times, he had felt the blood, enjoyed the release; it was *very* real. So then, where did this guy go? *Drip.* The sound came from down the hall. *What the hell was that?* Grabbing his knife, he edged around the corner, waiting to see the man standing there, dripping the precious blood onto the floor. The man wasn't there; however, there was one beautiful, tiny drop of blood in the middle of the hallway.

Tom looked around, then cautiously went to the blood. Just as he went to touch it, another drop fell. Looking up, he thought of the hundreds of movies and TV shows he had seen where someone investigates a drop of blood only to find a body or be attacked by the killer. He took caution and brought his eyes to the ceiling. The round glass dome that held the light had a stunning trickle of red running down it, pooling at its tip, building up and falling off to the ground. Tom was in such shock at its beauty, he almost forgot that he was searching for someone, someone who was most likely hiding in his attic, the one place he didn't think of looking.

Knowing there was no way out of the attic, Tom sat down in the hallway and watched the dripping blood for several minutes. It was just memorizing. The blood would leisurely flow from the base of the light down a slick line to the end, and slowly build up until it couldn't hold on anymore, then one beautiful drop of blood would let go and fall to the floor. Its impact sent a splatter of

blood in a two-foot radius, making the white floor look like a Jackson Pollock painting, with one concentration of red right in the center. Each drop that fell made him smile more, especially as the puddle grew in size.

Drip... Drip... Drip... Drip... Drip... Drip... Drip... Drip... Tom counted the drips, not wanting this spectacular show to end. It was so magical, so perfect. It reminded him of... it was just out of reach of his memory, but whatever it was, he knew it was wonderful. By the seventy-eighth drip, the puddle was the size of a small pizza. The walls were now getting splattered and the floor was speckled with so much blood, it looked as if someone's throat had been slit in that very spot. With that thought in his head, suddenly the memory came back much clearer than ever before... his mother.

The memory was fuzzy, quick and jumbled, but parts of him could remember his mother, naked on top of him, how warm and wonderful she felt... but then the knife... the hole in her neck and how the blood felt on him. A loud cracking noise in the attic took him out of his memory, the memory he had been searching for for years. This infuriated Tom and with one quick movement, he was up and running to the spare bedroom closet where the entrance to the attic lay. The man had stopped his memory and for that, he would pay. Tom believed the man had lost enough blood that he would not be much of a threat; besides, there was nothing in the attic except insulation, so it wouldn't be hard for him to find him. He just had to be sure the man didn't attack him the second he popped his head up.

Hard as he could, he thrust up the small piece of wood that plugged the top of the square hole in the ceiling. There was only a small stepstool and some coats in the closet, so he was impressed the man was able to get up there with his wound. Keeping his head down, he waited for the attack, but nothing came. Stepping on the stool, he readied his knife and stuck it up in the air, swinging it around the opening, hoping to catch the scrawny man. Nothing happened. The man had to be passed out; this was his chance. Stepping on the top step, he quickly popped his head up into the hole, knife by his face. Spinning his head around, he saw the man lying on his stomach about twenty feet away. Perfect.

Climbing into the attic, he carefully stepped on the support beams, making sure to not step on the insulation, as he would fall right through the ceiling if he did. The man was lying right across the beams. All Tom had to do was walk over, stab him once in the back, then drag him to the hole, throw him through, and clean the mess up. It would be a pain in the ass, but at least everything was going to be all right.

Even though the man was still, Tom approached carefully, in case he was playing possum. With his feet balancing on the thin two-by-fours, Tom steadied his knife and swung it down at the man, who quickly rolled away. Tom couldn't stop his motion and went flying forward, the knife stabbing into the pink foam. Without the body to break his fall, Tom crashed right through the sheetrock ceiling. As his arms broke through, he dropped the knife. Just as his head followed his arms through the hole, Tom forgot the trouble he was in. Instead, he was

thinking, *wow, the hallway looks odd from this angle, and look at the sheetrock dust on the floor, mixing in with the blood: it is ruining the blood, the perfect blood!*

Before his mind could clear, before he could think about pulling himself out of the hole and defending his life, the knife was in his throat. Stuck in the hole in the ceiling, his arms and head dangling down into the hallway and next to the light that was so beautiful minutes before, Tom felt the hot pain skid across his throat, followed by the beautiful warmth of the blood flowing over his chin, then his cheeks, and finally his eyes. It quickly got hard to breathe or even move. Tom didn't bother to try to do either. Instead, he wanted to watch the wonderful red liquid, his-- HIS blood, fall to the floor. He had to blink a few times to clear his vision, but once he did, he got to see the stunning shower of red falling to the floor. There were dozens of drops hitting at once, splattering and making wonderful art against the floor and walls.

Tom smiled, enjoying the warmth on his face and the wonderful show in front of his eyes. As his vision faded, he cherished the sound of the blood landing... *drip, drip, drip... drip.*

TIME LOCK

There were two days left before Kristof had to lock himself in the box. He always got a bit depressed around this time of the month. The nights in the box were hard, miserable, and exhausting. They were necessary, though. It was routine for him to go into the basement, make his way through the hidden passage, and check out the box days before the lockdown. It was ten feet by ten feet of solid steel with no windows and only one door. The door itself put most bank vaults to shame. Like the walls, it was over three feet thick. It had an advanced digital timer on it that ensured that once a time and code was punched into it, the door would shut on its own, lock, and not open, no matter what, until the timer ran out. Not even Kristof, the only person with the code, could open it. That was one of the main things he had programmed in when they designed the system. It was of utmost importance that nothing could get in or *out* for those few nights.

Part of the preparations was putting adequate food inside his temporary home. Kristof would always lug down several boxes of protein bars and other nonperishable food items. He knew most of them would get destroyed, but they needed to be there so he didn't get sick from hunger. He would place the boxes on the shelf

above the solid steel bed. Next, he would run the water in the sink to make sure it was working and flush the toilet; both were made from metal and virtually indestructible. Outside of the box he had a few shelves of supplies. There he kept a year's worth of bed sheets and pillows, one set for each month. Though he knew they would be shredded, he still liked to have them on the bed for some comfort beforehand.

Making the bed was when the depression would really set in. The days in the box were miserable. He'd be manic, raging, thrashing at the walls, trying to break the unbreakable, scratching at things uncontrollably, for hours on end. The days were filled with exhaustion, uncomfortable bouts of sleep and non-stop cursing of his damn burden. The few moments of clarity, which usually came around mid-day, were usually the most depressing as his mind was clear enough to think about the "events" that had happened before the box was built. The TV did little to sidetrack those thoughts, yet it was a lifesaver as it did occupy his thoughts for a few wonderful seconds every day, distracting him from the horror that his life was. Thinking of the television, he checked to see it was working. It was a thirty-two-inch flat screen that was built into the wall behind six-inches of bulletproof glass. Several times he had to have the glass replaced due to scratches, but the cost was worth it as books wouldn't last and it was his only form of entertainment. Also built into the wall, behind six inches of metal, were the speakers. The long tube the sound was forced out of resulted in a hollow, tinny sound, but at least he couldn't break them. Finally, there were the large steel buttons (somehow, they

had yet to be destroyed) to change the channel and volume.

With everything in order, Kristof set the timer for the correct cycle, double checked it, and left the basement. He would always pour himself a scotch at this point. It calmed him yet did nothing for his depression. *Three days*, he would tell himself. After those three days his depression would lift, he would be in a good mood, and life would be good until next time.

Slowly sipping his liquor, he sat in a high back leather chair in the stuffy library of his mansion, looking like a ridiculous snooty millionaire from some 1950's horror movie. He hated looking and feeling like that, but he had no choice but to take his family's money. He had a love/hate relationship with this old place. It was a dark, cold, and lifeless home. Yet it was free and his family's money provided him a good life. Life without the money would be intolerable, mostly because he wouldn't have been able to make the box. Without the box, he wouldn't be able to live with himself. After three more scotches, he would go about putting his affairs in order for his monthly "vacation."

The day Kristof was to go in the box he ate mounds of food. A huge breakfast, a hearty lunch, and at dinner, he stuffed himself so full he felt sick. He did this because the change made him famished, as the amount of calories burned in the conversion was astronomical. If he didn't have enough in his stomach, he'd have to live off the bars, and he would be angrier and crankier than normal. Around six that night, after his huge meal of several kinds

of grilled meats, he sent his staff away for three days. It was essential for him to have no one in the house when he was in the box, for the sounds would raise too much suspicion. Thankfully, his staff thought that the time off was nothing more than their boss being kind. That particular night, the crew was gone by seven. Kristof wandered the house, shutting off lights and closing windows. He got changed into his box clothing--a pair of cheap sweat pants, socks, and a t-shirt, all disposable. As he went downstairs to put on the alarm system, the doorbell rang. Kristof checked his watch; he only had a few minutes, so he ignored the ringing. Technically, he should be in the box earlier, but he just couldn't stand any extra time in there than was necessary, so at times, he cut it too close.

Sneaking past the massive frosted windows, he opened the alarm pad and started to punch in the numbers. That was when the pounding started.

"I know you are in there. I can hear you. Please answer the door, Sir. It's I, William." William was his head butler. He must have forgotten something.

"William, I'm in a hurry, but I have to go. I'm sorry." Kristof turned and started to walk away from the door. The banging became rapid.

"Please, Sir, please!" Kristof checked his watch-- less than five minutes. He raced to the door, shut off the alarm, and opened it.

"What is it William? I'm in a terrible hurry."

William, who was younger than Kristof, was winded and disheveled.

"What is wrong with you?" Kristof asked, a bit worried about him, but more worried about the time.

"Sir, I, I'm so sorry to bother you." William started to take off his coat. Kristof immediately grabbed him.

"Speak now or get out!" William's face was in shock and he stammered. Kristof looked at his watch. "Forget it: lock the door on the way out!"

Turning, Kristof started to run. He had less than two minutes to get locked in the vault. At thirty seconds, the door automatically started its slow swing shut. Racing through the halls and down the stairs, he was furious. He knew he shouldn't have answered the door. In all his years since he invented the box, this was the first time he had to rush. He was getting sloppy in his old age; years ago, he would have been in the box an hour before it shut. Now he only went down with five minutes to spare. He had been foolish.

Reaching the room, he saw the door was just starting its journey to being closed. The tension in his chest eased up a bit as he knew he would make it in. He slowed down, slipped into the room, and headed to the sink. Bracing the sink, he caught his breath. Relieved but still angry that William was in the house alone and needed to lock up, he would ask questions of his servant later.

"Ahhhrrrg." The sound behind him startled Kristof. Looking up into the mirror, he caught a glimpse of his sweaty face. Then he saw a figure that just squeezed past the closing door. Kristof spun around to see William looking at the shut door with curiosity and a bit of panic in his eyes.

"Sir, what is this?"

Kristof raced to the door, even though he knew there was no way to stop the massive gears from finishing its locking sequence. As his shoulder slammed into the steel he felt a blast of pain. It was too late.

"William, you fool! YOU FOOL!" He turned to see William tight to the wall, looking scared but baffled. Kristof wanted to punch the man, to tear him to shreds for his idiocy, but he knew a much worse fate would befall him in a few hours. Instead, he swallowed his rage and sat down on the edge of the bed, his hands in his face.

"Sir… I'm, confused. What is this place? I have never seen it in all the years I have worked for you."

Kristof kept his hands over his face, trying to ease the tension.

"You might as well sit down, William." Kristof could hear shuffling and knew William was sitting down on the floor. He had nowhere else to sit. "I hope you kissed your family good-bye today." Kristof said softly as he finally looked up and into William's wide eyes.

"I'm sorry, Sir? I don't understand."

Kristof nodded his head. "Well, William, I'm sorry, but you won't make it out of here alive."

The two sat in silence for a few moments. Kristof did not want to tell the truth. He did not want to face the inevitable. Kristof lay back on the bed, looked at his watch, and sighed when he saw there were less than two hours left.

"Sir… what is this room? What are you protecting yourself from?"

Kristof took his time answering and when he did, he didn't bother to sit up.

"William. I'm not protecting myself from anyone. I'm protecting everyone from me." Kristof could hear the man stir uncomfortably. Part of him didn't know if the words would come out, but he knew he had to tell the truth. The truth that was hidden deep inside, that he was raised to keep secret.

"I'm not like normal people. I... change. I become dangerous... at times." There was a long pause as he let William absorb what he said.

"So, you lock yourself in a room? Are you bi-polar? I don't get it."

Kristof let out a laugh. If it were that simple, he would be in heaven.

"It's a bit worse than that." Kristof got out of the bed, paced for a second then stopped to look at one of the deep gouges in the wall. He reached up and touched it. "It's a curse I have William... I'm a Werewolf." It was the first time he said it out loud in years: he wondered if dramatic music would play out of nowhere. *Dum, Dum, Dum.* While he was not expecting a scream, the response he got confused him, William simply laughed.

"Sir, are you trying to play a trick on me?"

Kristof glared at him, and the laughter subsided. Kristof rubbed the gouge in the wall; it caught William's eye. He got up and looked at it, then around the room.

"You are not kidding me, are you?" William said, astounded.

"No, I'm not. I lock myself in here every full moon so I don't kill anyone."

"But, but werewolves, they are…"

"Don't bother with the thought."

William sat down on the bed; Kristof took a seat next to him. The bed was small and the two were awkwardly close to each other. The room was built for one. William had worked for Kristof for years; they gave each other Christmas presents and cards on birthdays, but they were far from friends.

"Sir, if… if you are in here to protect people, what does that mean for me?"

Feeling more uncomfortable, Kristof got up, walked to the toilet, and sat down.

"It means when I change, I will most likely kill you. I have no control over the animal in me. Most of the time, I don't even remember what happened. It is why I created this box. It is absolutely impenetrable from the outside, and more so from the inside. I figured if I locked myself in something, then I wouldn't be able to hurt anyone. It has worked for almost a decade now."

William's face lit up.

"And that is why you send us all away once a month, not to go on a mini-vacation, but so you can lock yourself in here and no one would know."

Kristof nodded in response. "Yes, but now all of that will be over. Someone will know you came here. I will be investigated for your disappearance. They will find my box, ask questions, and all hell will break loose. I have been terrified of a day like this. The last time I didn't have my box…" He took a deep breath. "Thirteen people, William. Thirteen. I could barely live with myself. It was that very next day that I started work on this box.

If I get it taken away from me, a lot of lives will be lost." Kristof kicked at the floor lightly. William stood up for a second, but sat back down.

"William, what was so important that you followed me down here?" Kristof looked at the man's face. It turned red and eye contact was avoided.

"Nothing of importance."

This set off Kristof. "Not important!" He jumped up, raced over to the bed ready to hit William, but held back, knowing the pain he would feel later would be much worse. William cowered on the bed, covered his face, and curled into a ball.

"Tell me the truth: why did you come here tonight, why did you follow me?" Kristof backed up, giving William room to unroll.

"It, it was a dare, Sir. There had been rumors about your vacations for years. No one ever saw you leave the house. There were all sorts of crazy stories, though none as crazy as you being a werewolf. Jackson, who works in the kitchen, bet anyone five hundred dollars that no one would sneak in and find out what you do on these days. My son needs new braces and we can't afford them, so I took him up on the bet."

Kristof wiped his face; a stupid bet was going to end in another life lost.

"You could have asked me for the money. I would have given it to you. Now… now you are going to die because of a bet."

"I'm sorry, Sir. Really, I am."

"You don't have to apologize to me, apologize to your family, for they will be the ones to grieve you." Kristof saw a tear come out of William's eye.

During a stretch of silence, Kristof turned on the television to the local news. He kept the volume low, and the two just stared at the flickering image so they didn't have to stare at each other.

"How did you become a... werewolf?" William almost whispered.

Kristof said, staring at the television, "It runs in the family. My grandfather was one. It skips generations. When I turned ten, my father used to tie me up in the basement every full moon. For five years he did this and I never once changed. It was horrible, being a child tied down for days at a time. I hated him for it, but he was just being cautious." Kristof kept his vision on the flickering screen. He never told anyone his story, but maybe it was time. It would be good to get it out. Besides, William wouldn't live to tell it.

"After I hit puberty, around fifteen, that was the first time I changed. It was horrible. The first time the bones distend, grow, and snap, the first time the hair sprouts, it is insanely painful. Back then, my father used rope, not thinking I would be that strong at that age. When the transformation was complete, I snapped the ropes and nearly killed him. I raced upstairs-- at least this is what I was told... I remember nothing but the pain that night— and headed for my brother and sister, but grandfather had changed too. At his age, he was in control of his beast. He stopped me." Kristof finally broke his view of the

television, but only to check his watch. Time was running short.

Kristof saw William stiffen out of the corner of his eye. Instead of a scared, trembling man, he started to take on the posture of someone stronger, angrier.

"Sir, what happened as you got older?"

Kristof knew he was being humored, but he felt like getting the story out some more anyway, so he did.

"From then on they used iron chains. They kept me locked tight. My grandfather kept an eye on me during those times. He tried to teach me ways to control it, but I never could. I wasn't mentally strong enough yet. When I was twenty-two, my grandfather died. I no longer had a guardian. My father tried, but on the nights I broke my chains, he couldn't get the courage to shoot me, even though I wouldn't die from it." Kristof paused to take a drink of water from the sink.

"Your grandfather… how did he die?"

Kristof shut the tap off.

"We are not sure. One full moon we heard him off in the woods howling, and he never came home. Anyway, when I got older, I got stronger. My father made cages, I broke out of them. We tried sleeping pills and prescription tranquilizers, but nothing worked. He even shot the wolf version of me with animal tranquilizers. Still nothing happened. He said I just pulled them out and threw them at him. The first few years, my family would find me after the moon, naked in the backyard, covered in blood. I was only killing animals then." When Kristof looked at William, a quick peek, he saw the man fidgeting with his coat.

"I killed my first person when I was in my late twenties. When I awoke and found out, I tried to kill myself. That is when I found out that a werewolf can't kill himself or even die unless it's at the hands of a hunter and his silver. I'm not sure why that is and I don't give a shit: it's just a curse. Hell, I'm not even sure how it is possible for my body to transform like it does. It makes no sense, but it happens. I've spent millions having people research this crap, but all of them thought I was nuts and found nothing."

Looking at his watch, he realized only minutes were left.

"I don't have time to tell you my whole life story. Suffice to say, I realized I had to keep myself hidden on those nights. That is why I created this room. I haven't hurt anyone in years. And now, now I'm going to end up killing you."

"Is that why you created all of the charities that you run, to make up for your sins? For all those you have killed?"

Kristof nodded softly in response.

"Yes. It will never make up for what I have done, but it's something. You only have about a minute or two left before I change, William. If you're a praying man, I would pray now. I am truly sorry. Just know I will take care of your family financially: your grandkids will never have to worry."

"Thank you, Sir, but that won't be necessary."

Kristof could feel his gut twist and expand; it was the first sign, the beginning of the transformation.

"Don't... be silly. They... will be taken... care of," Kristof got out between gasps of pain as he fell to his knees. His vision started to get cloudy as he looked up. His eyes were always the next to switch. After they turned his vision into a sharp, stretched view, he would normally lose consciousness. He could hardly see William's legs approach him as he felt his skin start to bubble.

"Sir, I am sorry about this. Just think though: you'll be free after tonight."

Kristof forced himself to look up at William as his back legs snapped and stretched. He did his best to show William he didn't understand, though when he saw the large wavy silver blade William pulled out from his coat, he understood more.

"I'm a hunter, Sir. I was assigned to work here, the references you got on me were not a coincidence all those years ago. I was put here to watch you, to monitor you. I never thought I would get care about a monster like you, but you're a good person, Sir. I fought really, really hard on your behalf, but with the numbers of your kind dwindling, they decided to make the final blow and exterminate the rest of you, even the ones that don't hunt. Believe me, this is hard for me as well, but I have my orders."

As Kristof's vision turned gray and sharp, he saw the knife swing down in a low swoop, then up into his chest. The blade felt insanely hot. He could feel the transformation suddenly stop. As he fell to his side, he looked at his hands: there was no hair on them. He had changed back to himself. Trembling, he looked up at

Gore

William, smiled gently, and did the best he could to say, *thank you.*

THE JOGGING PATH

It happened when I went for a jog. I do a four-miler every day. I leave my house, take three rights, and then cut through the woods and end up at the opposite end of my street where I do a cool-down walk. I have been doing this for years. I see countless people as I go: some I know, some I don't. When I cut through the woods, usually I make it through without seeing anyone. There is a solid dirt path that is used often but still seldom enough that passing another person was not common. That day, as I entered the small path off of Elm Street, I thought about what to cook for dinner. Being a bachelor, several ideas that required little or no cooking came to mind. Ahead in the path, I saw a small child; he was maybe ten, twelve at the most, walking and slapping a stick at random objects. For some reason, my heart sped up.

Before that moment, I had never had anything like that feeling before: no impulse, no thoughts of... It was new to me. I passed the young boy who was wearing blue shorts and an Iron Man t-shirt; he said a shy *hi*, obviously nervous to have run into someone alone in the woods. I assumed he was just taking a shortcut home, one his parents probably told him to never take. Passing him, I suddenly stopped in my tracks, which was odd since I never stopped during, except when I was waiting

to cross a street. I felt like I was going to throw up; I hunched over and dry-heaved a bit. Out of the corner of my eye, I could see the child had stopped as well.

"You alright, mister?" I nodded my head and saw a thick stick in front of my face lying in a tuft of grass. It was as if it was put there, as if this was planned. Without thinking, I picked up the stick, gripped it with both hands, and took two quick steps forward. I swung hard enough to hit a home run out of the largest of ballparks. It was a direct hit. The kid's ear split open in a burst of red; I saw an eye dislocate and teeth fly as the boy fell to the ground. I didn't wait another second; I slammed the stick down onto his head five, six, maybe even eight more times. It was just a pulp of red hair, blood, and teeth when I was done. Looking around, I didn't see anyone, so I continued my jog. I kept the stick with me until two-tenths of a mile later when I passed by the pond that led out to the road. There I tossed it into the center of the water and waited for it to sink: thankfully, it was heavy enough that it dropped to the bottom fast. With that, I jogged out onto the road and resumed my run like normal.

The path came out on the dead-end road that I lived on. Three of the houses worked late, one retired couple was in Florida for the summer, and the other house's inhabitant was in a wheelchair and I never saw him. That day was no different: I saw no one. As I got to my house, I never even thought of what I had done. I stretched, took a shower, and checked my emails-- my normal routine. As I microwaved my dinner, I stared at the black tray spinning around. A red bubble of sauce perked up

and splattered. It was then that I realized I had just killed a kid.

I thought I was going to be sick. My stomach gurgled and I leaned over my sink ready to vomit, but as the microwave dinged, I realized it was merely hunger. As the wave passed, I pulled out my tiny meal of frozen spaghetti and ate with an appetite. I found I was so hungry I cooked two more meals-- another first for that day. As I was cleaning my fork, my gut fully extended, I heard the sirens. I looked out the window to see two cruisers go down my street, and I could tell others were on the other side of the woods. From my calculations, I figured the boy's body was about a half a mile from my house, and I would be interviewed soon.

After seeing a few of my neighbors come out of their houses and head to see what was going on, I figured I should as well. After exchanging polite greetings and asking what was going on, I stood staring at the mouth of the woods with the others, pretending to not know what had happened. After about ten more minutes, a rumor that a body was found started to circulate. It was followed by gasps and hushes. Another few minutes passed and our group grew to fifteen or so, and a news truck showed up. My neighbor Bill was picked to be interviewed, probably because he looked like the "average guy." After a while, I was getting bored and so were some of the other people, as they started to leave one by one.

An hour after I got home is when the police started to make their rounds and ask questions. My living room

looks out at the end of the street so I could keep an eye on everything that was going on, and I saw the cops going to the doors. Seeing this, I stood up, ready to panic, yet for some odd reason I felt nothing in my stomach. No butterflies, no nerves-- I felt as if I had done nothing, that I was not the cause of this. The fact that I had no remorse and wasn't scared at all was worse than the idea that I killed someone. I sat back down and un-muted the television, though I didn't watch it. When the knock came, I casually took my time getting the door; my pulse stayed steady.

"May we ask you a few questions?" the officer said. It was actually a woman wearing a pant suit, and she was pretty attractive, I must say. I quickly found myself playing the role of the curious bystander, asking what was going on: *Did they find a body or something? That was what everyone was saying.* She played it down, of course, and said she couldn't say much about the case just yet but asked if I had seen anyone suspicious or any vehicles come or go. That is when I dropped the bombshell.

"Man, it's weird. I jog through the path in those woods every day. I even did today at four and I didn't see a thing. Then again, I usually just focus on the path and run with my head down. My god! Did I run right by... a body?" As it came out of my mouth, *I* believed what I was saying. The comments perked her ears up a bit. She asked exact times, which way I entered the woods, what I saw, was there anything out of the normal.

"I passed a young kid. He was nice: 'got out of my way and stood on the side when I ran by. Shortly after, I ran by an older man, salt and pepper hair. He was walking

with a big stick and hardly got out of my way. That is the only reason I remember his hair color: I was pissed he was so rude and I looked back at him." Within a few minutes I had more detectives in my house along with a sketch artist and other people who I didn't know what they did. I politely offered them all coffee, which they accepted. I broke down at the appropriate time, when they told me the kid was dead. I sobbed: why didn't I think of looking out for the kid? Why didn't I pay attention? I could have saved him! They gave me tissues, patted my back, and told me I had no way of knowing, but that I could now help by getting the bastard who did this.

An hour later, I had given them all the information I could, they had a sketch (that later that night I saw on the news), and the woman who interviewed me, Carla Manson, gave me her card to call if her if I remembered anything or needed anything. I could tell she liked me, and with her not having a ring on, I knew I would call her soon. As I went to bed that night, I wondered if there was a reason I killed that kid. I prayed that it was a higher power that made me do it. Maybe it was so I would meet Carla? Whatever it was, I didn't lose any sleep over it.

Six years went by after that. The crime was never solved: rewards were never claimed. A memorial stone was put where Keith's body was found. (Everyone in town knew his name the day after I killed him. Everyone still does. There is a memorial golf tournament in his name every year.) During the months after, I started to date Carla, and two years later, we were married. I love

her tremendously and don't keep any secrets from her, except for one, which is hard because it is the only unsolved murder our town has (and it's pretty much the only murder our town has had in the past thirty years).

I never felt any guilt about the murder, which is why I knew it happened for a reason. A nice story kept me happy in my head. God made me kill Keith because he would have grown up to be a serial killer or a school shooter or something. Anytime his name was brought up, that was what I thought. His death had a purpose; it was what gave me the life I had: if I hadn't killed him, I would have never met Carla, the love of my life.

All those years later I still jogged that same path. When I ran by his marker I never even thought about what I did. Even the few times I used it to step on while I tied my shoe, it never crossed my mind. Not even when I met his parents in the months afterward. Not even when I volunteered at the call center to catch the suspect. I never felt the guilt, and I never thought something like it would happen again. That was why when I jogged past a tough-looking teen smoking a cigarette six years and three months after I first killed, I was shocked when that feeling bubbled up inside of me again. This one was a bit more difficult though. The teen ducked under the first swing of the stick, fell backwards, and tried to run away. Luckily, my running experience and running shoes enabled me to catch up to him and his heavy black boots before he reached the entrance of the woods. The smack I gave him in the back of the head knocked him down, but he tried to fight still. I had to swing twenty times, breaking his forearms, shattering his hip and collarbones,

before I finally got to his face. I hit it over and over again as if I was on autopilot, until his face was non-existent and I knew without a doubt he was dead.

Once again, I ran to the pond, threw the stick in, and watched it sink. This time though, I knew I couldn't get away with the same story, that I just missed the guy. So, I ran as fast as I could, to make up time, out of the woods and to the first house (since I never ran with a cell phone). I banged on the door and Leo (the guy in the wheelchair) opened the door with anger on his face.

"For fuck's sake, what do you want!?" Seeing me, he shut up; it was then that I looked down and saw that I was covered in blood splatters. Before I could open my mouth to ask to use his phone, I turned around, saw no one in sight, and kicked hard as I could at Leo's chest, sending him wheeling back into the house. It was a bit of an unfair fight, the man was old and a cripple, and I wasn't even in my forties and in good shape. I didn't use anything to kill him except my shoe. As he tried to crawl away, I stomped on his back, then his head, over and over again. Amazingly, my heart rate never rose: I knew this for a fact because Carla got me a Fitbit with a heart rate monitor for my last birthday. When I finished killing Leo, I looked at it and saw that my pulse was still at my steady jogging rate. Impressive.

Killing the teen, I knew I left minimal evidence; Leo, on the other hand, was going to be a mess. I would have more time though, being that he was indoors. I stood above his body and thought. DNA was going to be everywhere; my clothing was covered in both the kid's and Leo's blood. I was in a tight jam. The only way I felt

I could buy some time was to start a fire. It would take days before they realized he was murdered, and then there would be nothing to connect me to it. I lifted Leo back into his chair and looked around the house for candles. I found one on top of the television set that looked like it had been used often. I then wheeled Leo into his bedroom, placed him on the bed, and gently pushed his chair out of reach. After a second thought, I pulled Leo until he fell out of the bed, to make it look like he tried to get up, but fell and pushed the chair too far out of reach. I then went to the front of the house, looked outside, and saw no one around. I could make it across to my house in less than thirty seconds at full sprint.

I set a stack of magazines next to the candle, placing one a bit too close to the flame; thankfully, it wasn't a glass jar candle. I lit the wick and watched as it quickly burned and caught the magazine on fire. I waited until the curtains caught before I made my exit out the back, careful to wipe prints and lock the door behind me. Peeking around the house, I saw no one once again and sprinted. Making it safely behind the house, I took off all of my clothing, tossed it on our grill, and lit it. There was some awful smoke but I knew it wouldn't get seen, and if it did, people would think it was the house on fire down the street. Standing naked with only my sneakers on, I made sure all of the pieces were burnt, scooped out the ash, and let it blow away in the wind. Then I sprayed off my body and sneakers with ice cold water from the hose and went inside. Once inside, I tossed my shoes into the washer and hopped in the shower.

Before I got a good lather going I heard the phone ring, I had the receiver on the bathroom sink so I reached out and answered it, knowing it would be Carla. In a panic, she told me she was on her way, that Leo's house was on fire. I perfectly faked panic, telling her I was in the shower but that I would get out right away and try to see if I could get Leo out. Shutting off the shower, I carefully looked in the mirror for any blood spots; satisfied that I was clear, I threw on some shorts and a t-shirt, grabbed a fire extinguisher, and ran to Leo's. As I kicked in the door and sprayed foam, I heard the trucks approaching down the road. To make it look good, I raced into the fire, brushed against the charred walls to get dirty, and tried to make my way to the back room. I took big gulps of smoke, hoping to get mild smoke inhalation: that way, I would look heroic. As I made my way to the back bedroom, I was thrilled to see Leo already had a good char on him. For good measure, I pushed the bureau over and onto him, crushing his head, hoping that it would cover up my tracks even more. Then I pulled it off of him and started to drag his body to the front of the house, only the way was blocked by falling debris. I dragged his body into a front room that looked like he used for an office and broke the window. A fireman helped me get out and looked in at Leo's body.

As I collapsed to the ground, I screamed *Save Him, Save Him!* It was perfect timing too: a crowd had formed and Carla was racing over to me. I had to spend the next two days in the hospital, for I had taken in more smoke than I had hoped for. The other body was found, of course. It was another media sensation. Carla had to

work on it and hardly found time to visit me other than to interview me. This time, I told her I saw nothing on my jog. She believed me but did ask why I had washed my shoes. I told her I stepped in dog shit and laughed. I knew she believed it. Someone in love can be blind to evidence of wrongdoing.

Now, it was either bad police work, help from above, or just dumb luck, but no one ever connected Leo's death to the other one, and in fact, no one suspected anything but an accident. The bureau falling had covered up the smashed skull just fine. The final report assumed he fell out of bed, tried to pull himself up on it, and instead pulled it back on himself. The crush to the head was the final cause of death. This last-minute idea saved me, because if not, I realized his death would have been ruled suspicious because there would have been no smoke in his lungs. Funny how things work out. Carla told me that he died before I made it in the house to make me feel at ease for not being able to save him. She was proud of me, though: she told me that over and over again.

The crime went unsolved, and I got away with it once again.

Jump twenty-three years later and we are in the present. Carla and I had two children, both in college now, a few hours away in upstate New York. We moved when we had kids to a bigger house, but it was only three streets over, which allowed me to keep almost the same run for years. Thankfully, I had no incidents over the past two decades. I had almost all but forgotten them until recently. It was two days after my sixty-first

birthday when the message came to me. I don't jog anymore-- bad knees-- but I walk as often as I can. As I was walking through the same jogging path as two of my previous murders, a strange thing happened. I wasn't thinking about anything in particular, and then all of a sudden, I stopped, dropped to my knees, and used my finger to write in the dirt. *First National Church, Sunday, Ten A.M. All Must Perish.* I didn't question what I had just written; I knew I had to do it. I brushed away the evidence and went about my walk, trying to figure out how to kill so many people at once.

Though the order (at least that was how I was looking at it) seemed odd and harsh, I knew there must be a reason behind it and that I would not get caught. I was merely a warrior for God, doing his dirty work. With only four days until Sunday, I scoped out the church. It was only a few miles from my home and I had driven by it countless times, but I had never been inside. It was a massive brick building set far back from the road; in fact, you could only see the top it from the street as the massive property was littered with trees. I drove down the long drive, making metal notes of the land. There were no security guards or even cameras that I could see. That was good. I drove around the building and saw nothing as well. I also noticed the back exit that lead out into a residential street. It would be a perfect area to get away.

I parked and went inside the church. Being mid-day, it was pretty silent in there. I saw just a few old ladies praying alone. A quick flash came into my head about how I would have to kill them Sunday, but I forced it out.

The church, though beautiful, was typical, to say the least. Pews, aisles, and an altar. Pretending to pray, I sat in a pew and looked at all the exits; there were too many. I couldn't barricade them all. Part of me wanted to just set off some explosives and hope for the best, but the sentence kept nagging at my head. *All Must Perish.* That meant that I had to kill *everyone.* What if even one got away or lived? Would I be punished? Would I get caught? It was a horrible thought. After thirty minutes, I felt I had enough information and left to prepare.

It was hard to get away from Carla the next few days, but with our anniversary coming up, she thought I was planning a surprise, so she let me out of her sight more than she normally would. That was a good thing. I took out cash and drove hours away to hardware stores to buy the items I needed. I even stole a large U-Haul truck from a lot about four hours away from our house the night before. That same night, I slipped some sleeping pills into Carla's ice cream and went about working. I loaded the truck with one hundred and ninety propane tanks and bags and bags of fertilizer. The hard part was loosening the heads on the tanks so that one good thrust and they would pop off while keeping them tight enough for them to stay on in the drive. That night, I also snuck to the church and sealed all the emergency exits shut with nails and steel bonding compound. I hid an extra thirty propane tanks in the thick bushes all around the church, hoping they would catch from the initial explosion.

My next task was a bit harder, but I got it done without being noticed. I welded shut all the fire hydrants

within a hundred-yard distance of the church. By then, I was exhausted but still had some time. I took a ladder and climbed up to the roof and plugged all the gutters up tight and then poured gallons upon gallons of gas into the gutters. When the building blew, that should help ignite the fire some more. I may have been going a bit overboard, but I wasn't supposed to let *anyone* live. At four in the morning, I parked the U-Haul two streets over, walked home, snuck in the house, showered, and went to bed. Four hours later, Carla and I were up and eating breakfast like any normal day. We had plans to go visit the kids upstate, so to get out of this, I faked a horrible bout of the runs and told her to go without me. It took a bit of convincing, but she finally left around nine, just in time.

At ten of nine, I snuck into the U-Haul and drove to the church parking lot. There were dozens of cars. A few people mingled outside and several rushed from their cars to make it in time. At ten on the button, the doors shut tight. Seeing no one around, I sprang into action. With a screwdriver, I popped every gas tank in parking lot open and pushed in a rag, letting it hang out just enough to light it up. It took me a solid half hour to do it, but it would be worth it; if anyone got out and took cover by the cars, they too would go up. Back behind the wheel, I was not nervous at all. I merely drove the truck up over the grass and right in front of the main doors. I got it tight enough that no one could get out if they tried. Then I rushed as quickly as I could to knock off a few of the propane tank tops in the back. Shutting the back door, I lit a flare and placed it on the bumper, and lit another one

and threw it in the cab. Then, on my bad knees, I ran like I used to.

With another flare in my hand I ran around the parking lot and lit as many of the rags as I could before the truck blew up. The explosion was massive. I couldn't help but watch it go up. Of course, being that there were so many tanks, the explosions kept coming and coming, one after another. The gutter lit up just as I hoped. A massive river of fire surrounded the church roof and quickly ate its way up it as the tanks in the bushes started to blow. By this time, the first few cars that I lit were exploding and getting closer to me. Tossing the flare, I ran for the bike I had stashed in the bushes and hopped on it. I also had planted a small Dunkin' Donuts bag with coffee and donuts in it. Within a few seconds, I was in the neighborhood riding around just like any old man on a Sunday, getting coffee and donuts.

Three blocks over, I heard the sirens and saw the smoke above the treetops. I decided that any normal man would be curious and ride over, so I did. There was a massive crowd a few hundred yards away; I joined it and watched in silence just as everyone else did.

"Why isn't anyone coming out of the emergency exits?" Someone finally whispered to no one in particular. No one responded. Looking away from what was once a church and was now merely a pile of fire and bricks, I saw the firemen trying comically to open the hydrants, and I had to bite my cheek to not laugh. Feeling confident that everyone inside would die, I got back on my bike and started to ride away when I heard a scream.

"There are people alive! Look, look!" I turned to see several people jump down from the stained-glass windows. They were so high up I never even thought of protecting them; I don't even know how they could have gotten to them. Seeing firemen running to the three people who made it out, I knew I had to make sure they died. Leaving the crowd, I peddled as fast as I could to the people who were now lying in the grass, hacking. A cop tried to stop me, but I screamed that I was a doctor and he let me pass.

You better protect me if I do this. I said out loud as I jumped off my bike and ran to the side of one of the victims. It was a young woman looking at me with terror in her eyes. Her hair was melted to her scalp and her cheek had been ripped open. Since she was the one in the best condition, the firemen were helping the other two. Dropping to my knees I put my hands on her neck and choked her. I didn't look up; I didn't want to see if anyone saw what I was doing. As I saw the light go out in the woman's eyes, a hand grasped my shoulder and pulled me back. She was dead though, and that was all that mattered. I was filled with fear and rage for the first time, as I knew I had to kill the other two or I would be in trouble. I felt hands on me, voices screaming, but I ignored it all and fought to make it to the next body. Though I had hands pinning my arms down, I was able to bring my heel down on the man's throat. I felt a snap and knew it had worked.

The last victim was too far away and the arms on me too strong: I couldn't make it to him. As I was thrown in the back of a cruiser, I kept my eyes on the body on the

ground. The person was burnt badly and might not make it. I screamed for them to die as I hit my head against the glass of the cruiser. I needed that person to die.

Three hundred and sixty-seven people died that day, a third of whom were children. Only one survived; I failed by one. The bastard was in ICU for six weeks, and now I'm in jail for life. I begged for Carla to kill him in the hospital, to pull his plugs, but she didn't believe me. She didn't believe that if he died I would be innocent and let go. No one believed me and I knew why: I had failed God, and therefore, he had abandoned me.

Four years later, I become a model inmate. A television movie was made about me, four books were written about my life, and countless television specials interviewed me. I told the truth and nothing but it. Everyone in the world thought I was crazy. Then, one day, I got a letter from the one survivor, Richard Landis. He wanted to see me to tell me he forgave me for killing his family and friends and for disfiguring him for life. It seems he became a motivational speaker, promoting overcoming adversity and devastation through the power of the Lord. When the day came that he visited me, I was able to not be cuffed, as I was deemed non-violent and not a threat, though, of course, there was a guard standing by.

Richard looked like a mix between Two-Face and Freddy Kruger. He was disgusting looking, and my anger that he was alive made him look even uglier to me. I did not hear his voice as he talked non-stop for fifteen

minutes. I simply concentrated on the burn marks on his neck. Then, suddenly, he took my hands and asked me to pray. We both got on our knees, which made the guard nervous. As he started to ramble off a prayer, I reached up and grasped his head and snapped his neck faster than the guard could get to me. With Richard dead, I suddenly felt this light fill my body; I had redeemed myself in God's eyes, and I knew he would get me out of prison… I just knew it.

Less than a month later, during a prison riot, I slipped out of the gates along with thirty other prisoners. Every one of them got brought back in, except for me. They didn't know I was missing. My cell had burned along with a few dozen others, and they found a body inside and assumed it was mine. I was too old to have escaped, after all, and the twenty-year-old who was missing wouldn't have been in bed sleeping during a riot, so it had to be the old man. I was a free man, thanks to God.

I now live a simple life in Canada, running a small clothing store. I await my next orders.

WRONG NUMBER

Sam dialed the number fast without really looking. He had dialed the Noon Deli a hundred times; as it was ringing, he wondered why he hadn't put it on speed dial yet. Shuffling through some papers at his desk, he heard the phone being answered. It was a woman, not Larry like normal: he must have the day off. Without waiting for her to go through the normal spiel, *If it's noon, it's time for the Noon Deli! Thanks for calling, what delicious sandwich can I get you?*, Sam started to order.

"Yeah, I'd like a Reuben, extra sauce. Order of onion rings and an M&M cookie. You can put it on Sam Dye's account. I'll pick it up in fifteen." He started to jot down a note on an expense report while waiting for the woman to reply.

"Umm."

Sam sighed at the woman's response. "Do I have to repeat the order? Where is Larry? Are you new?" Sam finally looked away from his work and focused on the phone. He heard giggling on the other end. He was annoyed that the woman wasn't taking her job seriously.

"You do know that is not the most healthy of lunches, right?"

Sam couldn't believe someone whose job it was to take orders dared critique his lunch.

"Alright, what is your name? I'm talking to Larry about you."

"Marissa."

Sam leaned back in his chair. For some reason, her voice sent a little chill of excitement down his stomach. "Well, Marissa, I would like my order put in, and I when I pick it up, I will be talking to Larry."

"Alright, you tell Larry, but I'm not putting your order in. You should be eating a salad," the woman ended with a giggle.

Sam could feel his face get red. "That's it. I'm coming down there." Sam stood up, about to hang up the phone.

"Okay, but I won't be there."

Hearing the response, Sam paused. He smoothed his tie. He wanted to ask why, but then he looked at the phone's screen. He had dialed the wrong number: a seven instead of an eight at the end.

"Oh man. I'm so sorry, I dialed the wrong number, didn't I?" Sam laughed.

"I was wondering when you would catch on." The woman burst out in laughter.

"Well, I apologize. Have a nice day," Sam said, feeling a bit stupid.

"Wait!"

Sam paused at this response. "Yeah?"

"Why don't you have lunch with me? I'll make you a salad. The Noon Deli sucks anyway. I'll meet you in ten minutes in Phelps Park. The bench by the big tree. I'll have on a pink scarf."

Sam's head spun. *Is this really happening?* "I'm sorry, but we don't know each other."

"Yeah, so? That is the point. All friends were strangers once."

Sam listened to her voice. He fantasized about what she might look like; then he looked at his wedding picture on his desk. "I'm sorry, but I'm married. I don't think my wife would like me having lunch with a strange woman."

"I won't tell her if you don't."

Sam turned away from the wedding picture. He could feel a tingle in his crotch at the excitement of another woman, *any* woman, giving him some attention.

"Well... this is nuts! We don't know each other. I mean, are you coming on to me? You don't even know what I look like. I'm sorry. This is weird. And I've never met a stranger for lunch before." Sam's head started to fill with ideas about how he could have accidentally called an ugly cat lady or an old woman.

"I haven't either. I'm just a bit bored and lonely today. And I'm not coming on to you; for all I know, you could be old and ugly. I'm just looking to have lunch with someone... harmless. Lunch will be on me. What could you lose?"

Sam loosened his tie a bit. He thought of how his wife hadn't touched him in over two months. "Phelps Park? Okay..."

"Great, see you in a few minutes."

Sam walked by the Noon Diner and almost instinctively went inside. He saw Larry working the phones through the smudged glass and laughed to himself. *What am I doing?* The whole concept was crazy, but for the first time in ages, he was excited. Butterflies

flitted around in his stomach, his groin was slightly swollen with excitement, and his mind actually wasn't thinking about work. Even if nothing came of the lunch, if the woman was an ugly dud, he would still have had some excitement of doing something different for once.

The park was a small, one-block square in the middle of skyscrapers. A dog park was in one corner, and an X of a walking path cut right through the park and small playground in another corner. Benches and people were everywhere. Most were eating on their lunch breaks; others were walking dogs, and a handful of nannies in the playground stood with spoiled children. There was a massive tree in the middle of the park; it had been there years before the city was founded. In fact, the park was created because no one wanted to cut the tree down. A circular bench surrounded its ancient trunk. As he approached, he saw a slew of people sitting in his favorite spot: three couples, two businessmen, a bum, and one woman all by herself... a very, very old woman, feeding pigeons. It couldn't be her? Then he remembered the scarf; thank god: she didn't have a scarf. She wasn't here yet.

Sam slowly circled the tree, crunching the fall leaves under his black dress shoes, waiting for a spot on the bench to open.

"Sam?" Spinning around, he saw a young, beautiful girl. She had dark hair and a tan face, and she was half his age, probably in her late twenties. His mouth fell open when he saw she was holding a bag and wearing a light pink cashmere scarf. *It was her.*

"Marissa? How did you know it was me?"

115

"Well, you are the only one circling the bench and looking nervous. Plus, you look like you'd match the uptight voice on the phone."

Sam smiled, embarrassed. "Nice to meet you." Sam stuck out a hand, suddenly nervous and angry at himself for not bringing flowers. It probably didn't matter anyway because there was no way a young beautiful woman would find him attractive. Maybe in his youth, but now, he had graying hair and the start of a bulging belly. She took his hand gently and shook it. Her skin was so smooth. Sam couldn't help but wonder what it would feel like on him: what she would feel like, and look like, under the bulky gray sweater she wore.

"Let's find a bench." Sam let her lead the way, hoping to get a glance at her behind in the tight jeans. He felt a bit uptight in a suit. When she wasn't looking, he yanked off his tie and shoved it in his pocket.

Marissa sat down at an empty bench and patted the spot next to her. Sam sat down with a goofy smile. He knew nothing about this girl, and yet, he was in love with her already.

"Alright, Mr. Sam: I got you a spinach green salad with Gorgonzola cheese, walnuts, pears, and a roasted sesame vinaigrette!" Marissa said in the cutest voice he ever heard. He took the plastic container and looked at it. His wife had tried to get him to take a salad for lunch for years and he never did; now he was eager to eat one from a stranger.

"Looks amazing."

"Yeah, and ten times healthier than your Reuben." She looked him in the eyes when she spoke. They were a

beautiful green. Sam had a hard time finding words. Marissa handed him a fork, napkin, and bottle of water. Sam opened the water and started to take a sip to wet his quickly drying mouth.

"A healthy lunch makes for a healthy mind and body. Besides, you do know that what you eat affects how your semen tastes right?"

Sam choked on the water and spit up on himself. He grabbed his napkin and wiped it up as his face turned bright red. Glancing over at Marissa, he saw that she was smiling at him.

Not knowing how to respond, Sam took a bite of his salad. He couldn't tell if it was because of the company or because he actually thought it tasted good, but he loved it. Marissa smiled when he told her.

"See? Healthy can be good. You just got to branch out." Sam wanted to ask so many questions. *What did she do? How old was she? What was her last name?* And yet, for some reason, he found that nothing came out. *Was he that nervous?* He couldn't remember being this shy around anyone since grade school.

"Not much of a talker, are you, big guy?"

Sam could feel his face blush. "Sorry, it's just… this is a bit weird. And I didn't expect you to be so… pretty."

"It's nice though, isn't it?"

Sam nodded his head. He yelled at himself in his brain to come up with something witty and interesting so this angel wouldn't just go and run off on him, bored to death.

"So, tell me about yourself, Marissa. What do you do for a living, besides meet strange men who call wrong numbers?" Sam felt a bit of confidence coming back.

"Sam?" The girl asked almost solemnly. Sam paused mid-bite and looked at her.

"Look, let's not get into this whole family past, jobs, likes, dislikes, and whatnot. We know each other's first names: that is all. Let's keep it that way." Marissa's voice was a bit harsh. It took Sam off guard: he *wanted* to get to know her.

"Oh, alright. Well, then, what do you want to talk about?" Sam asked, now confused on top of his nervousness.

"Let's just watch the pigeons, eat our salads, and then you can call work and say you won't be back for a few hours. Make an excuse. Say you're sick or something. Then I'll take you back to my place and please you in ways your wife couldn't even imagine."

Sam stared at the salad on his fork. There was no way this was happening. It was a wet dream scenario, some cheesy porno he had watched and now was a dream he was having. Yet he knew it wasn't; he could feel his groin pulsating with the desire for this woman. Sam put his fork down, closed the lid, swallowed hard, and threw it in the trashcan next to him. He stood up, smoothed his shirt, looked back at Marissa, and offered her his hand. His face got hot as he felt passion and confidence he had not in a long time.

Marissa's apartment was close by. They walked side-by-side, silent. Sam could feel people's eyes on him. He

knew they were either wondering how the hell he got a girl like that, or they thought she was his daughter. In the elevator ride up, she took his hand. It was the first time he noticed how much he was trembling.

"You do this often?" He couldn't help but ask, wondering if he was just today's lucky schmuck or if she actually was attracted to him.

"No more questions. But to answer you: this is the first time. I need something to spice up my life." As the doors opened, Sam wondered if he could walk through them, if he could go through with this. He wanted more than anything in the world to sleep with her, but he was married, even if unhappily. What if he got caught? What if she got pregnant? What if he got a disease from her? He started to hyperventilate. Marissa walked through the doors; Sam stood still. She turned back to him and gave a nod of her head towards the hall, but he didn't move. Slowly licking her lips, she strolled over to him and put one hand on the back of his neck and the other on his hard crotch.

"I have no diseases, I'm on the pill, and I will never tell. And, I will make you come in sixty seconds. After that, you'll be relaxed and I can take my time fucking you all afternoon." Sam's brain shut off. He followed her out of the elevator, down the hall, and into her apartment.

Two hours later, Sam laid on an uncomfortable futon with a huge smile on his face. He had come three times, more times than he had in the past year with his wife. As he watched the rickety ceiling fan spin above him, he could have cared less if the world exploded at that

moment. It was the best sex he had ever had. She was the most beautiful woman he had ever been with. He was in love. He didn't care about anything. He would leave job, kill his wife, kill the president for this woman, and he didn't even know her last name. Sam could not believe it was possible to have a high, this high, but he did.

Looking up, he saw Marissa come out of the bathroom. She was stark naked and strutted like a runway model. Her breasts jiggled just a bit, her tan body glistened, and her smooth groin was so tempting Sam felt himself get hard again. He couldn't believe it: the last time he was able to go more than once in a day, he was seventeen. Marissa saw that he was hard. She licked her fingers, brought them down to her crotch and rubbed herself, then sat down right on Sam. She felt so amazing he grabbed her hips and forced his head back in the pillow.

Marissa was a like a time warp. It felt like he was only there a few hours when Sam noticed the sun was setting. A twinge of panic filled his head, but then he looked at her. She was still naked. *Let the wife worry.* He was in heaven and didn't want to leave it for anything. When his cell started to ring an hour after the sun went down, he took it out of his pants pocket, pulled the battery out, and threw it in the trash.

"Good boy." Marissa said, rubbing his chest as she lay back down. It seemed scientifically impossible for him, but he felt his penis begin to swell once again. Eight times in one afternoon? It made *Penthouse* letters seem

boring. It was almost like this woman was some sort of alien sex monster that could control his penis.

"I don't ever want this day to end," Sam said, looking at Marissa, his heart speeding up at the sight of her pinching her nipples softly.

"It doesn't have to; we can do this for eternity, Sam." He closed his eyes at the thought of never leaving the lumpy futon. They could take showers, have sex, and get take-out until they died.

"I wish," Sam said before leaning in to lick the nipple her fingers were still on. She pushed him away. It felt like a knife in his chest: it was the first time she had denied him anything.

"I'm serious, Samuel. I can make that happen. We can please each other for eternity, in this room. I can make that happen."

Sam let out a small laugh as his hands went for her hips; he wanted her again, badly. Again, she pushed him away. It felt as if the wind was knocked from him.

"I'm making you an offer, Samuel. Eternity with me, or back to your miserable life pushing papers and living with your wife, Janice, who won't even sleep with you."

Sam was hardly listening-- he just wanted to be in her again-- but hearing his wife's name snapped him out of his lust. "How, how did you know my wife's name?"

Marissa got up and stood naked next to the bed, staring at Sam. "It doesn't matter. Nothing matters more than us being here, forever. I just want you to agree to be with me." Marissa put one foot on the bed, giving Sam a perfect look at the place that brought him more joy than anything ever had. Though he was confused, he felt a

wash of calm come over him as he looked at her naked body. He just wanted to be with her one more time. He needed to be.

"Yes, yes, I want to be with you, here in this room, forever, but I don't know how it's possible."

Marissa smiled big, licked her lips, and grabbed Sam's hand. She placed it over her crotch, pushed his two middle fingers inside her and then pulled them out. She put her leg back down on the floor, moved his wet fingers to her stomach and drew a circle around her belly button with her juices. With the circle complete, she dropped his hand and backed away.

"Icsaw, Untormachant, fincula, ZANTU!" Marissa chanted. Sam smiled at her, thinking she was playing some cute game. It was cute, but he just wanted her to get back on the futon with her. He sat up a bit and patted the bed. Suddenly, the small studio apartment started to shake. The window behind him rattled; the door bounced.

"Christ, I think it's an earthquake!" Sam tried to get up but the force of the shaking knocked him off his feet. "Marissa, get in the doorway: that is the safest place!" Sam yelled, trying to get up. Marissa didn't move. She put her arms straight out to her sides and her head back. Sam looked to the door as if trying to will her to go to it. What he saw made no sense to him. Thick brown gunk was flowing out of the top of the doorframe, pouring down the door. A sewer pipe break? Sam turned to the window. It was no longer there: the entire wall was covered in the brown gunk. Turning back to the door, he saw that the wall, too, was now covered; it seemed to be

hardening as well. Sam couldn't find words, couldn't find logic to what was happening.

The shaking started to subside. Sam put his hand on the futon to try and get up, but it was cold and sticky. As he tried to lift his knee, the floor stuck to him, pulling back like brown taffy. Sam let out a scream and looked to Marissa. Her feet were welded to the ground by the gunk; her body was covered in veins of brown slime. Sam got up, wrapped his arms around her, and tried to pull her free. Marissa's arms wrapped around him, squeezed him tight. He could feel the cold gunk climbing up his legs, encasing his testicles, and sealing his body against hers.

Sam tried to pull away from her but couldn't budge an inch. He looked at her face. It was still beautiful but the brown was climbing over it. Marissa smiled and went in to kiss Sam. He couldn't help but open his mouth and accept the kiss. It was a wonderful, but he felt the gunk climb over their heads and seal them together.

After a few moments, he could tell both of their entire bodies were covered. The gunk was hardening. He didn't understand it, he couldn't move an inch, he couldn't see, but he could feel Marissa's body against him, her tongue stuck to his. She came through on her promise, he didn't know how, why, or what was going on, but it didn't matter. He liked the feel of her body against his and was grateful that he had dialed the wrong number.

LEROY

Leroy was a loser. He was born a loser, grew up a loser, and still is a loser. He was the weird kid in elementary school that everyone teased about the dirty clothes he wore. In high school, he was practically invisible, except when a bully needed to take out some aggression. In college (community, that is), he was the student that showed up a few minutes late to every class and sat in the back. The one that sent shivers down other students' spines. The student that the teacher went out of his way to be nice to in case he ever went on a shooting rampage. Leroy was the guy that everyone expected to turn out to be a serial killer or future child molester, and people were not wrong.

After college, which he passed with straight Cs, he got a job as a night janitor in a high school, putting his degree to no use. The first week at the job, he cursed himself for wasting time going to college-- hell, even high school-- when he needed no experience to do the job. Especially since he liked the job. He had a set list of tasks to do on his own wing of the school: empty the trash, sweep the floors, and various other cleaning tasks. Besides, when he checked in and got his supply cart, he didn't have to see anyone. It was just him and the empty rooms. He liked it that way: no one bothered him, no one was there to pick

on or judge him; he was content for the first time in his life.

Leroy never had friends, let alone girlfriends. Lonely and with the lack of female companionship, most of his time off of work was spent watching internet porn and eating frozen meals in his studio apartment. It was a nice routine, and though he was only in his early twenties, he could see himself doing this for the rest of his life.

His shift started at three in the afternoon and ended at eleven at night. By the time he arrived at school every day, most of the students had left. There were always a few sports teams or academic club students wandering around, but he was practically invisible to them. They never paid attention to him and he liked it that way, especially since he could watch the girls from a distance without them really noticing or caring. One night, while looking for Hector to get the key to the boiler room since he forgot his gloves in there the other day, he found the other janitors in an interesting situation. They spent the first few hours every night hiding in the darkened athletic director's office that was perched above the gym. It had glass windows that surveyed the floor below. They would all sit there, silently passing around a pair of binoculars, watching the girls' gymnastics practice. When he found them, Leroy went on to turn on the lights and they all yelled, mostly in Spanish. When they let him borrow the binoculars and Leroy focused in on a tight rear end bent over stretching, his world changed.

At first, he played it off that he didn't care that much: they were hot, but not his type. He didn't know why he did this because in fact, he wanted to be in that room

with the other guys, he wanted to watch every stretch and tumble those girls made. That first night when he went to his wing, he shut one of the classroom doors, made sure the lights were out, and stroked himself. He had jerked off many times while at work, but this time was different. Usually he thought of the porn he watched, but this time, he was thinking of the girls that sat in these rooms all day. With his hand on his erection, slowing its pace, he fell to his knees, shuffled over to the first desk and sniffed the seat, nothing. The next one had slight smell but it was sweet, like juice. Finally, the fifth seat he smelled had a salty, tangy sent that he just knew belonged to the girl had saw stretching. Sniffing, then licking, he finished himself off in a burst of pleasure that was better than he ever felt before.

The next hour he spent lying on the floor, his head spinning with the amazing idea that he could do this every night. He was excited for the first time in a while. All sorts of ideas came to his head, places he could sniff and taste. He had never smelled or tasted a real woman-- he always wanted to, always thought of getting a hooker but chickened out-- and now, now he could have it, he could have something close to it, for free and without any consequences. Getting up, he cleaned up his mess and finished his duties for the night.

The next evening he didn't go to watch the girls with the other guys. He was too worried he would get aroused in front of them, and besides, he wanted to keep his distance from them so they couldn't start to pick on him. Though he wanted to go watch-- *desperately*, instead, he

went to his wing, knowing he was going to be alone. He went through three classrooms until he found one that the teacher had put up senior pictures of the students next to the desk. He looked them over and found the most attractive girl, pulled it off the wall carefully and sniffed each chair until he found the one he just knew was hers. Again, he did his routine, only this time looking at the picture, and again, it was amazing.

Over a year went by and every single night he did this: sniffed, licked, and jerked. After a while, the routine got stale and he needed more. He started to sneak up into the office with the guys a few times a week: he found that the different seasons meant different games. Sometimes it was the volleyball team letting their perky breasts bounce; other times, it was the soccer team practicing indoors when it rained, but the gymnastics were always the best. The viewing was great, but he needed to be closer to them, to smell and taste them. It had been a while since he had started to lick the girl's toilet seats clean at night. They gave him more flavor than the desks and excited him more since he knew their bare skin was on them. The act turned him on so much he had even gone so far as to put a dirty tampon in his mouth. At first, it gave him a thrill, but when he closed his lips, the acidic taste was too overpowering. While it was all amazing and new experiences for Leroy, he needed more. He needed to *see* one of these girls... naked.

Using the Internet, he took three weeks to do research on how to install hidden cameras. He went to a specialty store an hour away from his home and bought tiny cameras with cash, to not have any traces back to

himself, but the desire to touch them for real became unbearable.

For three months he devised plans, scrapped them, then finally decided on one that might work, and if it didn't, it would sure as hell be worth the shot. There were three girls' bathrooms in his wing, some of which were locked on certain days during school hours to keep kids from skipping class and messing around. This was the key to his scheme. The night before his plan was to be set in motion, he installed a slide-bolt lock on the first-floor girls' bathroom. This one was locked three days a week. Next, he practiced climbing out of the window. It was pretty easy, and the window faced the back woods, so if he followed a careful path, no one would see him go out it. With both of those set, he was ready.

That night, after work, he left like normal with the other guys, drove home like normal, parked like normal, logged onto the internet like normal, then locked his door from the inside and slipped out his back apartment window. Dressed in all black, he walked the two miles to the school. Making sure no one was around, he slipped in the back door he had left unlocked; thankfully, the school had no alarm system or cameras besides the ones in the cafeteria and office. He then took up position inside of the bathroom and waited and waited. He took a nap on the cold tile floor and woke up at six using his watch alarm. The next hour he spent sitting on the toilet in a stall as his heart pounded.

When the first bell rang, he put his feet up and tried his to breathe silently, he had put up *Out of Order* sign on the stall, so no one should try to use it, keeping him safe.

Several girls came in at once, gossiping and yapping to each other. He heard two of them pee next to him. Knowing they were there with their pants down gave him an erection that hurt so bad he had to stifle a whimper. When the bell rang, the bathroom emptied out in a hurry. Now was when his plan was going to start. All he had to do now was wait. It only took about ten minutes until the first girl came in. Leroy leaned forward and looked through the crack. She was a fat girl and didn't interest him. She left and five minutes later, a dream walked in-- it was one of the gymnastics girls. He couldn't stop shaking at the sight of her. As soon as he heard her shut and lock the stall next to him, he sprang into action. Leaving his stall, he flushed the toilet to avoid suspicion, walked to the door, slid the bolt lock shut and returned to his stall.

Hearing her flush, he took a deep breath, watched through the crack as she washed her hands, and got ready. When she turned to the paper towel holder, he sprung out, grabbed her from behind and covered her mouth.

"Shhhhhh…" His stomach did flips as he held the girl tight against his body. It felt so good, she smelled so amazing, he thought he might faint. Using his body weight, he pinned her against the wall and pulled out a cloth from his back pocket.

"Now listen, girl, you are locked in here with me. No one can get in and I have a knife. If you scream, even one peep, I will slit your throat and I am not kidding." Leroy had no intention of killing her and didn't think he could even hurt her if it came down to it, but according

to all the movies he watched, he knew that he had to threaten her to get her to do what he wanted. He pushed the cloth into her mouth. She cried and screamed through it, but he was satisfied it wasn't that loud, especially since the walls were made out of concrete.

"I'm going to fuck you. There is nothing you can do to stop me from doing that. And I'm going to warn you now, if you try to fight me off, I will beat and kill you. If you just stay still, it will be over in a matter of minutes and you can get back to class." With the cloth tight in her mouth, he wrapped another cloth around her eyes and one around her wrists, keeping her hands tight behind her back. Satisfied she was secured, he took a moment to look her over and take in what he was about to have. She was short, maybe five feet, with dirty blond hair, an ass to die for, and tiny ripe breasts that stood at attention. She was wearing a tiny t-shirt and shorts so short they screamed for her to be banged. He leaned in and smelled her, took in her essence: it was the sweet perfume of heaven.

Spinning her around as she screamed, he grabbed her hair hard and pulled it back with a violent tug.

"Scream again and you get a knife in the gut." The screaming stopped but she cried heavily. Leroy ignored this and focused on her body. He lifted up her shirt and shuddered with joy at the sight of her flat, smooth, tanned stomach. There was even a little surprise; she had a sapphire belly button ring. Before he could even pull his dick out of his sweat pants, his body convulsed and he came. Part of him started to enjoy it, the other part panicked as he hadn't even gotten to touch her yet and he

was done. Time was of the essence and he needed to be able to come again! Pulling himself out, he wiped his stickiness on his pants and was amazed to see he was still hard, he could do it again… maybe he could do her several times?

Not wanting to waste any more time, he lifted the shirt higher, saw her pink bra, pulled it down and let the first pair of breasts he was ever going to touch fall in front of him. They were amazing, perfect, and tasted so sweet. He licked them long and hard and fondled, squeezed and pulled, plucked and nibbled them. They were better than he ever imagined. And if they were so good, he couldn't imagine what her crotch was going to be like.

Kneeling down in front of her, he slid his fingers under the waistband, stretched out the elastic, and pulled them down with one quick movement. She was shaved, so young and she was shaved! For a moment, he wondered if he was going to be her first as well, *they would be each other's firsts.*

"Ever been fucked before?" he asked with excitement. The girl didn't answer, there was snot coming out of her nose and her face was pale. He ignored her non-response and leaned in to smell her. With his nose pushed into her, he inhaled deeply and knew for the first time how wonderful a woman really smelled. Not being able to take it, he grabbed her and set her down onto the ground. He was going to use a condom but the excitement was too much, he needed to feel what a real vagina felt like on his bare penis. As he

grabbed himself, before he even got a foot away from her, he came again.

"Son of a bitch!" Leroy yelled, frustrated and yet feverishly excited. He collapsed on top of her, felt her skin against his and he cried, it was amazing. Even if he spent the next ten years in prison, even if he hadn't gotten inside of her yet, it was worth it.

As his penis shriveled he tried not to look at her body, for he knew it would grow again and he would want to spend more time with her. They were probably already wondering why she was taking so long, he had to get going. He got up, wiped up what he could of his semen, stood up the girl, helped her get dressed, searched her pockets and found her school ID, looked at it long and good, then put it in his pocket, then untied her hands

"I'm going to leave you now. You better count to a hundred before taking off that blindfold and gag. If you don't, I'll come back and kill you. And if I were you, I would keep this to yourself. If you tell anyone you got raped, I will kill your family and trust me, I know where you live and where your parents work. I have your ID, I know everything about you. I will kill them all and let you live to go to their funeral. Just tell your teacher you got sick: that is why it took you so long." With that, he raced out the window, paused to hear if she was going to scream and then ran his heart out.

Back at his apartment, he jumped around the place as if he had won the lottery. He was a new man, after all: he had touched a girl! Life was great-- he just had to be careful that they don't figure out it was him. Hell, he

planned it out enough that no one should ever figure out who did it... that is, if she even reported the crime. He had an alibi and that was the most important thing in a crime. As long as he didn't become a suspect, he would be safe, but if he did and they took a DNA sample, he would have to run and run fast. His junk was all over the room, even if he did wipe it up. Though maybe he could make an argument that he jerked off in there at night....

The rest of the day he spent running over what happened in his head. Replaying every second. He touched himself more times that day than any other in his memory and every time it was good, too good. So good, in fact, that he knew he was going to have to do this again. As long as he didn't get caught, he could. Going into work that night, he was more than nervous. *Cops are going to be everywhere.* But they weren't. In fact, it was no different than any other day when he arrived. The entire night he sweated, wondering if it was a set-up, if they were just waiting to take him down at any moment. Yet nothing happened. When he cleaned the bathroom where the incident took place, he found his cloths in the bottom of the trashcan. She didn't report it! If she had, they would have taken these as evidence. He could do it again, the same way, the same plan! There was a light step in his walk and he whistled as he worked the rest of that night.

If he hadn't been worried about getting caught, he would have done it the next day, hell every day, but he wanted to be cautious. He should wait a month, but his libido wouldn't let that happen. A week and a half was all

he could wait. He went through the same routine and set up all the necessary details to go through with it again. This time, he was calmer, even more excited, and ready.

Again, he waited with his feet up in the stall, the out of order sign on it, and looked to see how cute the girls were. He was pickier this time: he rejected several girls until he saw one that got him excited enough and was alone. Ready for action, he made his move. This one put up a bit more of a fight. He had to hit her a few times, which he didn't like, but it did the trick to keep her from fighting. With this girl, a cute little redhead with a bit too much chub on her hips, more than he expected, he took his time. The only other addition this time was that he brought a camera. While the girl was gagged with all her lovely parts exposed, he clicked off a few pictures, digital of course. Again, he came twice but never got to enter her: stupidly, he hadn't watched the time closely enough. After his second orgasm, there was only three minutes left in class. He had to hurry. Quickly, he took her school ID and gave her the same talk about how he would kill her and her family if she told anyone.

When he arrived at work that night, he was nervous, but he felt confident that she wouldn't talk as well. Again, he was right: there were no cops, no media, and no one said anything about anything out of the normal. He had gotten away with it once again! That night, he went about his normal cleaning routine, only this time, instead of masturbating in the bathroom, he sat at his favorite teacher's computer and downloaded the pictures he took from earlier in the day. Seeing the flesh that he tasted earlier made him come in seconds-- three times that

night. It was amazing, life was amazing. He hid the files on the teacher's computer in a folder buried within a dozen other folders that also held the hidden camera pictures. He was confident the teacher would never find them. Doing this allowed him to not have to bring the flash drive to work every day. He could simply log on and look at the pics in privacy without the fear of losing the drive.

Holding off for another week was going to be hard, but he had his pictures and memories to tide him over. A mere two days went by and he thought about doing it again, but that would be too soon, he thought. When he arrived at work the next day, his heart dropped to his feet as he saw two cops talking to his boss. His boss pointed at him as he walked in, and for a second Leroy thought about running, but he knew he wouldn't get far. He was better off lying. The two officers, with straight, scary serious faces, approached him and asked if they could talk in private. He nodded yes and went into one of the classrooms.

"We need to ask you some questions about one of the bathrooms you clean, the first floor one." The bigger of the two said while crossing his arms in a menacing way.

"When you clean the toilets, have you noticed anything… strange attached to the seats?" Leroy knew he might be a suspect, but he shouldn't show his cards too soon. He might be able to get away from them now, go home and get what he needed to pack, and then run with a head start, so he played dumb.

"No, nothing that isn't usually there, you know, besides chunks of shit and tampon blood. Why? What should I be looking for? Drugs being tossed?"

The officers looked at each other. "What about the door? Have you noticed anything about that out of the normal lately?"

Leroy pretended to think for a minute. "Yeah, actually there are some holes in the door, below where the lock is. The showed up about, a month ago I guess. Figured one of the day crew was going to install new locks or something." Again, they looked at each other. Leroy was thankful he was smart enough to remove the lock after each crime.

"What about the trash? Anything odd in it ever?' Leroy shrugged.

"Honestly, I don't ever look in it. I just pull up the bag and toss it. I learned quickly on this job not to look in the trash, it's disgusting." The one officer licked his lips, nodded, and motioned to the other guy.

"Alright, that is all we need. Thank you for your time." Leroy was confused. They didn't seem to be blaming him for anything.

"I don't get it, what is this about? Should I be looking for anything in particular? Is there something I can help you with?" The officer looked friendly for the first time.

"No, no, this will actually be resolved tonight. Nothing to worry about."

The rest of the night he spent looking over his shoulder, constantly nervous that they were about to

tackle him. Half of his wing was blocked off by police. He was told to not clean it just yet. He had never sweated that much in his life, especially when he went home. He expected them to be waiting for him there, yet there was nothing, nothing at all. That night, he packed an emergency bag of essentials that he could live off of in case he had to run. As he went to sleep, he wondered if it would be the last time he would ever sleep in his own bed.

When he awoke, he switched on the television like normal, only *The Price is Right* wasn't on: it was Breaking News, live from in front of the school. He bolted upright, shook the sleep from his head and moved to the end of the bed to get a better view of the television. He listened intently to the balding reporter he had grown up watching:

Again, details are sketchy at this moment but inside sources say that a teacher was arrested after nude pictures of students were found on his computer. There are also rumors that he is the suspect in two rape investigations that the police have been quietly investigating. To recap, the arrest was made this morning as Mr. Miller was entering the school. The students will have the day off while the faculty figures out how to address the students on this matter. We will be following this story closely as it unfolds…

Leroy started to laugh hysterically. Someone else was getting blamed for his doings! Of course, Mr. Miller would deny it, but the evidence was on his computer. He never even thought about that. It was perfect. He jumped up, did a little dance, and then suddenly stopped

as he realized that it wasn't perfect, that it was horrible. Yes, he was safe for the first two, but he couldn't get away with it again, for if he did it again, they would know it wasn't Mr. Miller. Leroy started to curse up a storm, throwing things and sobbing as he realized his good thing was gone. It took him an hour to settle down. When he did, he talked himself into realizing it wasn't the end of the world, that he would find other ways to get the girls.

Arriving at the school that night, he saw the countless media trucks along with police keeping them back from entering the school or bothering the janitors as they entered. There was even a podium set up for what looked like a press conference. Leroy felt his insides tingle with electric excitement. He had caused this, he had caused *all* of it. How exciting! Part of him wanted to walk up to that podium and admit it, admit that he touched those sweet bodies and that no one would have ever caught him. He wanted to rub it in their faces, wanted to show the world he was a man, a man who had hot chicks. So many men would be jealous of him for having those fine pieces of ass, he would be the cool guy for once.

The idea was tempting, but going to jail was not. Holding back a small smirk he rushed passed the questioning crowd and into the school. All of his co-workers were standing in the lobby watching the crowd, he joined them. They were all silent for a while, then one after another they spoke, to no one and everyone at once.

"I'd like to get my hands on that bastard."

"Yeah, I'd rip him to shreds."

"Fucking pervert." Leroy couldn't believe what these guys were saying. They sat everyday watching these girls with hard-ons. They went home and banged their wives thinking of those girls. And yet, they would want to kill someone who actually got to have one of them? Though he didn't understand this logic, he chimed in to "be one of the guys."

"Asshole, I'd tear his limbs off." He felt stupid saying it, but the guys all nodded as if what he said was a good idea. It took about another thirty minutes of watching people who were watching the school before they went to work, all mumbling under their breaths. Leroy was pulled aside first and told not to clean the bathroom or Mr. Miller's room, as they were still under investigation.

The rest of the night was uneventful and by the time he left at eleven, some of the trucks were gone while others were doing live broadcasts. Part of him hoped someone would run over and try to interview him: he'd get a kick out of seeing himself bash an innocent man on television, but no one came to him. Going home, he smiled to himself, enjoying the cool night air and thinking about how he was going to get the next one in the bag. Maybe the next one he could keep at his place, use her for a few days…

When he slipped the key in the lock his stomach suddenly started to tighten. He couldn't figure out why, but when he felt a hard thud against his head as he went to flick the light switch on, he knew why.

When he felt a cold breeze against his body, he awoke, realizing he was naked. He tried to jump up to

cover himself and to run, but he couldn't move. His arms and legs were tied to his own bed. He was spread eagle, completely naked. Looking down at himself nude and tied up, he momentarily felt aroused, especially when he saw the two girls he recently licked enter the room. The idea of a threesome ran through his head, both of them all over his body, kissing and sucking him. His penis stood up, splitting his vision of the two girls. One was on each side of his penis… the view was fantastic.

Leroy started to laugh, he couldn't believe he pleased those girls so much they went out of their way to find him and wanted to be with him again. It didn't take him that long to realize how stupid that thought was, especially when he saw that both of the girls had hunting knives in their hands.

"What's going on here, ladies?" he asked in his most casual voice. Watching them intently, he saw the two of them look nervously at each other before they walked up and took up stances, one on each side of him.

"You know what this is about," the girl, the first one he smelled, barked. The other girl chimed in even louder.

"We did our research. With the lack of evidence we have against you, you would get a maximum of five years in jail with a chance of parole in two. And that is *if* we could get you charged. That is unacceptable!" Getting more worried, Leroy took a look at his rapidly shrinking dick, suddenly feeling really uncomfortable with the knives so close to it.

"Ladies, I don't know what you are talking about. Your teacher, he, he is the one who did it. There is more than enough evidence to prove that," Leroy pleaded. He

looked to the girl who made him a man with puppy dog eyes. She looked at the floor, almost as if she might throw up. It made him feel a bit confident that she might not do whatever they planned on doing with those knives. The other girl, though: she did not look so worried; her face was beet red instead of pale and she held the knife at his waist as if ready to plunge. Catching his eye, she spoke again.

"You realize neither of us has slept in weeks. That I shower ten times a day to get your filth off of me. That we both can't let anyone touch us, not even on the arm, without jumping?" The knife slashed at his hip. He felt the blade cut into his skin, through his thin layer of fat and finally hitting the bone. As she dragged it across his hipbone, he arched in pain, sending the knife deeper across his body. Screaming and thrashing frantically, he prayed she would stop.

"You bitch! Holy fuck, that hurts." Catching his breath, he spoke more.

"You do realize that I have pictures in my apartment. You call the police and they will find them, it would prove it was me... then you could put me away for a long time!" Leroy belted out in the hope that they would realize this and not kill him. Jail was a much better option than those two knives. For a second, he thought he might have gotten them thinking, for they were silent.

"We already thought of that. Problem is, the maximum sentence you would get, since you actually never entered us, is nothing compared to what we suffered. We decided we couldn't chance seeing you on the street before we even get out of college." The girl

stared at his cut the entire time she spoke, then walked around the bed to the other girl. She gave her a quick hug and spoke again.

"You see, you having the pictures doesn't prove much, as we never saw your face. You might not even get convicted if we turned you in. We can't live knowing you are out there, especially with the fact that you threatened our families. And worse, the thought of you doing this to others... I won't let that happen."

Realizing he wasn't going to talk his way out of this, he started to look at the knots on his hands to see if he could pull out of them quickly enough to fight the girls off. No go. They were good knots. The next thought was to scream his head off: he had neighbors, they'd call the cops. He'd get arrested, but hell, he'd be alive. As he started to scream, he felt a burning hot pain shoot through his calf. Looking down he realized the girl had slashed him again.

"Every time you open your mouth, you get a new cut." Leroy felt tears squirting out of his eyes as he held back screams of pain and help. He couldn't believe such a young innocent girl was capable of this. That was it, that was the route he had to go.

"Look, you don't want to do this. You kill someone and it will haunt you the rest of your life. Besides, it will make you no better than me. Killing is worse than rape. I'm sorry for what I did. Just let me go and I'll turn myself in." His vision of the girls was a bit blurry from all the tears... the silent girl couldn't be laughing, could she?

"So, you admit it was you! That was what we needed. We were eighty percent sure it was you, and now we

143

know. Now we won't have guilty consciences." Leroy started to thrash, knowing it was useless, but he had to try something to get away.

"And just to let you know, it was the rags that gave you away. They were the same red, dingy things I have seen only one other place, hanging out of your pocket when you clean. I'm on the chess team. You always walked back and forth with your fucking cart as we practiced, those red rags hanging out of your back pocket." Leroy couldn't believe he was so stupid, he was meticulous with everything, everything, but one fucking detail got him.

"And we are not going to kill you, you fuck: we are just going to render you useless. You see, we are part of a new generation of women, ones who don't hide and stay quiet. We fight and claw back so this shit stops... permanently." It took him a moment to realize what she meant, and just as he did, he was being gagged.

The screaming and thrashing were useless. He stopped moving altogether when he felt two pairs of hands on his dick. Though he knew what was about to happen, he couldn't help but feel that familiar feeling of blood flowing into his best friend. The feel of it getting warm, hard, and ready for action. The hands on him felt amazing, even if they were just grasping it to get a good hold. As they squeezed him he felt an amazing, wonderful feeling he knew so well, a release he would never feel again. Just as the hot whiteness squirted out over the girl's fingers, he felt the searing pain at the base of his dick. For a split second, it felt good. Then it was followed by the most pain he had ever had in his life.

As blackness started to creep around the edge of his vision, he saw his dick right in front of his face, closer than he had ever seen it before. The beautiful, delicate hand holding it was covered in red and white goo as she cut the head of his friend off, then cut it into thirds as if preparing hot dogs for a child to eat. He felt the warm wet splats on his chest as they fell on him. Sitting up to look at it one last time, he saw he no longer had a crotch; there in its place was just a tiny stump with a geyser of red shooting out of him like a giant red orgasm. Starting to pass out, just as they were going back for his balls, Leroy realized, he had never really lost his virginity... and now he never would.

M.E.

Chris loved his job. If asked why he got into his line of work, he'd give you some in-depth mumbo-jumbo about science, when in reality, he just liked to play with dead things. This was true even as a child. He was eleven when he dissected the family dog after he found it dead in the backyard. From there he moved on to other animals, and finally, in medical school, to humans. Science was always his cover. He just had a strong desire to know how things worked, at least his cover story mentioned that. Becoming a medical examiner allowed him to play with dead bodies all day… and get paid for it. He'd been at the job for over twenty years and never once did anyone suspect that something was… off, in him. As for himself, he never thought anything was wrong either: he just liked bad things. He never once hurt a fly: so what if he liked to play with dead people's guts? Hell, his fascination had solved many murders. Things were just fine.

Fine that is, until one particular body came in. At first it was nothing out of the ordinary. Sixteen-year-old girl, suicide, slit writs, just one of dozens. After the clothing and hand examination, Chris would cut the clothing off, bag it, and finally, place the cadaver on the table. During this process, he did his best to not look at

the body as a whole, for that was always his favorite part. If he did it just right, he could not look at the body as he placed it onto the table. Then, when he was ready, he'd look up and take the whole thing in. He'd always stand there for a few seconds, breathe in the acrid air of the examining room and just stare at the corpse. Mostly he worked alone, but at times, when the director or someone else was in the room, he still did this, only he would explain he was bonding with the dead, letting the body be a person before he treated it like meat. Doing so, he would explain, wouldn't let him forget that it was a *person* he was working on. In truth, he merely was savoring the moment before he dove into the body.

That day, the body on the table-- Trinity Sands, so said its sheet-- didn't look any different than the countless teens he had seen dead before. The smooth young flesh and tiny breasts before him did give him a little tingle of sexual excitement, but he was always professional: never, ever had he crossed that line, at least at work. As if on autopilot, he went about doing the normal tasks he did with every body: weigh it, examine the wounds, draw blood, record all birthmarks and abnormalities, and place the body block under her back. Everything was normal, everything except for an odd itch in the back of his thigh. Having to keep his hands sterile, he struggled to itch it with his knee, but it would not go away. Ignoring the irritancy, he checked his tools, and got ready to dive in, and that is where the real fun began.

Cutting the typical Y incision along Trinity's torso, he sighed with pleasure at the sound of the flesh tearing open. As he peeled back the skin and muscle, the itch

behind his leg started to spread. Breaking protocol, he grabbed a scalpel and used the back of it to scratch the spot. It felt wonderful, but didn't soothe it. Once again, he tried to ignore it. Grabbing the large shears, he cracked each rib one by one with the popping crunching sound he loved so much and exposed the organs. His breath started to become strained; he usually got excited at this point, but the adrenaline he was feeling was more than normal. He took a second to try and catch his breath, but doing so made him want to scratch the tickle that had now spread up his leg and over his butt cheek. His mind started to become a bit cloudy, but there was no way to stop mid-autopsy, so he pushed his way through.

He removed organ after organ, took tissue samples, and weighed them. Then, as he started to remove the stomach, he nearly fainted when it moved in his hand. The movement startled him to point of dropping it back in the body. He took a few steps back and held in a scream. In the thousands of bodies he had taken apart, this had never happened. Being a logical man, he tried to think of good explanation… frog, she swallowed a frog or some sort of small animal and it was still alive. Or maybe, Alka-Seltzer. Yeah, that could be it, she swallowed one still in the wrapper, and it took a while but the bile finally ate through the wrapper and now it was fizzing, filling the stomach with gas. That had to be the reason. Slowly approaching the body, he watched the stomach wiggle, inflate, and deflate… maybe it wasn't gas.

Grabbing a knife, he approached the pulsating stomach as if he were a hunter sneaking up on prey. With the knife pointing at it he quickly grabbed the stomach

with his other hand. It was slippery and the movement inside went frantic as he grasped it. He felt something through his gloves on the palm of his hand: it was like he was being kicked by a tiny foot. Not wanting to hold it anymore, he tossed it into the stainless-steel bin next to the scale. Once there, it stopped moving a bit. Chris wiped sweat from his brow, wondering what to do. Curiosity made him want to cut it open, but fear of what was inside, of letting it out, was keeping him from slicing. The thought of getting someone else to witness this crossed his mind, but he didn't want anyone in his exam room... just in case this was only in his mind. That and he didn't want to share Trinity with anyone: she was too good looking. Though the stomach was moving a bit, Chris found himself looking at the young girl's breasts, which were on the side of her body, facing the floor in the most unnatural way possible now that her chest was cracked open. *Cut them off, take them home.* The thought bubbled in his mind as an urge. As he reached out to touch one, the steel bowl tinked and was nudged toward the edge of the table by the stomach. *Take care of the stomach first, then touch and keep what you want.*

Another wipe of sweat and Chris felt ready to attack, kill, or examine whatever was making the stomach move. As he took a step closer to it, he couldn't think of anything but the girl's perfect nipple that was touching the table. It looked so, so tasty, squished flat against the steel. He shook his head. He had never had thoughts like that, at least not this over-powering. Raising the blade up high he knew he had to stab the stomach, that he had to get it over with so he could get to those... *beautiful mounds.*

149

Thinking again of the breasts, he dropped the knife and went after them. Grabbing the sides of her exposed ribs, he pushed the chest cage back together and watched the breasts jiggle as they moved to where they once were. Leaning in, he puckered his lips and placed them around the soft nipple. He had tasted a lot of skin in his life, and it usually tasted like nothing, but this nipple, it tasted better than anything he had ever eaten in his life. It tasted so good he had to... bite it. He wanted to chew it, to swallow it and feel it in his stomach.

A tingle of nerves telling him not to do it shot through his spine, but it did nothing to stop his teeth from clamping down. He had to move his teeth back and forth a few times and bite harder and harder, but it finally popped off. Standing back up he chewed the gummy nipple over and over again. His mind raced to compare the amazing taste to something he had eaten before, but there was no comparison. The flavor that was dancing around his mouth was so intense he thought his body was going to spasm and orgasm right then and there. As he swallowed, the sensation settled down. He had to have more: it was too good not to. Leaning down to bite the other nipple, he realized he had forgotten about the stomach. With one hand on the fresh breast, he was no longer scared of the moving body part. Using his free hand, he picked it up, felt it squirm in his hand, and laughed. He had no idea why, but he now liked what was moving inside, so much so that he wanted to protect it. And there was only one way to do that: he needed to swallow it so it could hide in his warm stomach.

With large surgical shears, he snipped off the end of the stomach. There was no curiosity left inside him, which meant there was no need to dump the stomach's contents out on the table. Instead, he held the sack up to his mouth and started to pour the half-chewed food, bile, goo, and whatever was moving, into his mouth. The bitter bile almost made him gag as well as the oddly familiar chunks of food. He held strong though, and swallowed all he could without chewing, wanting-- needing-- to get the thing inside of him. Squeezing the last drops out of the sack, he finally took a breath, sucked in air and realized he needed to wash the bile out of his mouth. Rushing to the sink, he turned on the faucet, filled his mouth, swished, and spit a dozen times before suddenly becoming overwhelmed with thirst. Gulp after gulp, he swallowed until his own stomach felt like it was going to burst. The thing was thirsty.

The movement in his stomach felt odd, like a case of the butterflies, only, much, much stronger. He liked the feeling and found he kept patting his stomach as if to show his love for it. As he headed back to Trinity's body he realized how delicious her flesh looked. He had never seen anything so delicious looking. Picking up a ten blade, he started to cut long strips of meat off the girl's body. One after another he gobbled them down. After his twentieth piece, he was amazed that he could keep eating. He would have, too, if he didn't hear the door open behind him. Turning, he knew he was in trouble; there was no way he could cover the body and clean his face fast enough, but at least he had a knife in his hand.

"Chris, sorry to bother you but the girl's dad is here, throwing a fit about wanting to see... Jesus Christ!" Chris wiped his mouth with his sleeve, gripped the blade tighter, and smiled at the in-take manger.

"Jonathan, I never realized how delicious you look." Chris was ready for a chase, but it wasn't necessary; the skinny man just stood there with his mouth wide open and face going pale. When the knife plunged into Jonathan's chest, a scream finally released. Chris just laughed as he cut the man's throat, stopping the scream. As the body fell to the floor, he tried to decide what body part to eat first. Getting to his knees he decided on the meaty part of Jonathan's thigh when he heard the door burst open. It was followed by a howl of a cry, some clattering, and a sob. Chris was annoyed that his meal was being interrupted, but he tried to cheer himself up at the thought of even more food. As he started to stand up, he heard an all-too-familiar loud buzz coming from near the autopsy table.

Standing up, Chris saw a young man, looking like he saw the most terrifying thing of his life, holding his cranium saw. This must have been the girl's dad. He hated when people touched his stuff: he was going to make this man pay. Looking at his knife, he knew he needed something bigger, something that would stop a blade that could cut through a skull like butter. The stainless-steel pan next to the girl's body might stop the blade, but to get to it he'd have to get by the man who looked ready to attack. The movement in his stomach started to speed up to a frantic pace, and it made him feel sick.

"What...what?" Chris asked the thing in his stomach, wanting to know if it wanted him to run or to attack the man. When another giant flip hit his stomach, he couldn't keep the flesh he had just eaten down. Hunching over, he started to vomit violently. The taste of the hardly chewed skin and meat leaving his throat was horrible. The vomiting was hard and long, and he had to gasp in tiny breaths of air to keep himself from passing out. Hearing footsteps approach him, he tried to find the blade, but he had to sift through the red pile of chunks to find it. The slick bile made it a bit too slippery. Just as he managed to get it in his hand, he heard the familiar buzz right at his ear, followed by tearing sounds. The pain followed.

As he laid on the ground, he watched his own blood mix with the pool of vomited flesh. Starting to lose consciousness, he realized the feeling in his stomach was gone. It made him upset: he had failed the thing. Then, near his now useless hand, he saw movement under a large strip of un-chewed flesh. Seeing the movement made him smile. At least it wouldn't die with him. Just as his vision started to go dark, he saw the man who had just killed him scoop up the pile where the movement was... and bring it to his mouth. Everything was going to be all right.

THE LOSS

He lost her. When he lost her, he lost everything. The world suddenly changed. It got darker, even more pointless than it already was. There was no meaning without her anymore. The worst part was that he knew it was his fault. A stupid glitch in his brain, a malfunction of the wiring. It was a tiny, simple glitch, but one that caused him endless grief and stress his entire life. Day after day, he thought about how different his life would be if this defect weren't there, yet it wasn't until he lost her that he knew he had to change, for he lost the best thing he ever had. The one thing that inspired him. The one thing that made his cold, dead heart wake up. Without her, his heart would go back into the musty box, the door would shut on it, the chains would be replaced, and it would slowly start to freeze once again. Seeing her leave, he knew his heart was already placed in that box, but the lid was not shut yet; he had time to do something, anything, before it closed forever.

By the time Matt was in his mid-thirties, he had created a comfortable existence that side-stepped the quirks he held so closely. Plain and simply put, it was anxiety, mostly based off of social situations, or more so, anything that required him to leave his comfort zone of

his home or the movie theater. While he never fully addressed the anxiety until his early twenties, it ruled his life with an iron fist. By the time he was ready to face it, it was too late: the fist would never let go. At times, he tried to fight back against its grasp, but it merely laughed at him. While occasionally it would loosen a mere finger to allow him to do the most minor of activities, it quickly shut right after. Most of the time, Matt felt as if the hand crushing him was there for the sole purpose of messing with him. He truly wanted to be like others-- to go out and have friends, to go to parties, bars, and events-- but he simply couldn't. The hand would not allow it.

The worst part was that he always had the intentions do the things normal people did. In his younger years, he would be social and friendly with kids at school, and they would ask him to hang out; he would agree and they would make plans, but then the hand would start to tickle his brain with thoughts of panic. The night before he was supposed to go to a party, he would hardly sleep: he would be too nervous. What killed him was that he knew most people wouldn't even think about the party at all besides looking forward a bit to going. For him, it was a constant worry in his head. It would start as an itch of worry, then grow and grow until the fear covered his entire body like poison ivy. When the time for the party finally came, he would get dressed, try on outfits, finally pick one, then sit at the kitchen table and just think and think and think. The thoughts were not about being harmed or bad things that might happen; they were simply, *what do I do, who do I talk to, how do I act*: questions that normal people never had to think about, but Matt

obsessed over. In the end, so much time would tick by, he would use the excuse that it was too late to go and he would stay home. The next day, he would make up an excuse and then listen to the stories about all the fun he had missed.

While he had memories of being a child and hugging his mother's leg, refusing to play with kids his own age, it wasn't until one particular event in his last year of college that made him realize he was broken. There was a mixer for the graduating class to kick off the new year. It was a party thrown by the school and students were expected to attend, as the president would be there to give his "last year toast," something notorious for its laughs. They also gave out packs of goodies to all the seniors and raffled off dozens of computers and other fancy things that students his age could never afford. Classmates had talked about this party all through their undergraduate years, and they couldn't wait to go. It was tradition that whoever got the grand prize in the raffle would host the after party, with everyone going to his dorm room to have an all-night blow out to kick off the year. While Matt had not gone to a single school or student party his entire college career, he decided he *had* to go to this one.

The night of the party, he selected his best outfit, got dressed, and headed out across campus in the pouring rain to the main hall. The heavy golf umbrella thudded with what sounded like ball bearings hammering down onto it, yet the inclement weather didn't deter Matt: he was *going* to go. While his stomach was already in knots, he forced himself across the campus and finally arrived at the large stone building, where he simply... froze. It was

dark already, and he stood in the shadows of a statue of someone who was once important, his eyes scanning the bright windows with the countless blurred figures moving around inside. It was warm and dry in there; there was food and drinks, companionship, and prizes to be had. Yet Matt just stood there, fifty yards away, under his umbrella, his dress shoes getting soaked and ruined in the rain. The desire to go in was so deep, it was like a child looking at a Christmas present he had wanted all year long. But no matter how much he wanted to go in, no matter how much he wanted to be a part of the party, he simply could not do it. The hand would not let him. It was as if it let go just enough to let him walk there, then snapped its fist shut and forced him to just stand and watch as if to mock him. Thirty minutes later, his pants were soaked to the knees and Matt was still standing across the way, trying to talk himself into entering. It was then that the excuse of *I'm too wet to go in now* gave him a final reason to leave and return to his dorm room.

This cycle continued into his adult life, whether it was a party, helping someone move, or simply going over an acquaintance's house. He'd say yes, want to do it, and then not be able to go through with it. Over the years, he lost all of his friends this way and never really made new ones. There were a few people he kept in casual touch with from school, but not a single one he could call a real friend. He never once stepped foot into a bar or went to a function alone. While he knew he was different than everyone else, he just accepted it and lived his life how *he* could live it.

While this invisible hand controlled him, to the outside world, he seemed completely normal. In fact, he was downright charming. What no one knew was that the charm came out of insecurity. At a young age, Matt learned how to "act" so people would like him. He learned the right things to say at the right times and how to make old ladies blush and young girls swoon. He learned how to make mature men nod in appreciation and young men respect his politeness. In a way, he thought of himself as a robot, functioning on protocols programmed into him. While he never wrote them down or even really thought of them much, Matt learned to live by a set of rules and codes he created to help him understand the rest of the world. Meticulously he would watch and see what things people did that others liked. He would cheerily pick actions he thought he could replicate and do in order to make himself look like everyone else. And it worked. He was able to get through life without anyone noticing that he was not normal. He could always get a girlfriend and he was able to hold down jobs. But all of those things were done on autopilot, his mind running off the code he built, doing each step exactly as it was programmed to do.

Good and "normal" only worked for so long. Anyone who got close to him quickly learned that he wasn't really normal. It wasn't that they would see the robot underneath his skin, but they couldn't understand why he wouldn't do anything other than hang out at his apartment or go to movies and dinners alone. They wanted him to meet friends, go to parties, and meet their families, but he refused. He explained that he really

couldn't, and while they tried, none of them understood. One by one, the fights over these situations would start. It would boil down to them thinking he didn't care. He'd argue he did, but by then it would be over because he simply could not prove his feelings. Regardless of how each relationship ended, Matt always felt the same: relieved. Being alone was much easier for him. Alone was safe. Alone did not cause him stress. Alone was the only place he felt normal.

But his heart: that was another story. For years, he thought it was normal, that he loved like everyone else and that he felt things like the rest of the world. When he realized that his emotions were also a part of his programming, the depression set in. It was such a small thing, but it made him realize it was not just the inability to socialize that was wrong with him. His most recent girlfriend, one that was so quick and forgettable she was not worth even naming in his memory, was watching the news over his shoulder during a dinner at his favorite restaurant. She lightly put her hand on her chest and pursed her lips, and her eyes got watery. When he asked what was wrong, she said there was a sad story about a few hundred people who died in an earthquake in some foreign country he could not pronounce. Matt innocently asked why she cared about people she did not know halfway across the world. Her look instantly told him everything he needed to know: it shattered his pretense that he was normal. Her rant that followed (*how could he not care about them? how could he be so cold-hearted?*) started a domino effect of thinking in his brain.

159

That night, he did not sleep, not for a second; he didn't even close his eyes for more than a quick rehydrating blink. He laid in his small bed and went through his past memories. One by one, he realized he did not truly care if someone lived or died; he didn't care about *anything* really. Yes, he had things he liked: movies, books, sex, but other than that, he didn't care if the world exploded. *All* of his emotions had been acted his entire life: every single one of them. It was in that moment that he started to picture his heart as a block of ice locked in a box, sealed with chains. Depression set in that night and it never fully left. He did his best to ignore the fact that he didn't care for anything and was merely a robot following commands through life with an invisible hand crushing the possible humanity that was inside of him. He simply just existed. Life went on like this for years. He skidded by, day after day, no one the wiser that they had talked to a robot and not a real human. He dated women, went to family functions, worked his job, and felt empty the entire time. Until she came into his life.

It was at his new position, the second in four years, where he first met her. His job was to edit articles for several different boring magazines, ones like *Knitting Monthly* and *Hip Replacement Weekly*: periodicals he never knew existed until he was hired. The company gave him a small, dank, old office in the back of their building, and one by one, the managers would send him articles to edit. It was a job he could do at home, but for some reason they wanted him in the office, so he obliged and came every day, on time, to make sure he followed the rules.

Once a week, he brought cookies from a local bakery to show he "cared" about his co-workers, even though he never saw them in the back forgotten office that he rarely wandered from. It was in his fifth month when Brie from clerical knocked on his door, shocking him out of his stupor, as it was the first knock in over three months. When he looked up, he saw her smiling and blushing ever so lightly on her pale, soft, porcelain skin. Matt had met her briefly his first week and saw her occasionally on his way to the bathroom, but he had never had a conversation with her, even if he did find her to be rather attractive.

When it came to women, Matt never once approached them. Never in his life did he ask a girl out in person. He never kissed them first nor did he even attempt to try to sleep with them. Every girl he ever dated he was set up with or he met online, and they all fell madly in love with him because he was "sweet" and "gentle." Little did they know, the sweet was because he was scared, and the gentle was because he couldn't do anything to break his rules and make himself look bad. Looking at the beautiful woman in his doorway, he blinked, put on his robotic smile, and asked what he could do for her. She smiled lightly and said,

"I was walking in the back to get some paper and just realized I had never really talked to you. You're probably the only person here that I haven't had a conversation with. 'Figured I'd stop by and get to know you, if you had time that is."

Matt was taken aback by this, but he quickly stood up and offered the chair in front of his tiny desk. There was

only one tiny, frosted window in his office, but it was still cozy and comforting thanks to a small lamp he had brought in so that he could avoid the harsh fluorescent lights. Brie took the seat and crossed her legs, which Matt made a conscious decision not to look at-- he never showed his interest, and looked around.

"Your office is cozy, though I think I'd die without a real window. I need to see the sun."

Matt instantly blurted back, "I hate the sun." It sounded cold and not the correct answer he should have said. This woman had him off kilter. He didn't like that.

"You'd think I would, too-- I'm so pale-- but there is nothing I love more than to put the top down in my car and drive."

Matt nodded. He loathed convertibles and wind and the sun-- it sounded God awful to him-- but he acted as if it must be enjoyable. The conversation went on for ten minutes: typical getting-to-know-you and talk about work ridiculousness that Matt didn't care for. Most of the time, he thought of her breasts or of getting back to work. When she left, he thought of her as having the potential to sleep with, but he didn't know if a workplace romance was appropriate or not. He'd have to play it out.

Over the next few weeks, Brie started to come down regularly. At first, it was once or twice a week, but then it picked up until they saw each other every day. They would have a routine: she would come down during her break in the morning, and at times, come down at the end of the day and have Matt walk her out. While he typically didn't care much for conversation, he genuinely enjoyed talking to Brie and enjoyed that he could have a friend, at

work at least, for he knew he could not handle it outside of there. It would cause him too much stress. Their conversations were never dirty, but they were frank and loose. He imagined that this was what real friends were like and for the first time in his life, he looked forward to actually spending time with someone. Brie never asked him to hang out outside of work and he never asked her; he was comfortable with what they had and enjoyed it, but it soon all changed.

One day, he was asked to go to a yarn convention to sit in on some lectures about the intricate coloring of yarn because one of the staff writers couldn't make it. He didn't do much writing, only the editing, but they were in a jam and needed someone to cover it. Matt gave seventeen excuses to get out of going, but his boss put his foot down and said he had to go: all he had to do was sit in the back, listen, and take some notes. Begrudgingly, Matt went, which meant he was not going to see Brie that day. An hour into the most boring lecture he had ever heard, his phone buzzed in his pocket. He pulled it out and saw a text that read, *Want to hang yourself with the yarn yet?* Matt almost laughed out loud but stifled it and looked around. He did not have Brie's number in his phone, but he was positive it was her. He texted back, *Yes, just trying to pick what color to use.* For the next three hours, he texted back and forth almost constantly with Brie, and for the first time, their conversation veered towards things they never discussed in person, and that is when everything changed.

It was a text that read *I don't think I'm normal* that started it all. The second Matt read it, his cold, dead heart

163

beat a bit harder in his chest. He wrote back that he wasn't either, and the conversation bloomed. From that point on, Matt did not hear a damn word about yarn: he was focused solely on the texting conversation, waiting eagerly for each response, not being able to handle it when it took longer than a minute for her to reply. During this marathon texting session, Matt learned that Brie thought *she* was broken as well, that she had done things in her life just for the sole purpose of feeling *something… anything.* Matt wanted to run out of the building and into her arms; he wanted to consume her and be with her in a way he had never been with a woman before. He wanted to blurt out everything about him that he had hidden from the world his entire life; he wanted her to know his secrets, and he wanted to know hers.

The next day at work, he stared at the clock waiting for her to show up. When she did, their eyes met and connected in a way he had never experienced. It felt like they were staring into each other's souls and it made him more comfortable than he ever had been in his life. Deep down, he knew this was going to be different than anything he had ever experienced. When Matt opened his mouth that day, it was like a dam breaking: he couldn't stop. Part of him felt like he was saying way too much, way too fast, but he didn't care. It had all been inside of him so long, he needed it out and she, she was the one it was all meant for. Brie listened intently, nodded, and commented when appropriate. Matt told her how he felt like he was always a robot, not of the human race; that his heart, if it existed, was frozen in its box. She understood… she *understood*.

When it was her time to speak, she told of a similar story, but in not as much detail and not as deeply. She was holding back some, but that was alright with Matt: they had all the time in the world.

Less than a month later, on St. Patrick's Day, when the rest of the staff left early to drink green beer, Brie and Matt stayed behind and talked briefly, before silently making their way to his apartment three miles away. There, they kissed, it was like sliding into an old glove, warm and familiar and perfect. When Matt sat on the chair in his bedroom and she straddled him, reaching down and grabbing his penis, which was harder than Matt ever imagined it could get, the entire world melted away. When he slid into her, her gorgeous breasts against his chest, arms wrapped around each other, nothing mattered. It was as if their bodies were a matching set of lock and key. They smelled each other's necks, licked skin, explored with hands, and slid back and forth with utter pleasure. As the rhythmic movement sped up, Matt grabbed Brie's hands, intertwined his in hers, and told her to look at him. They locked eyes, and he pushed harder into her until a deep hot burst shot out of him and into her.

Afterwards, her head on his shoulder, Matt blinked hard. He was confused at what the small wet glob was on his cheek. Realizing it was a tear, a real tear: not a manufactured one, he enjoyed imagining his heart inside thawing just a little. It might not work like others', but he knew he had one inside of him now. It would have all been perfect, if only Brie weren't married.

Over the next six months, things were amazing. They had a relationship unlike either had ever experienced. They came up with the term, "shutting off the robots," when they were around each other. They didn't have to pretend to be the fake people they had been for the rest of society. They laughed, they fucked, and they talked about everything under the sun. But the most important thing in the world was that they understood each other. When they were together, the entire world would disappear. When they were not together, Matt thought of her constantly. He wanted to tell her everything, talk to her about stuff, show her things. They texted sneakily to avoid her spouse when they could and met at Matt's apartment almost daily. It became their sanctuary.

Matt was over the moon. He finally had a partner and, best of all, it didn't stress him out. He didn't have to go places, he didn't have to put on the fake show of going out of his way to do overly romantic things he didn't believe in just to keep the girl hooked; he simply just had to be himself. This, of course, meant he would eventually screw it up.

Little by little, the raw desire for each other grew and they wanted, needed, to see each other more often. Matt wanted to see Brie a lot more, to spend long days lounging in bed, exploring her body and talking incessantly, but his fears outweighed his desires. The all-too-familiar hand was back, clutching him when Brie began to ask him to do things outside of work. There were a few times she was able to get away from her husband, and she wanted to spend that time with him. Of course, *he* had the free time, but the damn hand would

always squeeze and create the excuses that soon became old hat anytime she asked him to do anything that was outside of his apartment.

When Brie's husband was out of town, Matt wouldn't go over her house because he feared the man might show up or that someone might see them. The few times she pleaded with him to go out with friends and co-workers, he said he would and then didn't show up, sending a last-minute text about how he got held up. Brie knew it was a lie and she understood his anxiety, but only to a point. The arguments started, the same ones he had had with all of his girlfriends: *If you really cared for me, you wouldn't let the anxiety win; you'd come see me when I had time.* Matt tried to overcome the fears-- tried hard-- but the hand squeezed his chest tight and forced him to ruin each plan they made. After Matt canceled for the third time a day they had planned to play hooky from work and get a hotel room, Brie had had enough. It had finally gotten to the point where she was done: done with his excuses, and done with him.

At this point, Matt was taking her for granted. He was comfortable and beyond happy with how things were, regardless if she wanted or needed more. When she hung up on him the day he canceled their plans, he knew he had to change. The next day, he begged her to give him another chance, but it was already his tenth, and they both knew he was not going to change. When Brie walked out of his office, his heart, the one he thought he didn't have, felt cold and started to drop back inside the box it had called its home for so many years.

That night, Matt was a maniac. He paced his apartment, screamed at the walls, and slammed his fingers on his laptop keyboard, looking for ways to overcome the damn invisible hand. There was a lot of stuff about meds on the internet, but he had taken them all in different doses. None of them did anything except make him tired and lose his sex drive. Other sites offered meditation training and baby-step processes that he did not have time for. He had to change, *now*. After typing in a thousand different searches using various keywords in the hope of getting different results, something caught his eye. *Get Rid of The Invisible Rope That Ties You Down!* As if his life depended on it, he frantically clicked on the link and started to read.

> *Anxiety got you down?*
> *Staying home when you want to go out?*
> *Don't let the monster keep you tied up!*
> *Break free and be a new person!*

Matt read the bold type with anticipation; he was shocked that someone explained their anxiety in a similar way to how he thought of it. The website itself was cheesy, colored in deep reds and blues with no pictures-- just print. It was like an early 90s website he remembered from his childhood, just text with an excessive amount of exclamation points and nothing else. Quickly, he scrolled to the bottom and found the copyright. It read 1997: he was pretty close. Regardless, he kept reading the infomercial-like statements, eager to find even the smallest tidbit of information to try.

When he finished reading the sparse six paragraphs, he sat back in his chair and rubbed his eyes. It was stupid, like all the other sites and ideas. It must have been written by a lunatic or as a joke. Then he thought of Brie and how she held his face when he had a panic attack and soothed him. He thought of her when he needed to be calm or to do something out of his comfort zone. He needed her; he had to have her back in his life. Pushing aside how stupid he felt, he stood up, walked to the middle of his room, took in a deep breath, and yelled.

The article claimed that it was not merely a chemical imbalance that caused anxiety, but a spiritual force that stuck to your soul and fed off of your fears. The more it stopped you from living, the more *it* could live. When you died, it took your soul so that it could be reborn into the world. Being an atheist and against all religion, Matt thought this was an appalling idea, but the possibility of confronting the monster that tortured him intrigued him. What if he stood there and yelled at the hand that always crushed him, faced it straight on for the first time and had a conversation with it? A symbolic showdown with his inner thoughts. He had read an article once about a boy pretending there were fighter jets in his blood attacking the bad cells that gave him cancer. His cancer had disappeared and the doctors could not explain it. Matt might not believe in magic and miracles, but he believed in the power of the mind, so why *not* scream at himself in the middle of the room? Fuck his neighbors!

"I'm done with you! You won't control me anymore, you goddamn piece of shit! This is my life, MY LIFE. You hear me? I control it! I get to decide what I do and

don't do!" Matt's throat instantly hurt from screaming so loud. He couldn't ever recall raising his voice that high. Of course, nothing happened, so he screamed again.

"Show yourself! You want to control me? You can at least show your weak ass life-sucking face to me! Because I'm not going to take it anymore!" This time, Matt made sure to not hurt his voice, but he still yelled loudly. On the outskirts of his peripheral vision, he thought he saw a sticky note above his computer move a bit as if there was a breeze, but that was ridiculous, and he laughed to himself. Then he felt a small pain in his chest. It was familiar: it was the start of a panic attack. It usually came with one tiny tick then slammed him to the ground like an elephant falling on him. He thought of his pills in the bathroom. They took twenty minutes to kick in, but just taking them would usually ease his thoughts. He took a step to the bathroom, but then stopped. No, no: he was going to face this panic attack head-on. Let it wash over him, let it bring the pain and suffering! He would *not* let it control him. Talking in a shaking voice, he yelled some more.

"Scared to face me, huh? Going to give me a fucking panic attack, you pussy? A real monster could confront me to my face, not just fuck with my mind!" As his chest started to tighten a bit more, his eyesight blurred, and he thought he saw something in front of him. No, no: he didn't *think*-- he *did* see something there...

There, right in front of him, a shadowy figure materialized. It was taller than him by four or five inches and at least three times as thick as he was. It was all gray and had no clothing. In fact, its body, arms, and legs

seemed to be made of one long piece of material. Its face looked like smooth stone with just the vaguest of human features carved into it. In a way, it was like a liquid statue. Shallow eyes, a tiny lump of a nose, and two thin, worm-like lips. Its head was smooth with what looked like a ripple of a cloak over his skull, but it, too, was solid and part of its body. The saying *couldn't believe my eyes* was never truer to Matt than in this moment. At first, he thought he must have be having a delusion or some psychotic break, but then the thing reached out to him, its hand bigger than the rest of its body; it clamped itself onto Matt's chest. The feeling of slow suffocation was eerily familiar.

"You, you can't be real," Matt gasped. The thing turned its head and then spoke directly into Matt's head without any of its facial features moving. The voice was wispy, almost echoing, and chillingly cold.

"You are mine… never confront me again or I will kill you."

Suddenly, it let go of Matt. He could breathe again. Part of him wanted to run, but he knew he could never get away from the thing; somehow, it was a part of him. Like a shadow, it was always there.

"No. I can't have you control me anymore," Matt stammered. "I'd rather die than live my life this way." Matt felt like a hero in some film, standing up to the evil villain before the great fight: it felt good. The creature seemed to swell to almost twice its size, and this time, both hands swept up and grabbed Matt's chest. It crushed him harder than he had ever felt. Reaching down, Matt tried to grab its forearms, but he could not

get a grip on them: he just kept sliding off, like the gray skin was covered in wet ice. Matt felt his feet come off the ground; he couldn't breathe at all now, and his entire body tingled like his limbs were falling asleep.

"Enough!" The one simple word echoed in his head in the thing's chilling voice, and suddenly, he was dropped to the floor. On his hands and knees, he sucked in air and watched the thing turn around and start to sink into the floor as if it were leaving. Taking a chance, Matt ran into the bathroom, grabbed his bottle of Ativan, which the doctor had prescribed him for serious panic attacks, and shook ten, maybe thirteen of the white tablets into his mouth. The pills always worked, so they had to do something to the damn monster. He turned on the water, drank a handful of it greedily, and washed the tiny pills into his stomach. When he looked up, the creature was behind him. While it still showed no expression, he could sense it was furious with him. Matt smiled.

"Let's see how you handle those, you piece of shit!" Matt let out a nervous laugh as he watched the thing transform its shape into something that stopped his laugh cold, a giant hand. It was almost as if the monster's head multiplied into five and then stretched long to form a sadistic, massive palm with five grotesque digits slightly curled into a claw-like shape. Seconds after it formed, it quickly swung down, grabbed Matt around his entire body, and pulled him out of the bathroom. He was suddenly being dragged down the hall, his lungs collapsing.

The hand brought him back into his tiny home office and slammed him against the wall-- once, twice, three times and then dropped him hard onto the floor. A strange sensation like a cannonball being fired into his stomach hit him, and he felt numerous ribs crack. It was one of the creature's fingers trying to get him to vomit. As it lifted Matt in the air to land another blow, he rolled over so that it couldn't hit him in the breadbasket again. The pain began to mix with nausea when the shrill tweet of Brie's text message notice filled the room. The sound seemed to confuse the hand, as it did not touch him for a moment, giving Matt time to get up, fight over the pain in his body, and grab his phone off the desk. Just as he clicked it on, the hand clasped around his waist again.

With his own hand clasped to his chest, Matt looked down at the phone and squinted to read the message.

I might not understand, but I think you are worth the trouble. Let me help you. I don't know what I can do, but I will do it. We have a Halley's Comet rare love and I don't want to lose that. No matter how much of pain in the ass you are.

As he read the text, he felt his face and body flush hot with passion and anger. It was as if he was Popeye and the text was his spinach. He took a deep breath, let out a guttural scream, and pushed his arms out like a wrestler breaking free during an overly dramatic championship match. The hand released him, and when he turned around, the hand was just finishing transforming back into the human-like creature. It looked smaller, much smaller this time. While in intense pain, Matt stood as tall as he could.

"My life. My life now. For the first time, I have something to fight for, something that is real and not fake. I'm not going to let you ruin that for me," he said with a crackling, almost slurring voice. Matt realized he was feeling a bit off, but it didn't matter: his words seemed to work. The thing started to melt away into the floor as if Matt had won the battle. Just as the head disappeared through the hardwood floor, he thought he heard a tiny laugh inside his head. Matt wanted to jump up and put his fists in the air with triumph, but his body collapsed under him. The pills...

As he fell to the floor, his broken rips screamed with pain. A vague memory of his doctor telling him to not take more than three pills, ever, came into his mind. Thirteen was more than fatal. Matt laughed out loud at the biting irony. Just when he was finally going to win his battle against anxiety, it beat him.

Lying there, dying, Matt desperately wanted to grab the phone to hear Brie's sweet voice more time, wanted to tell her how much he loved her, but he couldn't move his arms, he couldn't move anything. Instead, he said the words in his head and hoped she could hear them. And while an atheist, he whispered a prayer that his soul, the one he never thought he had, would not belong to the hand for eternity.

IT GIRL

The audience burst out with robust applause as the end credits stated, *It: Chapter One.* It was the movie of the year for horror fans like Jessie. In fact, it was a movie she had been dying to see for years. As the credits rolled and the creepy music played, a few tears spilled out of her eyes while others in the theater laughed and made their way out. Seeing the film was the closest thing to a religious experience she had ever had. *It* had been a part of her life for as long as she could remember; seeing a new version on the screen was like seeing Jesus come back to life in person. At the ripe old age of ten, she had seen the original version of the movie on television. Not only did it give her nightmares for weeks, it changed her life. It sparked her curiosity in horror, which grew over the years to an obsession. She read every single thing Stephen King wrote more than once. *It*, the book, she read over seven times, and as the tome was over a thousand pages in length, that was quite the feat. She could quote any and every line in the book, tell you the backstories of its characters, and even teach an entire lesson on the making of the films, the history of the book, and how it affected our culture.

On the day she turned eighteen, she was in a tattoo parlor at 10:04 in the morning, lying back in a soft leather

chair. She would have liked to have been in it earlier, but the place refused to open before then, even if it was her birthday. Through five hours of pain, the smile on her face hardly faded as the artist etched Tim Curry's version of Pennywise onto her arm. In the eleven years since then, she wore sleeveless shirts as often as possible to show the beautiful clown's face to everyone who saw her. While seventeen more tattoos-- all horror related, four based off of *It*-- had been added to her body since, Pennywise was still her favorite. When she was twenty-four, she discovered horror conventions. If she was asked, she would say seeing *It* the first time and walking into Monster Mania for the first time were the two most significant events in her life. It was at the convention that she made the first real friends of her life and where she learned there were others just like her. It was also where she learned about cosplay and that she could dress up like the characters, or more so, as the *character* she loved most, and people wouldn't think she was weird. In fact, people would appreciate it and *want* to take pictures with her.

Over the years, she went from dressing up as Pennywise to creating her own character in his image, one she considered to be his spiritual soulmate. It was a female clown that had matching colors but a much more feminine feel called Penny. With her short, five-foot frame, the baggy yellow, blue, and purple costume had her own embellishments like some jewels and girly bows on the front. The biggest liberty she took was hacking the hair color from red to a deep green; it was puffed out, frizzy, with a perfect little yellow bow sitting in the bird's nest of a mess. She never told Penny's story to people:

she let them guess if she was Pennywise's daughter or wife or maybe even a sister. In fact, Jessie didn't know the backstory herself and didn't care; she simply wanted to be a scary clown and freak people out. In fact, it became such an obsession that her life revolved around it. All her screen names were *ScaryClownGirlPenny* or variations on that. She got her own website and even started a YouTube Channel where she put up videos of herself scaring people and doing Q&A sessions with her so-called "fans."

She invested more money into what her family called a "stupid, disgusting hobby" than she made, but she was happy and doing something she loved; that is what mattered, or at least, that is what she told herself when she couldn't pay the bills each month. However, she was making some money from her online presences. It wasn't much yet, but she knew she could really, really start to rake in the dough and become famous if she got just one viral video. That's all it took. She had heard countless times about how YouTubers had become millionaires from their videos, and usually it all started with one viral sensation. Jessie's, or Penny's, page had a respectable ten thousand followers, but she needed to hit millions before she could make a fulltime living from it, and she knew she would, soon. She had plans that coincided with the release of the film she had been waiting her whole life for.

Sitting in the theater that Thursday afternoon, she swiped the tears away with a tissue that had bit of salt from her popcorn on it. The salt stung her eyes a bit, making her blink a bit more than she wanted to, but she

ignored this irritant and focused on how this day was going to change her life. It was merely two in the afternoon and she had seen the matinee of the film. She had loved it with more love than a mother seeing her newborn child for the first time. Jessie-- no, no-- *Penny*, today and every day after this, she was going to be Penny (she had plans to change her name legally after the fame really kicked in), sat so long after the credits that the usher had to ask her kindly to leave. Thankfully, the guy was a young stoner and nodded and laughed in appreciation at her tattoo; he didn't even think it was odd that she was alone. Penny briefly felt an urge to talk to him about the film, but she did not want to spoil the ethereal high she was feeling.

As she walked outside, the sun's glare shattered into her eyes, sending ripples of pain and confusion into her retinas, finally breaking the sense of wonder that had fallen over her. Closing them, she let them adjust under the shade of her lids. She took a deep breath and felt the warmth of the rays on her face (which she normally hated, but today was different). Finally able to open her eyes without pain, she looked around the parking lot. A few people were coming and going into the theater, but it was a mere trickle compared to what it was going to be that night. The thought of how many people were going to be there made her stomach bubble with excitement. While she had planned the night meticulously over and over again, she wanted to walk through it one more time: everything had to be perfect.

After twenty-five minutes of walking the path, checking the locations of where she was going to put the

hidden camera, and where and how she would scare her unexpecting victims, she giggled, looked at Tim Curry's crooked smile on her arm, lifted it, and kissed it lightly. "I'm going to make you so proud... Just you see!" The second half of her statement was said in a loud cackling voice: her Penny voice. A mere two minutes later, Penny went back inside of the theater and saw the 2:20 showing of *It*. She'd see the 6:45 as well.

Just before ten that night, Penny left the theater. She'd seen the movie three solid times and eaten two large popcorns and five boxes of Junior Mints, and she made her way to her car. Inside, she had to hold the steering wheel tight and take a few breaths: she was too excited and needed to calm down and get into character. Over the next hours, she made six trips from her car to various spots in the parking lot where she attached small cameras that cost her every dime she had ever made on her YouTube channel (and even then, she needed an extra four hundred dollars which she got from a fan after making him a *special* video). When all of the cameras were set, her heart thudded as much as the first time she saw the original movie in her bedroom as a little girl. It was time to get into costume.

Within seconds, she had masterfully slipped into the full body jumpsuit and shoes. She then put on the make-up. It used to take her an hour to apply and it would always vary slightly, but after the first two years, she learned to put it on flawlessly in twenty minutes. The contact lenses, which looked like lime green lizard's eyes, took her under a minute to pop in; the custom-made

sharp teeth, seconds. Last but not least, she slipped on the white gloves and the transformation was complete. When her hands eased into the soft cotton of the gloves, something always changed in Jessie: she *became* Penny. When the costume was on her, she stayed in character; no matter who she talked to, her high-pitched, demoniac voice was the only thing that came out of her mouth and the creepy facial gestures and movements never stopped. She considered herself a true actor and would never break character, at least that is what she told people. In reality, she didn't think she was acting: she believed Penny was the *true* version of herself.

Looking into the mirror, she gave herself a toothy grin. She loved the terrifying face that looked back at her; she had to fight crying tears of joy, as they would ruin the make-up, so she let out a maniacal laugh to snap herself out of the sappy sentiment she was feeling. Getting out of the car, Penny was sure to play up the creepy clown aspect, bobbing her head side to side as if she was listening to fun music, adding a light skip. She felt the movements added a spooky yet childlike feel. With a few hops, she opened her trunk and a dozen yellow balloons floated up (yellow was *her* color choice of balloons). She grabbed the bunch and started her skip again. One by one, she carefully tied each balloon around the parking lot, one to a sewer grate, another to a car bumper, one to a light pole, and another to a rock. Between each one, she kept up her light skip and hop: that way, the cameras would catch her and she could use the footage to cut into her viral video. She had meticulously planned the timing to ensure that very few people would be in the lot, if any,

as it was between showings. In a mere ten minutes, the lot would be filled with scared teens and adults leaving the theater, their minds still flush with thoughts of Pennywise.

With all the balloons placed, she quickly skipped back to her open trunk and grabbed her sledgehammer. Usually she walked around the conventions with a fake hammer as it got too heavy to carry a real one throughout the long days; tonight, however, she needed a real one to show the heft in the video. That, and she planned on smashing it into the ground a time or two when chasing someone away... to add that extra scare. Checking the head of the hammer, she was thrilled at how it appeared. It took her five tries, six sledge hammers, and countless hours to get it just right. She had spent one after another sitting in her living room, carving *Penny* into the handle and making claw mark scratches down the long wooden base. Almost every time, she had messed it up or it didn't look just right. Aging the head was even harder: she let it sit overnight in a bowl of Coke, hit it with another hammer countless times and even left it out in the rain for a week to rust. When she finally got one that looked just right, she added fake blood and chunks of what looked like human hair to the end of it. She leaned her head to the side and smiled, touched the tip lightly, then let out one of her laughs and shut the trunk.

Everything was set; Penny's heart started to slam-- it was show time. As she got into her place at the corner of the building, she briefly wondered if Tim Curry felt this jolt of excitement before filming his first scene in *It*. Within seconds, just as she planned, she could hear the

doors open and people start to walk out. Penny could hear the excited chatter or teens talking about the film and the parts they thought were scary and the others that were cheesy. With a deep breath, she raised her sledgehammer and ran around the corner, letting out a screaming laugh. The scare was beyond satisfying and was going to make a great intro to her video. There was a group of six kids, probably seniors in high school, who all jumped back in unison. The two bigger boys in the back turned and ran, two girls in the middle grasped at each other in a panic, and a skinny boy in the front turned to run and knocked down the girl next to him. The little blonde girl sat on the ground, her eyes wide in terror as Penny raised the hammer above her head. Penny let out a long, loud yell to give her a chance to move before she swung down the hammer. Just as the girl moved her legs, Penny slammed down the hammer, the pavement splattered open, sending up a small cloud of dust, which surprised her. Within seconds the group was gone, all of them running off in different directions.

A high like she had never experienced washed over her, goosebumps broke out across her body, pushing up under her make-up, like little white mountains suddenly populating the landscape. *That a'girl, more, more, more!* The voice, an all too familiar voice, one she just spent watching for six hours, suddenly whispered in her ear. An electric tickle shot down her spine. The words seemed so real: she couldn't have imagined them. Could she? *Fear keeps us alive.* The voice came back with a bit more giddiness in its tone. Penny spun around as quickly as the heavy hammer would allow her to. She desperately

wanted to see Tim Curry in full make-up behind her, but she'd take the new guy as well, but there was nothing-- just the parking lot. Just as she started to contemplate whether she was losing her mind or if her acting had ripped a hole in the universe, causing fiction to come alive, the theater door swung open again.

Out in the open this time, she was not able to take these ones by surprise. They stopped in their tracks at the sight of her: a group of ten young adults Penny assumed were around her age. A few laughed, others stood confused, and a few looked genuinely scared.

A tall young man who reminded Penny of Anthony Perkins in *Psycho* pointed at her and spoke loudly enough for her to hear: "Fucking freak." A few of the people in the group laughed, the few who were scared eased up and joined in the laughter. Penny turned her head, the best "creepy" turn she knew, twisted the handle of the hammer and let out a cackle, sure this would scare them more.

"Listen, loser, move out of our way or I'll kick the shit out of you," the biggest of the group said, puffing up his chest to show he was serious.

This was not right, Penny thought. She suddenly lost the amazing feeling of joy that had been circulating in her body. It was replaced with the old familiar feeling of not fitting in, of not being "normal." *They MUST fear you… if they don't… they win.* The voice came, serious and strong this time. Penny pushed away the urge to walk away and hide like she normally would have done. Instead, she quickly raised up the hammer, screamed like a maniac, and raced towards them. Every single one of them

scattered, even the tough guys, pushing each other out of the way to get to safety. This time, as she swung the hammer, she was not purposely trying to miss; something inside of her made her try to hit a young man that was skinny as death. Part of her wondered if he would just shatter into a pile of bones if she struck him, but she missed by a mere inch. She was so close, she saw the dark gray fabric of his hoody get pushed back by the rusty head of the hammer, leaving a tiny smudge of red from the blood she so carefully placed there.

As a child, Penny had seen a psychologist weekly. She hardly could recall the reasons or any of the sessions, but she knew it had something to do with a game she played with the family cat when she was five. From then on, she was on medication; at twelve she stopped the counseling, but she had stayed on the meds. Repositioning the hammer's handle in her hand, she couldn't quite figure out why a flashback of her therapy days came into her mind, but with it came a lot of anger, something she had not felt since she was sixteen, after she attacked a girl for making fun of her *Friday the 13*ᵗʰ t-shirt during woodshop. The memory was foggy, but there was blood involved, a new school, and tripling of her medication. The one thing that was not foggy was the memory of pure anger and hate, the memory of wanting to kill the girl for making fun of something she held so dearly to her heart. She didn't want to be understood. She just wanted to be left alone.

Picking up the hammer, she could feel her heart slam. It thudded in her chest so hard she actually paused a second to picture it inside of her, slamming against the rib

cage, a brief flash of it breaking through her and exploding flashed in her eyes and it made her laugh a fleeting little chuckle. When she turned back to the group she saw they were about thirty yards away, in a tight group, walking together, most of them looking back at her as they walked. She could hear snippets of swears being yelled at her. Without any conscious effort, she started to run after them, faster than she had ever run in her life. Not even her oversized shoes, which made a ridiculous tiny squeak as they hit the ground over and over again, could slow her down. She caught up to the group as they were rushing to get into three separate cars. Just as she was able to reach them, they started to peel out: two of the cars didn't even have the doors shut. Penny swung hard at a red Volvo, the closest of the cars, and was able to connect with the rearview mirror. It exploded into two hundred tiny pieces. She could have sworn the second it connected that she heard a loud laugh in that familiar voice.

As the cars sped away, with six middle fingers all sticking out of windows, Penny was no longer excited: she was simply angry. Gripping the hammer, she turned around to see she was more than halfway through the parking lot: nowhere near the doors, where crowds were now pouring out. Breathing heavy, she had a moment of rational thinking; someone was going to call the cops, she had to get out of there... but the anger-- this new, powerful, consuming anger-- was too intense. She needed to try and get one more. Part of her played over the word "get" in her mind. She didn't know what it meant: get a "scare" or get them?

185

Turning to head back to her vehicle, she saw one car near the woods: one lonely car in the packed parking lot. It was suspiciously all alone; it was a busy night, but the lot never filled up that far back. The windows were fogged slightly and Penny instantly knew why that car was there and what was happing inside. *They won't see you coming.* Penny licked the backs of the sharp fake teeth, thought for a second, then ran toward the car. After twenty seconds of sprinting, she reached the black Mustang and in one single leap, jumped onto the hood. Raising the hammer above her head, she did not hesitate to bring it down onto the windshield. The entire sheet of glass instantly went white with spider web cracks. As she lifted the hammer to swing again, both back seat doors shot open. From the driver's side, an angry thirty-something-year old man jumped out; his shirt was off; his dick, hard and straight, stuck out from his pants, and one shoe was off. Penny was about to leap at him when she heard a scream on the other side. Her head quickly shot to passenger side where a curvy, topless redhead was covering her breasts; her pants were unbuttoned, but she had both of her shoes on. Penny bore her large, sharp teeth to the woman. The woman screamed and moved her hands away from her breasts to cover her mouth. The woman's large bosom dropped down, revealing the most beautiful nipples Penny had ever seen. For some reason, the sight of this woman and how beautiful she was angered Penny even more: why did this man get to have her?

Snapping her head back to the man (who still had not put his dick away), Penny jumped off of the car. It was

an ill-planned jump, as she landed in front of the door, putting a barrier between her and her prey. The man, who looked more confused than scared, came around the door, fists clenched. Penny tried to pick up the hammer that had slipped out of her hands during the jump and was now precariously standing on its head between her feet. She was only able to lift it a few inches when the punch crossed her face. Flashes of light lit up her brain in brilliant waves; she had never been punched before, and this new sensation was one she never wanted again. As she fell to the ground, she grasped at the door, but missed the handle. She was able to grab the closest thing to it, however: the man's dick, which was oddly still erect.

With another new sensation of pain, her shoulder hit the ground, but she did not let go of the man's dick. Looking up, she could see the man's face and wished she could have had a still shot of it. The lower portion of her vision framed a gloved clown hand gripping a-- rather nice-- hard penis, and right above that was a man's face, purple with anger and painted with confusion. It was priceless. *Tear it off*, the voice demanded out of nowhere. Penny did not hesitate to comply with the demand. With all of her strength, she pulled and tugged; the man's hands grasped around her and a sick tug of war began. Using his dick as a lever, she pulled herself to her knees and without thinking, lunged forward with her sharp teeth bared. They might be fake, but they were more than sharp and easily sank into the underside of his penis, right where the shaft met the balls. Biting down has hard as she could, she felt a serious of gelatinous snaps followed by a rush of hot coppery fluid. As the warmth filled her

mouth, she had a flashback to junior high health class when she learned about what the boys called "the main vein" that carried the dick-hardening blood to a penis. This memory made her realize what she had just severed. The scream that followed brought back the tingly pleasure that she had lost a mere few minutes before.

The man's hands magically disappeared as she bit again and again all while tugging, pulling, and twisting. As the man stumbled backwards, his weight let the last vestibules of skin tear away, releasing his still hard cock permanently from his body. Penny let out a laugh as she spit out blood. It was just as easy as *Last House on the Left* made it look, she thought comically. Squeezing the rapidly softening member, she remembered the woman, who had been screaming through the entire ordeal, and ran around the car to her. She was still covering her mouth, bearing her breasts. Penny cocked her head at her, smiled wide, and threw the limp dick directly at her face. It landed with a wet slap on the woman's clavicle bone, leaving a red smear the shape of the Leaning Tower of Pisa before it rolled off her to the ground. "Sorry it's not the pearl necklace you wanted tonight, but at least it's a ruby one!" Penny said in a high pitched, perky tone. She was impressed at herself for making such a good pun while staying in character. A second later she watched the woman faint to the ground, her breasts smashing against the dirt, trapping the severed penis below them.

When Penny turned around, she was shocked to see there was a crowd of twenty people watching her, cautiously standing back; several were on the phone with whom she presumed were the cops, and half a dozen

others were filming her. *An audience! Take a bow, you deserve it.* Penny scurried over to her hammer, picked it up, then quickly curtsied and waved. "Next show is at midnight! Be sure to tip your waitress, Toodly Lou," she said before starting to skip away, worried they would chase after her, but knowing none of them would dare.

Penny applauded herself on a successful dramatic exit. Smiling to herself, she continued skipping away. Since her car was in the opposite direction, she had no clue where she was heading. It didn't matter, though: she knew the fear she had caused was more than real and it was more than satisfying. As she scanned the lot, wondering where to go, keeping up her skip, she suddenly felt a hot, searing pain in the back of her head. It was so hot and sharp, she stopped in her tracks, dumbfounded.

She reached up to her green wig, and right at the base of her skull, she could feel warm wetness. She didn't need to bring her hands forward like they did in the movies to look at her fingers and realize it was blood oozing out of her scalp (besides, her hands were already covered in blood, real and fake). *Looks like the show's over kid: you are on your own now*, the voice said with a laugh.

Penny screamed out into the air, "No, no, don't leave me!" Turning around, she saw in a millisecond flash the horde of people walking towards her, some with rocks in their hands, others with bottles and smaller weapons. Another rock hit her; this one, right on the bridge of her nose. The sound her nose made as it shattered disgusted her: it was a wet, crackling sound like a giant monster taking a huge bite of wet cereal and crushing it in his mouth with one hard snap of its jaws. The pain and short

circuit of flashing lights she saw in front of her eyes disoriented her, but mostly, it made her mad. They were *not* scared of her… they did not *fear* her anymore.

The third rock skimmed the top of her head, knocking her wig right off, making her appear to be instantly scalped. Penny had had enough. Gripping her hammer, she screamed, not in character this time, but with a real, deep guttural scream that came from the soul of Jessie, not Penny. With it, she started to run fast as she could directly at the crowd. As she approached them, screams still spilling out from her soul, several more rocks and even a bottle hit her, but she ignored them. Half of the crowd dispersed but a good dozen stood their ground, ready to defend themselves. One man, who looked like her high school gym teacher who she hated, did not move, and this made Jessie happy. Raising the hammer above her head, she yelled one more time and brought it down right above his head. The man's hands went up to protect himself, but he clearly had to think it was a prop hammer made of nothing but plastic or Styrofoam. In slow motion, Jessie watched as the man's hands were crushed underneath the weight of the steel head, each finger snapping, one by one. The man's face went from cocky and ready to fight, to pure shock and pain. His shattered fingers were forced into the top of his head, and within a second, they disappeared into the hole on the top of his head that the hammer caused.

It looked like some odd art piece-- two hands disappearing into the hole of a head. Jessie would have called it *The Mindless Man*. As she stared at the man's blank face, which looked as if it were trying so hard to

concentrate as what was left of his brain misfired, trying to figure out what was happening, she was happy. Pulling back the hammer released the flood of blood. It poured out of the hole and down the man's face like a water balloon being untied: all of the liquid quickly spilled out. Jessie turned away, readied her hammer, and looked for her next victim, but before she could even eye anyone, she found herself on the ground, pushed over by an unseen but very strong person. The hammer flew from her hands and skidded away, sending up a few tiny sparks as it glided across the asphalt. She was about to get up and go after it when a rock hit her lower spine so hard, her left big toe contracted and would not release, like the worst Charlie horse imaginable. Another rock smashed her shoulder, another hit her cheek, and a third, her right knee. *Rock fight.* The thought came into her mind: *Rock fight.*

Within a second, there were too many hitting her to count or pay attention to where they had landed on her ever-bruising and breaking body. Jessie didn't even try to protect her face: it was futile. Just as she was about to close her eyes, she saw one of the balloons she set out. It was floating above the storm grate, a mere ten feet away... only it wasn't yellow anymore. It was *red*. Her mouth fell open. How did it change, why was it red? Was... was *he* here, was he *real?* With all her might, she got to her knees and started to crawl to the balloon. Rocks still hit her from every direction, but she could no longer feel them, she no longer cared, she needed to get to the sewer drain and see if he was there, waiting for her. A mere three feet away from the grate, a rock hit her left

eye, popping it with the ease of a foot smashing a grape. Her vision was blurred, but she pushed forward the last three feet, grabbed the red balloon, and looked down into the sewer. With her one good eye, she could see a clown down below, smiling and waving her down. As she reached for him, she heard the words, *Penny, we all fl...* when a foot came down on the back of Penny's head. Her nose went between the grates as her cheekbones snapped against them and her head caved in.

Penny, not Jessie, went on to achieve her ultimate goal of fame. An unmanned source took over a dozen videos from the incident: patrons' cell phone shots, security footage from the theater, and clips from the cameras Penny set up (that was leaked from the police) were cut together into a terrifying five-minute video. A mere month after the incident, it had amassed over thirty million views. Fan pages for "Penny the Clown" were set up. Two months later, a Hollywood movie producer contacted her family for the movie rights. Three years later, there were four television programs dedicated to her story, five unauthorized books, a line of Penny merchandise, two novelizations of her life, a major film, and countless urban legends told about how she now haunted the sewers in her hometown. Penny the clown would live on for generations to come, and on every anniversary of the incident, a yellow and red balloon would appear on the sewer grate where she died.

RIPE

The stunningly red flesh was smooth and perfect, nature's purest form of perfection. Beatrice lightly glided her finger over the tomato, admiring how gorgeous it was. Seventy-one years working at the same farm stand, spending her entire life growing vegetables and yet she still got tingles and amazement looking at something so perfect, something that *she* grew. She harvested her own seeds and she planted them one by one, by hand, not like the modern farms: *she* tucked them into the soil like little children going to sleep. Watered them gently with her own hydration system she built forty years ago with the help of her long dead husband. Tended to them every day, watching them grow up towards the sun. In a way, each one of these beauties were her children. Her pride and love for her tomatoes (along with the six other vegetables she grew, but it was the tomatoes that made her known) fed a booming roadside farm stand. Sometimes people would be idling down the street, waiting for twenty minutes to park... all for some tomatoes.

Half of her customers had been coming for decades; she had watched entire generations grow up and bring their own kids, then grandkids, to grab a basket of ripe reds. They all knew her by name, and even new

customers knew her name by the time they left, for she was "the nicest old lady" they had ever met. She'd smile, make you laugh, ask how you were, give you a free sample, and always had something to give to a little child to make them smile. Hardly a summer week went by when a customer didn't make a joke about how "Ray of Sunshine Farm must have been named after you, because you certainly are a ray of sunshine." She'd always smile, give a wink, and nod a bit. Ray, her dead husband, was the real namesake of the farm, even though she owned it before she had ever met him. Regardless, she liked being associated with the name.

Day after day, year after year, she would sit at her small stand and sell her vegetables. At times, she would read a book in between customers, but mostly, mostly she just sat and watched the world go by. Car after car sped through town, going to jobs and dinners and sporting events for children. Most years, within one month of the season starting, she could chart the routine of the passing automobiles: which colors would pass going which way at what time. By July, she could easily recite the colors in order in her head: *red south, green north, two silver heading south, tan north*. One by one she would predict them in her head and was almost always right. The days a certain car didn't make its scheduled pass, she would sit and wonder what happened to *Mr. Red Car North* or *Ms. Mauve Car South*. Did they spill a coffee and run late that morning? Were they sick? Taking a vacation day? Have a meeting out of town? Or, perhaps was there a death in the family? When this last thought popped into her head, she would always smile and giggle a little. She'd even put her hand

up to cover her mouth as if someone would notice she was laughing inappropriately. She giggled because she always wondered if *she* was the one to have killed them.

Beatrice had seen people like her in the news over the years. They were mostly nurses who got caught killing patient after patient through administering overdoses or suffocating them with pillows. It never failed that there would be at least one story about an "Angel of Death" in the paper every year. She understood those nurses, but she did not approve of them being sloppy enough to get caught, because getting caught was not an option. Getting caught meant the fun had to stop. Beatrice never intended to get caught and she never planned on stopping either, not until the day she died. Death was just too much fun.

Sitting in the morning sun, baking her aged, handbag-like skin for the millionth time past her dermatologist's recommendation, she sat watching the dew dry on the field across the street. The cars started their morning routines. Ray never used to come out this early; he always said it was a waste of time, as ninety percent of the sales were from the after-work crowd grabbing a tomato or cucumber for that night's salad, but Beatrice liked the morning and would rather sit there where she could make a few dollars than sit in the house watching the *Today Show* like Ray did for four hours while the hired help did all the grunt work required in the fields. Beatrice was content sitting in her folding chair, soaking in the sun, and thinking. She did it then, she did it before she ever met Ray, and she did it now.

This particular morning, the smile did not leave her face as it was the first day of summer; the *season* was now officially open. One by one, Beatrice put out the baskets of tomatoes, the bins of cucumbers, the small decorations the local nursing home made that she offered to sell, and the jars of pickled items she made with the vegetables that were going to go bad. The routine took her exactly fourteen minutes, just like always. With last looks to make sure the best of the produce was showing and in place, she sat down in her chair, lifted her face to the sun and enjoyed the wave of heat that the early June sun granted her. Today was the day, the first of what she hoped would be a bountiful summer. Last year, she had a record of six, and this year, she was going for ten. With her years numbered, she wanted to pluck as many lives as she could before she kicked it. And who knows how many summers she'd have left: hell, this could be the last one. She had to *make it count,* as they say.

Around ten-thirty, the first car pulled up. It was a retired elderly couple she had known for ten years, ever since they had moved to town. With a light wave and a smile, she stood up, waited for them to walk over, exchanged pleasantries, and then told them what was the ripest at the moment. They bought a basket of tomatoes and a single cucumber, had some awkward conversation, and left. This couple would not do: they were too old. Killing the old is boring; they were going to die soon anyway. The deaths she caused had to be tragic. Her favorite choice of victim was a middle-aged husband with a family. It was always devastating to hear of a man leaving his family behind. *Poor young children-- to grow up*

alone with no father figure! So awful… and so, so rewarding. Last year, she got three middle-aged husbands, two teen girls, and two single school teachers who were retiring. Those last two were not planned; the man who bought the tomatoes had used them to make a salad for a retirement party at his school and the two hapless victims were the guests of honor: Mr. Johnson, sixty-five, who taught music for forty-three years and Ms. Blum, who taught English for thirty-eight years. That one did not give her much pleasure, though the fact that she got two instead of one certainly made her smile, and the newspaper clipping about how two retirees both died the same day in ironic twin heart attacks shot to the top of her memory pile.

She didn't realize she had this lust for taking lives (she thought of it as taking lives, not killing; killing was personal: what she did was more about playing God and choosing who lived) until she killed Ray. The son of a bitch was an awful, awful man who controlled her life like an evil dictator. When she so-called "fell in love with him," it was really just her deciding she needed to have a man in her life so she could stop listening to everyone tell her that she did. He was a decent man, at least he seemed so at the time, so she figured, why the hell not? Within six months of marriage, however, he started to get a bit rough with her in bed, and no matter how often she stood up and said she didn't like the things he did or wanted to do, he did them anyway. If she told him "no" and walked away, he knocked her unconscious and did what he wanted. In the first few years of their marriage,

this happened over a dozen times. In each instance, she would stand up for herself, then wake up the next day feeling like a herd of elephants had run over her head and a pack of wild dogs had chewed on her privates. It was beyond awful. When he changed the name of the farm to his name, Beatrice understood that she had to get away, for he had the power and was going to use it unless someone stopped him. This was in the days when a woman couldn't speak up, and if she did, even the law would have said it was a man's right to do what he wanted with his wife in the bedroom.

Four days after the shiny new farm sign reading "Ray of Sunshine Farms" replaced the "Beatrice's Bounty" sign, Beatrice hatched a plan to kill Ray. It involved a gun she had bought in town under the guise of a rabid fox eating the chickens. She was going to accidentally "shoot" good old Ray, thinking he was an intruder. There was a lot of fear, after all, with those farmhouse murders a few towns over the year before, the one that famous guy wrote a book about. She had a whole story planned about how she had read the book and was on edge and got *real scared* when she heard a noise that night. *What if it was the rabid fox, or worse, a killer?!* Of course, she had no clue it was Ray: she thought he had gone into town for a drink. *Oh god, oh god: what had she done?!* She thought it was good plan, but she was merely twenty-two at the time and not as smart as she was now. Looking back, it was the lack of practice with the gun that ruined it all.

The night she planned for the "accident" to happen was like any other normal night. Ray had just showered

and come down for his dinner: it had to be on the table by five sharp, or else she would be punished. When he came down to find no food on the table, Beatrice pleaded with apologies, saying the gas to the stove wasn't working and she needed him to look at the connection outside; maybe one of the workers had messed with it or something? She saw Ray ball his fist to hit her, but he looked around the kitchen and saw that all the food was, in fact, ready; it just needed to be heated. With a grunt, he went outside and around to the back of the house, right next to a back window where the gas pipe came in. Beatrice rushed through the house, threw the window open, grabbed the rifle she had hidden behind the couch, and took aim outside. It was a perfect plan: if she shot him at the back window, it made sense that she was scared-- why would she think Ray was there to begin with? After he was dead, she would clean up the food and pretend they had eaten earlier that night before Ray went out. She would say she had no clue what her husband was doing out back there.

When Ray's head came around the corner and into view, Beatrice snapped off a shot, but the second she squeezed the trigger, she knew she was way too early. Ray had hardly been in full view. The blowback of the gun sent her stumbling backwards, and as she spun, she could see him dart back around the house, moving faster than she had ever seen him move. Getting her footing, she raced to the window, sticking the barrel of the gun out first, looking around eagerly to try to see where he had run. In what seemed like an impossibly quick time, Ray showed up behind her: as she felt the hand on her

shoulder, she heard the screen door slam. As she spun around, she wondered how it was possible for him to get to the living room before the door had even shut. *That fucker could be fast when he wanted.* Before the thought could be completed, she saw stars as his fist hit her square in the face. The gun was then pried away from her fingers with ease.

Less than three minutes later, she found herself out in the back shed, her head pressed to the wooden stump that they used to cut off chicken heads. While the memory of that day burns the brightest and most painful of all of her collective thoughts, the thing that sticks out the most is the wood block and how it smelled. The years of dried chicken blood had created a metallic, rotting smell that was not all unpleasant. The feel of the stickiness against her cheek reminded her of Ray's hot sweatiness against her in one of his rages.

She probably could have gotten up, pulled her head away from the block as Ray shuffled over and gotten the axe, but she didn't see the point. She didn't want to go on anymore, and the block was a fine place to end. Besides, if she tried to move, she would just end back up on it, and in more pain than she already was. There would be no way for him to get away with *her* murder: he hadn't planned. How would he explain her head accidentally chopped off? He'd probably hide the body, but he was too inept and lazy to hide it well. Yes, he would get caught. In that moment, she was at peace, and she stared at the rings on the stump, each one representing a year in the life of this tree that had lived many years before she was even alive and each one was blackened with blood.

She thought it was sort of poetic, each of its years marked with blood stains just like hers.

As Ray stumbled forward, mumbling something about her being a bitch, she lifted her hand and ran it over the wood. The rough, sticky rings were soothing. She heard Ray scream at her to look up, to *look into his face while he cut her fucking head off*, but she ignored him. After his third demand, the axe flew down, cut the tip of her pinky off, a mere quarter of an inch, and dug into the wood so deep, Ray could not pull it out in the first three tries. The pain was insufferable as her blood spurted out onto the wood, but she didn't mind it. She watched as her blood quickly soaked into the wood, mingling with the thousand dead chickens' blood, becoming a part of the stump's gory history. There were more screams, but she did not hear a word of them until Ray's sweaty hand grabbed her shoulder and threw her back onto the ground. The rotting, dusty old ceiling of the shack filled her vision, snapping her out of the peaceful thoughts of death.

"No, no, you don't die… that's too good for you. You are my property, just like the fucking pigs," Ray said as stepped over her, blocking her view of rafters. Squinting, she noticed he was holding the rifle. The realization that she was *not* going to be killed did not sit well in her stomach. It meant there would be more pain, *much more pain*. And she was right. A second later, Ray put the barrel of the gun to her knee and pulled the trigger.

When she woke up, her face was back on the stump, her thoughts cloudy. She thought she had been shot, but she wasn't sure anymore. Why was she back on the

stump? Had she imagined that? Then she felt the stinging inside of her and Ray's hands on her back. Her cheek started to scratch back and forth on the stump, pump after pump. Even though she knew he was fucking her, she lifted her head to look back to see if that was what this man was really doing after all of this. Instantly, it was slammed back down onto the stump. Ray's hot hand held it hard against the wood, and she could feel the skin of her cheek scratch away with each of his thrusts.

"Remember this next time you try to kill me," he said with heavy breaths. It was then that she realized she *had* been shot, as when she tried to adjust her legs to ease the pain, she could not move her right leg, not even an inch. It was all but gone. "And try running now… you are not going to get far without a fucking knee."

Beatrice closed her eyes, and sobs spilled out of her as she prayed to bleed to death. The pumping stopped, Ray pulled himself out of her, and for a split second, she thought it was over, but she was wrong. Ray crammed himself into her again, only this time, not into her vagina. She could feel blood trickling down her thighs as he pounded harder and harder. Each thrust seemed to get more violent and as he sped up, he pushed her face down harder. Then, it was over. With the weight of him off of her, she took a deep breath. She heard him hack up a big ball of phlegm and spit. It landed on her lower back, towards her left side. The hot slime dribbled over her hip and down and around to her stomach, and the sensation of it disgusted Beatrice more than that of the liquids running down her thighs. His phlegm was all she could think about as she passed out.

The next day, Beatrice woke up in the hospital, almost forgetting what had happened. She as alone in the room. There were no flowers, and for the next six weeks, she did not have a single visitor, not even Ray. The rifle blast had destroyed her knee and severed her leg by 80%; they had to remove it. She now had a nice stump. It took weeks for it to heal and for the awful plastic leg to arrive, and it took her almost a solid year to walk normally, or at least in a new normal manner.

During her stay, she inquired about her injury, asking if the cops were going to come and talk to her, but the nurse explained they did come when she was unconscious and just said that a lady like her should "be more careful when trying to shoot a gun." Beatrice nodded, knowing Ray had gotten away with it. If she squealed on him, he would point out that she had tried to kill him. In that moment, she wanted to kill all of the nurses, doctors, and cops, for not a single one of them could have believed that a woman with such severe trauma to her groin and cuts and bruises on her face had shot off her own leg, especially with a gun that was too long for her to point at her own knee. But it was small town, and that's what small towns did: bury things under the rug.

The day she came back to the house, awkwardly walking on the crutches, Ray was sitting in the living room. He hardly looked up at her when he said, "It's three. I expect dinner on the table by five."

That night, after they had eaten the dinner she made, an activity that exhausted her, Ray slapped her, pushed

her to the ground, ripped off her fake leg, and raped her in the same position and the same way as the day he shot her, only over the living room ottoman. When he finished, he got up, grabbed her stump and looked at it carefully before saying, "Cover that shit up the next time I fuck you: it's disgusting. I almost lost my hard on."

That was how the next fifteen years went: farm work, dinner, and the occasional rape (though Ray said you can't rape you wife-- it's just her duty). When she had full capability of walking on the fake leg to the point where no one realized she had one, she once again worked on plans to kill him, but this time, she was terrified. Every once in a while, he would take her false leg and lock it in a cabinet to "remind her" that he was the boss and that if she ever tried anything again, he'd shoot off her other leg. She wanted to run away (which sounded like a joke in her mind, as she could no longer run), but Ray had put every bit of money they had in his name: she had no access. This meant that if she ran, she had nothing but the shirt on her back, and that was not an option. She had built and owned the farm; she was not going to let him profit from it while she ran away destitute. It was then that she started taking trips to the library in the fall, when farm work was light. Day after day, she'd peruse the botanical books section, grab a copy, and sit and read about all the poison plants that existed.

It took her a decade and seventeen attempts, but she was finally able to create a strong enough poison to kill Ray in an untraceable manner. The sixteen attempts leading up ended in various results; the first three times, nothing; next four, diarrhea; the next three, vomiting; and

the eleventh time ended with a bout in the hospital. At this point, she thought Ray would be suspicious, but she had spaced out the tests by half a year each time, so he never suspected anything. The twelfth and thirteenth attempts fell flat with a mild case of the squirts after dinner. The fourteenth again resulted in just puking, and the fifteenth caused Ray to sleep for two days straight, but not because he was sick or dying (though he did piss himself as he never got up for the two days). The sixteenth try she was sure was going to be the one, but Ray only ate half of his dinner that night and just had bad cramps.

On the seventeenth attempt, she baked the poison into a chicken pot pie. She even killed the chicken herself on the same damn stump she almost died on a decade earlier. The dinner smelled amazing and looked fantastic, and Ray ate it without a second thought-- ate the whole damn thing himself, not caring if his wife had any. An hour later, Ray started to slur his words; he grasped at his chest and vomited on himself. He kept pointing to the phone, pleading with his eyes for her to call for help, but she merely stuffed her hands in her apron, smiled, and watched him. Three times he attempted to hit her, but he couldn't raise his arms high enough or swing hard enough; she just kept moving back gently to avoid the weak attempts. When he grabbed for the phone on the wall, she unplugged it. After a long stretch of moaning, Ray laid on the kitchen floor, taking a few last gulps of air before he breathed no more. Beatrice knelt down and whispered into his ear. "Who owns who now, bitch? Enjoy hell."

When Ray stopped breathing, Beatrice got a knife, gripped it with both hands and readied it to stab the shit out of Ray's body. She had a deep, unsettling rage in her that she wanted to release upon his disgusting corpse. Her hands trembled as she fought the urge, the need, to take out the years of frustration, but she fought it successfully, for she wanted to be a free woman for the first time in her adult life. After a deep breath, she plugged the phone back in and called the police. There were no news trucks, no investigation: it was merely a man who had a heart attack in his kitchen after his loving wife made him dinner. The police officer noted, "At least he got a nice home-cooked meal before he went." She smiled kindly at that man, forcing down the Cheshire cat grin that wanted to burst out of her very soul.

That night, she went out into the field under the stars, and as she walked, the cool fall breeze welcomed her, and she felt a freedom and excitement she had never felt in her life; it was more than exhilarating. After a few minutes, she came upon the patch of indigo-hued flowers lightly moving in the breeze. She held out her hand and touched them, one by one, as if caressing a sleeping puppy she loved and adored. Her fingers started to tingle instantly and she giggled with joy. The plant was beautiful: it was no wonder Shakespeare used it in his plays to kill people.

Getting it had been easier than she ever thought it would be. Beatrice simply mentioned to an avid plant lover she did business with that she was having eye trouble and couldn't afford the dilation medicine the doctor prescribed. It worked almost too perfectly: the

eccentric, effeminate man squealed, saying he could help her out-- he knew of a plant they used for eyes, *Atropa Belladonna*, more commonly known as Nightshade. He grabbed a book, flipped through it, and showed her the pictures, and she acted amazed, even though she knew every detail of the plant by heart from her library visits. Within two weeks, her friend had ordered her a packet of seeds. Before he handed them over, though, he warned her to be *extra, extra* careful with them. Part of her always felt like he *knew* what she really wanted to do with the plant, but there was no way he could have ever imagined that she wouldn't stop after Ray.

Two years after Ray sadly passed away, she found herself happy but bored. The business did well, she had plenty of work to do, but in her down time, she was restless. There were many nights she found herself visiting her little plants as if they were the best company in the world. There was no need to take care of them after Ray was gone, yet she tended to them as if they were the most important crop on the farm. Night after night, she would go out to the patch and let them tingle her fingers. She even had conversations with them (one-sided ones, of course: she wasn't *crazy*).

One night, on her way out to visit them, her false foot got caught in a mole hole; she stumbled forward, her leg fell off, and she tumbled to the ground. It happened every now and then: when you can't feel your foot, it catches sometimes. Usually, she would pop back up and hop to her leg, put it on, and act as if nothing had happened. That night, she just laid there and looked up

at the stars. The thought that she must be a sight to see crossed her mind, lying there, her arms spread wide, and one leg ten feet behind her. She laughed lightly to herself and started to get up when the idea hit her. Poison the tomatoes. The thought came out of nowhere, as if a shooting star fell out of the sky and hit her with the notion. She could cook the Nightshade, distill it down to a potent form, then inject it into the tomatoes. This thought brought such joy to her, she jumped up, hopped to her leg, put it back on, and raced to her small patch of purple flowers.

Within an hour, she was in the kitchen, wearing gloves and boiling a pot of nightshade while humming a tune. After a mere ten minutes of boiling the small amount of liquid and large number of flowers and leaves, she was left with what looked like violet-colored applesauce in the pan. Using a potato masher, she mixed up the contents thoroughly, then got out a jar and spread cheesecloth over the top; it was the same method she used when making jelly to strain out all the chunks. With the care of a surgeon, she poured the liquid over the cloth, spoonful by spoonful, giving each ladle time to drip through into the mason jar. As each drop dripped down, she felt a ripple of excitement wash over her body. It was an intense, wonderful feeling she had never experienced, and part of her wondered if it was what an orgasm felt like.

At the end of the night, she had four cups of light purple liquid in a jar cooling on the kitchen table. Sitting in front of it, she sipped some tea and wondered what it would feel like to drink it, how quickly she would die, and

then the waves of pleasure washed over her body again when she thought of the people she could kill with it. The hard part would be guessing how much to use. It was then that an idea struck her, and she raced to the barn with the jar in her hand. Inside the barn, she hurried to the storage room and rumbled around until she found the "medicine" drawer where she kept udder cream and other medicines for the two cows she owned. Behind a pack of gauze, she found an old stainless-steel syringe from when the cows had an infection a few years back. Damn vet wanted to charge her fifty bucks a day for nine days in a row to come and give them shots; instead, she gave him a hundred for her own needle and the medicine and did it herself. Placing the needle next to the jar, she could see her hands trembling: she had never been this excited before. Trying to calm herself so she didn't spill any of the precious liquid, she unscrewed the jar, dipped the syringe into it, and drew two millimeters. Admiring the beautiful shine of the needle and the glorious color in the glass tube, Beatrice looked into the barn.

Two minutes after the needle was plunged underneath the skin of Helga, the oldest of the two heifers, the cow started to kick and moan. Beatrice stepped back, clenching the needle in her fist, watching with amazement and anticipation. Large globs of thick white snot came out of the black nostrils, foam started to pour out of her mouth, and the giant old girl started to buck and kick like a rodeo bull. Beatrice started to clap and do a light jump up and down as if she were cheering on a horse in a race. Helga let out a sound that sounded like a boat horn dying, then ran full speed at the barn

wall. The entire building shook as her head slammed into the ancient planks of wood. Dust fluttered down as the heifer stumbled, then collapsed. Beatrice let out a scream of victory. The next night, Beatrice had a large steak dinner, with the mason jar of her "night juice," as she had decided to call it, sitting across from her.

Over the next few months, Beatrice made more batches of her night juice until she had a gallon mason jar full and tucked away in her root closet. At the same time, she did math, a lot of it (*if X amount killed Helga, and she is X times the weight of an average man, then X amount will kill a man, assuming that he consumed the entire amount*). Having only a ninth-grade education, the calculations were a bit complicated for her, but she figured out the exact amount to put into a tomato. After practice injections using colored water, Beatrice figured that she needed to inject the fluid in one chamber of the tomato, by the stem. That way, even if the fruit were cut up and split, the poison would be concentrated in one spot, creating more of a chance for *one* person to ingest enough to die. Others who got a little of the poison would just get sick. When she perfected her idea, it was time to execute it.

Ever since that night when she stared up at the stars and the idea came into her head, life had been better. It had been exciting, and that week, the week of her first test, life was downright thrilling. She had a hard time sleeping at night, she was so excited, and she woke each morning believing it was going to be the greatest day ever. The morning of the first day of the test, she could not get the smile off her face, no matter what. Her customers

even noticed: a few of the regulars commented on how chipper she looked, and she just smiled bigger and nodded at them. An empowering sensation came over her as she tried to choose who to give the special "ripe" tomato to. It was as if she was playing God, getting to pick who lived and would die.

It was seven minutes after eleven the day that she picked her first victim. The second the man got out of his car, she knew he was the one; there was just something that reminded her of Ray in his ruddy, pissy face. He needed to die. As the man approached, she pasted on a fake smile and acted as normal as she could, all the while trying to hide her pumping heart that was rushing blood to her face. The man just nodded. He didn't even smile, which reassured her that he was the one. He quietly walked around, picked up some squash and a basket of tomatoes-- everyone got tomatoes-- and walked towards her. Beatrice had to clear her throat to make some pleasantries about the weather, but he just ignored her and asked in a rushed grumble, "What do I owe you?"

She always kept shears near the counter, originally for trimming plants when there was no one there, but then as a safety measure after the time after she was robbed by some kids in the early seventies (something Ray blamed her for). An urge to pick up the shears and plunge them deep into the soft part of the man's throat overcame her, and for a split second, she really thought she might do it. Most of the cars went by so fast that no one would ever notice what happened. Getting rid of the body, on the

other hand, now *that* would have been messy. So, a nice, ripe tomato it was.

Beatrice tallied up all the veggies first, leaving the tomatoes for last. She hesitated, her hand over the basket, then scooped one up and moved it close to her. "Oh, my. This one has a bad spot. Let me get you a better one," she said in a caring voice.

The man sighed heavily as if this was a waste of his time. She turned her back, smiled, and squeezed the perfectly fine tomato as she walked behind the truck to her "special" tomatoes. Lifting one up, she gave it a light kiss, and as she did, she could feel a slight tingle on her lips. When she reappeared in the front, she asked, "What do you plan on making with these?" A perfectly innocent question.

Again, the man sighed. "Sauce. My grandmother asked me to stop for her, made a point to say it had to be your stand," he said without much emotion. Beatrice's heart dropped. In a sauce, the poison would be so diluted, he probably wouldn't even get heartburn and that is if he was even going to eat it. She had to think fast. Holding back the bag as he held out the money, she asked who his grandmother was. She did not recognize the name, but instantly said she did and came up with a quick lie.

"Well, tell you what, since she has always been a good customer, I want you to try a new type of tomato I'm growing and if you like it, you can take some home to her, on me."

The man half rolled his eyes, but then looked down at Beatrice who was giving her best *please, for a lonely old lady*

look she could muster. "That would be nice of you," he said, again without much emotion.

Beatrice quickly hobbled behind the truck, took the syringe, and shot it into a pear tomato, which was a bright yellow and was all but two inches in size. It dripped out a bit and her fingers instantly went numb, but she had to act fast. Grabbing a pint of the yellow pear tomatoes she walked to the front, smiled widely and held out her hand with the beautifully yellow tomato.

The man looked at it with hesitation, "Haven't seen one of those before," he said, with actual emotion for once.

"They are to die for." Beatrice let out an inner cackle and couldn't believe she had said a line that an evil villain in a movie would say.

The man popped it into his mouth and bit. He winced slightly, probably at the sudden strange taste and numbing of his mouth. Beatrice then worried he might spit it out, so she flashed him a hopeful smile, showing him that she hoped he liked it. He coughed lightly into his hand, but swallowed and forced a smile back. "It's great. Thank you so much... hmph... I really need to run," he muttered. Beatrice just smiled as she handed him the bag.

She had never experienced an orgasm in her life. She had engaged in whispered conversations about them with some lady friends in town, read things in books she wasn't supposed to read about them, and was even told by Ray that "no one will ever make you cum like I do," but she had no clue what they felt like. Part of her didn't really care, at least she told herself that, but as she watched the man walk away and stumble into his car, as

he skidded out and swerved down the street, she felt a wave of pleasure rush over her body that made every inch of her cells burst with pure, uninhibited joy. When she heard the loud crash a mere twenty seconds later, she fell to her knees and yelled out in ecstasy. She looked up at the cloudy sky and laughed and laughed until she heard the sirens and knew she had to get up and "act" like a concerned neighbor. The cops didn't even bother asking her many questions after the man died; in fact, the only question they asked was how much the tomatoes were.

Four day later, she went to the man's funeral and, in fact, did recognize the guy's grandmother. She held her hands and said what a nice boy he was, that he talked so glowingly about her when getting her tomatoes. When she saw the man's two children, probably six and nine, sobbing and hugging each other as the casket lowered, she had to bite her cheek from smiling. A wave of amazement hit her like a train out of control at this reaction: she literally had *no* feelings for this man or *anyone* there, or hell, anyone in the world. Part of her wondered if Ray had broken everything inside of her or if she was born this way. She couldn't recall ever feeling much, but she also blocked out a lot in her life. With a small shrug to herself, she decided she didn't care. She was having fun and that was what mattered.

Beatrice found herself the center of attention at the get-together after, everyone wanting to know *what were his last words, did he seem sick, was he acting off?* To entertain herself, she made up various stories about what he said and how wonderful he was and that no, he looked just fine, but he did rush out of there. If she had a dollar for

every time she heard someone say it was a shame someone so young should have a heart attack or "you just never know, do you," she'd have taken herself to the casino afterwards. It was an exhilarating day. The only thing she did make a note of that night was to no longer give anyone the juice at the farm. It acted too quickly. If people kept dying within a mile of her place, she'd definitely get caught.

Year after year, Beatrice did her routines and picked her special "ripe" tomatoes for all kinds of people. Every year, she was careful to not do too many and raise suspicion, especially after the summer of 1986 when a nosy detective got a bit too suspicious (he, of course, just happened to have a heart attack the night after interviewing her for a third time). That next year, she killed no one and went into a severe depression. She even thought of injecting herself with her night juice that winter, but she made it through, telling herself she would kill double the amount that year and if she ever got caught, she'd just eat a tomato before they put the cuffs on.

There were times she would experiment and put the juice in other foods, bigger tomatoes and smaller ones, but sure enough, she always came back to the classic beefsteak tomato. It worked about fifty percent of the time. After each one she would give out, in the next four days following, she would scour the newspaper and hope to see a "death" report, but often times, she didn't. In the times there was no death, she would wonder what happened. Did they end up in the hospital or just get really sick? Did they cut it up into too many pieces or

maybe never even ate it? That was half the fun, though: never knowing if it would work or not. It was kind of like hunting. You can take a lot of shots at a deer, but you don't always get a hit.

That morning, after the elderly couple left, she sat there and waited, waited for her first victim of the summer. The excitement was bubbling as usual, but part of her felt like she needed a bit more this year. Yes, she had set a new goal of ten victims, not really caring if people got suspicious anymore, but part of her wanted something bigger. If only she knew when she was going to die. If she got terminal cancer, then she would go out in a huge bang, see how many she could get, maybe inject every item she had or maybe just kill everyone who came and throw their bodies in the back. She had plenty of room to hide the cars and bodies; hell, she could probably go at it for a few days before anyone figured out what was going on. She could do it too, if she weren't in her seventies, had one leg, and weighed about a hundred pounds. With a big sigh, she sat there, hoping cancer would creep into her body that winter, and waited.

As she was eating her daily tomato sandwich at one o'clock sharp (she loved the irony, but she also loved the taste of crunchy toast, a dash of salt, gobs of mayonnaise, and sliced, fresh tomatoes), a mini-van pulled in. She wiped her mouth and sighed. No victims yet. Kids were boring, and there was no guarantee they would eat their vegetables. Two kids-- they looked to be twins, probably around eleven-- wearing matching orange soccer outfits jumped out of the side door a solid minute before a

frumpy mother got out and yelled at them to wait for her. The poor woman looked so disheveled and miserable, Beatrice wanted to give her a tomato on the spot to put her out of her misery. The two kids, like many annoying children who had visited the farm over the years, ran around and touched shit they shouldn't, moved things they shouldn't. Beatrice sighed and smiled at the mother who returned a "sorry" look. She waved to the mother as if it was no big deal, even though it pissed her off to no end seeing the kids squeeze and bruise the beautiful vegetables. The boy with the bad butch lesbian-like haircut—their hair was probably the only way the mother could tell them apart-- actually popped his finger right into a beautiful Cherokee Purple Heirloom tomato. This was a death sentence… literally.

The mother did not see what the kid did, and Beatrice was not going to point it out; she just watched as the boy shook the seeds off his hand and grabbed another tomato to pantomime throwing at his brother, who was making an obscene gesture with a large cucumber. She thought of giving them samples. It was against her rules, but she wanted to see these kids die right in front of her. *Could she pull it off as maybe a tomato allergy?* It was tempting, but being the start of the summer, she did not want to get caught. If these two morons died right here, the place would be swarming with cops and even reporters, and no one would come anymore. They'd have to take it home and she'd have to risk the mother or father (if the bastards had one) eating it instead. A death was a death, but she really, really wanted *them* to die.

The mother came to the counter with a large basket, an odd array of vegetables that she obviously had no plans to get. It was probably an impulse or a "sorry my kids are assholes, so I'll buy extra stuff" purchase. The woman looked as if she was going to cry when she set down the unique assortment. "Some days I just can't control them. Do you have kids?" she asked almost desperately.

Beatrice shook her head, looked down and answered, no, she never did: her husband had died young. She was playing it up, something she realized she was always doing with other humans, but she figured it would instill a bit of shame in the woman.

"Oh, I'm so sorry… well, maybe you are lucky. These two drive me to drink," the woman said, trying to make a joke but instantly realizing she had been insensitive. She started to apologize, but Beatrice again waved it off.

"Tell you what. How about I give them some tomatoes to sample. Do they like them?"

The woman smiled and nodded before yelling over her shoulder for the boys to come over to the counter. They pushed each other and laughed but arrived quickly. Beatrice looked them up and down and smiled. "I bet you boys are good at soccer," she said. Dyke Haircut laughed and said he was, but his brother sucked. The mother told them to cut it out and Beatrice laughed a fake chuckle to seem as if she cared.

As she bagged up the items and rang up the cash register, she saw Dyke Haircut out of the corner of her eye, popping another tomato. This sent anger up her spine like she had not felt since she wanted to kill Ray.

"You know what, let me get you boys a special tomato to try," Beatrice said, knowing instantly that she could not, should not, kill these kids. If she gave them the night juice now, they'd be dead before they got home and it would be all too obvious what killed them. While she told herself that she could not do it, she found herself on autopilot, going to the back of the booth and grabbing the familiar cold syringe. As she picked up a small grape tomato, she squirted enough in it to kill a boy of their size. She set down the tomato and picked up another one, but just as she stuck the needle into the ripe flesh, she heard a voice behind her.

"What is that?"

She froze. No one had *ever* come back there and seen her, no one had even come close. With the needle in one hand and the tomato in the other, she turned and saw the kid with the awful haircut looking at her. When he saw the needle, his eyes opened wide and he let out a half-hearted laugh.

Beatrice had no clue what to say or do, but she quickly stammered, "Oh, uh, this is a flavor enhancer, like a salt solution; that way you don't have to put salt on it."

The kid's face changed quickly to one that seemed much more mature than his age. He simply said, "Bullshit."

Beatrice thought about lunging at the boy and sticking him with the juice. She could get away with it, say he had a seizure or something, but while he was merely eleven or so, he was still probably stronger than her. "Will that kill you, if you eat it?" the child asked, shocking her to the core.

Whether it was the need to share her decade-long secret, or a recognition of something in the boy's eyes that she felt akin to, she replied simply, "Yes."

A large, sick smile grew across the kids face. "Give me a normal one, give Nick that one. How quick will it work?"

Beatrice did not understand what was going on or how she had gotten into this position, but she listened to the boy. She took a fresh tomato out of the basket and handed it to him and kept the poisoned one in her hand. "What's your name?" she asked in a soft voice that she did not recognize.

"Tim," he answered. "Let's do this."

She followed the boy back to the front where the mom was scolding the other child. When she saw Beatrice, she said, "I'm so sorry he went back there. Sometimes he just, I don't know. I'm sorry."

Meanwhile, Tim walked over to his family and showed them the small tomato. He popped it in his mouth and said to his brother, "She has one for you, too, dork."

Beatrice was in a daze, not really sure what was happening. Part of her stomach bubbled with excitement (someone like her? someone who she could share her secrets with?) but the other half of her stomach dropped with the fear of getting caught. Without thinking, she held out her hand and dropped the small tomato into the other boy's palm. The kid popped it into his mouth, chewed, and swallowed.

Beatrice looked at Tim. The boy was smiling big, too big. Seconds later, the mother started to walk her family

to the car. Beatrice couldn't let the boy leave; she needed to talk to him some more. "Wait a second!" she yelled after them. The mother turned, but the boys kept walking to the van, pushing each other back and forth. Beatrice hobbled her way towards the Mother who looked curiously at her. "I'm all alone here. I do pretty much everything myself. I could use some help, under the table, manual labor, moving things, digging holes, good character-building work. Might be perfect for your boys if they'd be interested. I could give them ten dollars an hour, just a few hours a week after school."

The mother's mouth opened as if taken aback by the idea of her children working, but then she smiled. "You know, it might be good for them, but I'm not sure you'd be happy with how they work. I can't even get them to mow the lawn."

Beatrice waved her hand as if it was no big deal. "When money is involved, you'd be amazed with what a young person can do. More than a few wise asses have worked here and left polite men." She then gave the lady her number and told her to think about it. The woman gave her the most genuine smile she had ever seen, thanked her, and rushed off to the van.

Beatrice could not sleep that night, not a wink. She was too excited at the prospect of the one boy dying and the fascination of the other child being... *like her.* She knew that if the boy died, and the chances of him living were astronomical, the mother would never call her as she would spend the rest of her life grieving and not worrying about getting the other son some summer work. This

thought terrified her. She had to talk to this boy, she had to talk to this boy *now*. Then again, what if when the kid died, Tim told on her? Maybe he didn't really believe her, maybe he thought it was make believe. But the look in his eye: it was too damn cold. The entire night, she paced the house and finally went outside and walked through the fields, desperate for connection, needing answers, and just not knowing what to do with herself. Of course, she ended up at the patch of her special flowers. She lightly tickled them but was concerned when she couldn't feel the usual tingles in her hand: the poison always tingled her fingers. A panic set over her-- was this the start of the end? With her left hand, she clasped a flower in her fist and squeezed it hard as she could, crushing the purple petals so forcefully that she could feel her nails cut into her palm. She still felt nothing.

The next day, Beatrice found herself standing by her mailbox at five in the morning, a cup of coffee in one hand, the other clutching her robe closed. She had no clue when the paper usually came, but it was always there by breakfast, so she was going to wait for it. She finished her coffee and forty minutes later, the sun started to rise. She watched the stunning rays dance and light the sky with a pallet of oranges and reds, yet she felt nothing about it. She had seen plenty of sunrises. Then she heard it, the low hum of an engine approaching, and two minutes later, a small green car raced by her and threw the paper out a window, twenty feet away from where she was standing. How could they not have seen her? Beatrice wanted to chase them down and shoot whoever was in the car with five shots of night juice.

After a painful hobble from standing so long, she grabbed the newspaper, slipped it out of its orange plastic bag, and unrolled it. Thankfully, she didn't even have to flip it open, because there on the front page, in the lower right corner, was a picture of the boy she met yesterday. It wasn't the one she wanted to talk to; it was the stupid one, the one she gave the tomato to. Right above the photo read the headline, *Local Boy, 13, Dies From Heart Attack*. Beatrice read the article six times. There seemed to be no suspicion of foul play or even a mention of them visiting the farm stand that day. Tim hadn't said anything. Beatrice wanted to jump up and down and yell for joy, not because she wasn't getting caught, but because she had found someone that was like her, someone she could talk to or even train one day. She just had to figure out *how* to see him again.

The funeral was private, she could not attend it, and this upset Beatrice to the point of her throwing a tomato against a tree. Ruining something she grew was against her morals, but that's how angry she was. After calming down, she put together the most beautiful basket of vegetables she had ever made (with not a single one having any night juice injected), wrapped it in a green cellophane, put a bow on it, and wrote a sweet card about how she saw the paper and recognized the child, and offered her deepest, deepest sympathies. Of course, she made sure to make the offer for Tim to come and work, to "clear his mind" on the farm. It was her best hope. Then she sat to wait and hope.

A mere two poisoned tomatoes and seven days after sending the basket, a van pulled in. She recognized it

instantly. Tim got out first, and Beatrice couldn't help but smile (for real) at the sight of him. The once disheveled-looking mother followed, this time looking almost like a homeless woman. She wore dirty gray sweatpants, her hair in a loose ponytail, and donned an *I Love Bermuda* t-shirt that looked like she had worn it for five days straight. Her face didn't have a stitch of make up on. Beatrice lowered her smile and changed her face to a classic, sympathetic look. The kid arrived first, stood looking at her with a bored glaze on his face, and Beatrice tried not to stare at him and instead attempted to lock eyes with the mother. She couldn't: the woman had put on sunglasses.

"Um, so, we appreciate the basket. Are you serious about the job… for Tim?" she asked. "We, he, could use some time away from the house."

Beatrice instantly shot around the counter, put on her full act of sympathy and told the woman, of course: he could work and stay here all he wanted; she would take care of him and it would be good for his soul. A few seconds later, the van pulled away, leaving Tim behind, and as she watched it crunch on the gravel, Beatrice realized the woman hadn't even said goodbye to her son.

Beatrice walked back to the stand where Tim was playing with a cucumber, pretending it was a gun. He said to her, "I can't believe you actually killed him."

Beatrice let out a laugh and replied, "I can't believe you kept your mouth shut about it." The two then laughed heartily. She felt an excitement in her bones she had never felt, a feeling she wished would stay forever. "Take a seat, kid. I think we have a lot of talking to do."

The kid walked around the counter and hopped onto one of the stools; Beatrice followed and sat next to him. "I don't like to talk much," Tim said, flipping the cucumber up into the air.

"I don't either, kid, but you know what? I think you and I will have a *lot* to talk about. Let me guess. You don't talk much because you find you don't think and act like others. Other people feel like aliens to you, right?"

The boy caught the cucumber and stayed still. He stared at the vegetable in his hands, shrugged, and then answered her. "Yeah... exactly. Everything I say and think, people say is wrong. Is that how you feel?"

Beatrice felt her cheeks turn red. "If only you knew, kid."

Four hours later, Beatrice had told the boy every single secret she had. The boy listened, asked questions, and never once seemed bored, acted like an idiot, or was rude. It was like talking to an adult; the calm coolness, the smart questions, and the intrigue in his eyes shocked Beatrice to the core. *How could a thirteen-year-old be so damn smart and understanding?* The thought burned in her head, but she didn't care. She had a sounding board for the first time ever. The two went for a walk, and she showed him the flowers. He touched them lightly and giggled at how they tingled. She showed him the jars of night juice and even her newspaper clipping collection, all of which he found amazing. A few customers came and went; they politely served them and the boy acted like a true gentleman, carrying bags to cars for old ladies, giving

change to mothers, and offering free samples to kids. Tim was being good because he wasn't bored.

After a while, Beatrice finally asked him what *he* felt and if he had ever done any bad things. The boy just smiled wildly. "I think of lots of really, really bad things, things I could never tell anyone. Well, maybe you. As for bad, I've learned I can't do bad and live a good life, bad things make it hard to blend in. Unless I do the bad when I'm alone. I've killed a few animals, but I don't really like it. They don't have feelings, and I want to the pain to hurt in their brains too, not just in their bones."

Beatrice suddenly grabbed the boy's face, pulled him close and kissed his forehead before starting to sob. "I never thought I needed anyone, but I just realized I've waited my whole life for you, a mere boy." Tim gave her an awkward smile. She knew he didn't understand, he hadn't been alive that long, but the chance of two monsters like them finding one another were like winning the lottery, getting hit by lighting, finding a cure for cancer and seeing a shooting star all in the same day: astronomical, but possible.

When the day started to get long and their conversation dwindled a bit, the boy seemed nervous. He picked at the sandwich she had made for him, and finally he asked, "Could we, poison someone today?"

Beatrice licked her lips, held back a smile, then looked at Tim. "'Long as you keep your mouth shut, of course we can kill someone. You pick the person, and I'll let you inject the tomato." The boy jumped up from his seat as if something had shocked him. She could see the

excitement on his face and couldn't help but feel proud and excited as well.

Four customers came and went, but Tim just shook his head no to each one. Then an older man who reminded Beatrice of Tom Selleck walked up to the stand wearing an old newsboy hat. Tim looked at Beatrice and raised his eyebrows; she smiled and nodded back. After a few minutes of browsing, the man brought up several baskets of tomatoes, five different varieties in all. Beatrice started to chit chat and asked the man what he was making. The man replied something about a tomato salad, but she really wasn't listening; instead, she was watching Tim out of the corner of her eye. After a few seconds, she scooped up a small yellow tomato and said, "Tim, sweetie, this one has a bruise; go in the back and get a nicer one for the man, please."

Four minutes later, the man had paid and was pulling away. As soon as the taillights disappeared, the boy ran out to the parking lot and jumped up and down, hooting and hollering. Beatrice wanted to join him. She knew she couldn't do the jumping, but she could do the yelling, so she did: she let out a loud howl that surprised herself. Tim talked a mile a minute after that, asking tons of questions like how quickly would they know, what if he didn't eat it, and if she normally felt a rush like he was feeling. She nodded and gave all the answers she could and promised to show him the paper if the man died if he could talk his mom into bringing him back again. An hour later, she gave him sixty bucks and his mom came to pick him up. As he was about to leave, he stopped, gave her a hug, and said it was the best day of his life.

227

Beatrice never found an article about the Tom Selleck look-alike dying, but it did not disappoint Tim. They tried again and again and together, they ended up killing nine before the end of that summer. By the fall, they had formed a bond stronger than anything Beatrice had ever had. When winter came and the fake "work" he was doing theoretically dried up, the boy's mother still brought him daily, offering him up to do "stuff around the house." Beatrice didn't mind that the mother was using her to get rid of her child after school every day and for hours on the weekends: she wanted the boy there, she needed him there after a while. The two would watch horror movies in bed together, go out to eat, play board games, or go to the mall and sit on a bench and play their favorite game, "How," where one would point to a person and the other would have to come up with a crazy way to kill them. Everything was perfect and stayed that way for two years.

When Tim was about to turn sixteen, he had grown several inches and developed thick ropey muscles on his body, something Beatrice couldn't help but stare at; she noticed that he was getting antsy with just "poisoning" people. He started to talk about kidnapping and brutal, physical murder. It appealed to her deeply, so much so she found herself aroused by it, but she worried about Tim getting caught at such a young age. If she got caught, she wouldn't care: she'd die after a mere year in jail if she was lucky. They discussed this countless times until he finally wore her down. They came up with a plan to kidnap a customer and dispose of the car in a lake five miles away. They would then come back and take their

time killing the person. When they made this decision together, Tim grabbed Beatrice, pulled her tight to him, and gave her a quick kiss on the lips. He said *thank you* to her five times. It could have been in her mind, but she thought she felt that the boy was hard.

The next day, the plan went off without a hitch. A middle-aged woman, plain-looking and full-figured, pulled in but never pulled out. Tim asked her if she wanted to see the special supply of tomatoes behind the shed, and she followed him without hesitation. After he knocked her out, Beatrice tied her legs while Tim gagged her and tied her hands. Together they put her in a wheelbarrow, brought her to the back barn, and tied her to the rafters. Then, wearing gloves, Tim drove the woman's car (Beatrice had given him lessons beforehand) and she followed behind. They got it to sink without a problem and then drove back to the farm together, holding hands the entire time to calm their trembling bodies.

Back at the farm stand, they sat on their stools and waited on customers for the next five hours, just like normal, to avoid any suspicion. When, not if, the cops came around, they would have been gone for only twenty minutes total, a mere lunch break like normal: nothing suspicious. No one would have seen them with the car: they obsessively picked a route with no traffic or security cameras at all. When they closed the stand at six, they both practically ran back to the barn, like teenage lovers racing to lose their virginity. As they opened the doors and saw the woman, covered in tears and what had to be urine staining her pants, they both looked at each other with big smiles.

"Remember, Tim," said Beatrice. "We can't do this as often as we do the night juice, it's too dangerous, so take it slow and enjoy it." Before she could even finish the sentence, Tim ran up to the woman, grabbed her bobbed, brunette hair, and slit her throat. Blood poured out in a sweetly beautiful flow, and Tim was soaked by the artery spray in the process. Beatrice felt a bit of shock and sadness at the suddenness, but also a sense of arousal like she had never experienced. *The blood was fucking beautiful.*

Quietly, she came up next to Tim and slipped the knife out of his hands. He seemed to have forgotten she was there. She then quickly thrust it into the woman's stomach hard and fast, over and over again. Tim stared at Beatrice with a goofy smile, then leaned over to her, grabbed her face and kissed her hard and long on the mouth. She could taste the blood and feel it smearing on her cheek. She moaned against Tim. Then she pulled away, wrapped his hand over her hand that was holding the knife, and together, both holding the blade, they started to stab the woman over and over again. Beatrice was sixty years older than fifteen-year-old Tim, but in that moment, their souls were one and ageless together.

When they woke hours later, both completely nude, covered in drying blood, there was no awkwardness. Tim had lost his virginity to a senior citizen and Beatrice had her first orgasm covered in a dead woman's blood. The passion and ecstasy still lingered in the air and between them. Beatrice, feeling like a nineteen-year-old girl who had just experienced the greatest night of her life, looked at the pieces of body strewn around the barn and smiled. There was a foot nailed to the wall, intestines hanging

over the beams like sausages drying in a smoke house, part of a torso on a hay stack, a leg in a bucket and the woman's head nestled, face first, on Tim's crotch. The thought of cleaning up exhausted Beatrice, but they had time and besides, they would have more fun, at least as much as they could before it started to stink.

After several showers, a bonfire, and several dozen laughs later, the party was over and the mess gone. Their relationship had gone from mentor and mentee to partners in crime. Tim suddenly wanted to always hold her hand and was treating her like a girlfriend. The age difference grossed her out for a mere second, but then she realized that the world would think that every aspect of what they had was wrong. It didn't matter. To them, it was perfect in every single damn aspect.

A month after Tim's nineteenth birthday, seventeen "in person" victims after that first night in the barn, Beatrice got the news she had once begged for. She had cancer and a mere half a year to live. Tim's face was like stone when she told him the news. He sat for a solid five minutes after hearing the word "cancer," hardly shifting in his seat or making a face. Beatrice finally leaned in and asked what he was feeling.

"You are all I know" was his only response.

She cried softly and said, "I know, and you are all I know. But everything must end. I have already made out my will. You get everything, and you can keep our traditions: you just have to promise me to never get caught. And who knows, maybe one day you'll find another partner like me."

231

Five fat tears rolled down Tim's cheeks. Beatrice stood up, took him in her arms and whispered in his ear. "I'm not going to let cancer kill me: *you* are going to kill me."

True to her word, less than a month later, when she began to feel the ache in her bones and the exhaustion had begun to take its slow toll, Beatrice took Tim's hand in hers. It was time, she told him.

They waited until the sun had set. Together they walked past the barn and out to the fields. They stopped in the patch of purple flowers, and Beatrice leaned down, pulled off her fake leg, and threw it away from her. She held onto Tim for balance, looked into his eyes, and said, "I'm ready."

Tim smiled, leaned in, and gave her a small kiss, and pulled her into his body. Beatrice laid her head on her partner's shoulder and breathed in his scent for the last time. She hardly felt the needle stick into her neck, a mere pinch followed by a wave of tingles.

My night juice, my beautiful night juice, she thought as Tim placed her gently down amongst the flowers. She felt her heart start to dance in a way she had never experienced, and she stared up at the night sky, squeezed Tim's hands in hers, and cried softly.

Just as the stars started to blur in her vision, Tim leaned over and whispered into her ear. "I love you, and don't worry, I will treat this farm just like you did. I will grow the ripest tomatoes you have ever seen, and I will continue your work for as long as I can." With this final thought falling softly in her head, Beatrice closed her eyes. She never thought it would come, but she had

found happiness in her life, and all because of a beautiful, ripe tomato.

FOUR HALLOWEENS

The sun was setting; an uneventful, boring sunset, as Molly took Chet from house to house. His pillowcase was getting full of candy and her feet were getting tired. Being a nurse, she had worked a twelve-hour shift before starting off on this night of trick-or-treating. Being a single mom, she had to do what she had to do.

"Only a few more houses, Chet, then we have to go back before it gets too dark and cold, alright?" Molly sighed.

"Mom! Don't call me Chet!"

"Sorry, I mean… Captain Fire!" Looking down at her son, she could tell he was smiling behind the plastic mask. At first, she was upset to dress him up in a store-bought costume-- *her* mother always custom-made her outfit for trick or treating-- but after realizing how easy it was to just take something off the rack and have Chet jump into it, she was fine with this decision.

Being rather early, there weren't too many people on the streets yet, only other groups like her, Moms with the really young kids. Chet himself was only four. His bedtime was eight and it was already almost seven-thirty, which meant with all the candy he would eat at home, he would not be going to bed on time. She needed her own

sleep, so she was going to have to bribe him with the offer of a few extra pieces tomorrow to go to bed tonight.

"Mom, that lady gave me Reese's!"

"Your favorite! Awesome!" Molly answered on autopilot as they walked away from the house and headed for the next. This one had some rather high bushes by the front door, but other than that, it looked just like any of the other houses on the street with the porch light on, which meant it was fair game.

"Alright: let's hit this house and the next two, but after that, we are heading home, got that Captain Fire?!" Chet waved his head back and forth, complaining silently.

The routine was for Molly to push the doorbell so Chet could do a good superhero pose while waiting for the door to open. Using her pudgy finger, Molly jabbed the glowing orange circle. The same instant that the bell chimed inside, the button sent a shock up Molly's arm. It scared her more than it hurt, but she'd still have to make a point of telling the homeowner about it: it could be dangerous, especially for the little kids.

With Chet in position and Molly rubbing her finger, the door opened to reveal a small round man with a balding head, glasses, and sweater vest on. He had one of the most pleasant smiles on his face, a smile that Molly rarely saw in her line of work.

"Trick or Treat!" Chet said on cue with his best deep voice impersonation, which sounded more like a chipmunk losing his voice.

"Wow! Captain Fire! I love your comic book. And look at that! You're covered in flames." The man reached out and touched one of the cloth flames on

Chet's shoulder, then quickly brought it back with a yelp, pretending it was hot. They all giggled. Molly thought about how this man must be a good father while she tried to keep the thoughts of Chet's father out of her mind... *bastard*.

"Well, a superhero gets to pick whatever candy he wants!" The man said as he produced from next to the door a bowl filled with an assortment of candies. Chet immediately dug his hand in and searched for another Reese's. As if he had a Reese's magnet in his hand, he found one instantly.

"Thank you, sir," Chet chirped, forgetting to use his deep hero voice. The man smiled and nodded back as he placed his hand on the door to close it.

"Oh sir! I should tell you: when I ran the bell, I got an awful shock. You might want to cover it up with tape or something so no kids get hurt tonight."

The man's face scrunched up with concern. "I'm so sorry, I had no clue." He leaned out of the door to look at the bell, and the bowl of candy slipped from his hand, dumping dozens of sugary delights everywhere.

"Oh, darn it!" The man cried, looking down at the candy. Chet instantly started to pick it up for him.

"I'm sorry," Molly chirped, as if it were her fault, then bent down to help. When both of her hands were full of candy and her head was facing downward is when it happened. The man, out of nowhere, grabbed Chet's tiny body and threw him into the house like an old duffle bag. Molly's motherly instincts didn't hesitate: she rushed after him. She ran right past the man to Chet, who was starting to get up and crying, not realizing she fell right

into the man's trap. The second she passed the man, the door slammed shut and several locks snapped into place.

Picking up Chet, she felt a blast of pain slash through the back of her head before darkness took over her eyes.

When Molly's eyes opened, with pain she had only heard about, she had no clue how much time had passed, though she assumed it wasn't long, for she could hear the doorbell ring and child after child scream "Trick or Treat." Hearing the door slam shut, she shook the fogginess from her head and looked down at herself. She still had her pink scrubs shirt on, but that was it. She was naked from the waist down. Her legs were spread wide and tied to the legs of a chair she was sitting in. Her arms were bound behind her back so tight that she knew that if she struggled too hard, her shoulder would dislocate. Her mouth was also gagged with what tasted like a dish rag. She attempted a yell but could hardly hear it herself. Screaming was useless: it was Halloween, screams were everywhere on this night. No one would think twice.

Seconds later, the man she thought was so nice appeared in the room. This time though, he looked *much* different. He still wore the same outfit, only now he had a white chef's apron over it, and it was covered in blood. Both his hands had rubber gloves on and they, too, were spotted red. His glasses were also gone. Without them, he looked evil and menacing, as if the glasses had kept all his secrets buried inside.

"Oh, you're up! How wonderful! If you remember, your son asked for a Trick or Treat. Well, I'm giving him a trick. Would you care to see it?" The thought of this

man touching her child, in *any* way, filled Molly with feelings of vengeance she had never felt in her life. She wanted to kill this man, even if Chet was fine, even if this was all some sort of joke. The man walked behind Molly and pushed the chair. It scraped against the hardwood floor but moved smoothly on the tile through the doorway into the kitchen.

As her body passed through the threshold of that room, the world stopped spinning and everything in her universe ceased to exist. In that room, Chet's tiny body was laying on the kitchen counter, stripped naked, his stomach splayed open. Instantly, Molly vomited into her gagged mouth, sending the bile out through her nose and back down her throat, almost choking her. The man quickly removed the gag, allowing her to expel the early dinner she had eaten with Chet an hour earlier.

With all of it out of her, she wanted to scream, to thrash in the chair and run to Chet's body to try and put him back together. She was a nurse, she could do it. She could get him to the hospital in time. Subconsciously though, Molly knew there was no way for him to be alive. Instead of doing anything, she just stared at Chet's face which was pale and sickly looking. His eyes were open, staring at nothing, cold and dead. Her own eyes moved a few inches to look at his pillowcase full of candy on the chair next to him. He was so excited to get home to eat and eat until the treats made him sick. Instead, she was the sick one, physically and mentally.

Realizing the situation, Molly understood that at that moment, no matter what was about to happen, she, too,

was dead. Whether the man killed her or not, her life had ceased the second Chet's heart stopped.

"Please... kill me. Quickly-- so I don't have to look at him anymore," Molly recited in a barely audible voice, void of any emotion or feeling.

The man looked at her with a smile of pure joy. This was the part he loved: being able to kill someone without ever really touching them.

"Oh, dear, no. We have a lot to do and not much time to do it in. You can watch while I get to work. Don't worry: you don't have to do much." The man left her side and headed for Chet's lifeless body. He took up a position on the other side of the counter facing Molly as if he was about to give a cooking demonstration. And in a way, he was.

"Don't touch him," Molly barked through gritting teeth. The man ignored her and went about his work as she screamed until her voice went hoarse. Cut by cut, the man pulled chunks of meat and organs out of Chet's stomach, placing them on the counter next to his body. The man giggled as he watched Molly shut her eyes and hum to herself. The man joined in with a hum of his own as he pulled out Halloween goodie bags. Small orange bags will pictures of black cats, pumpkins and bats on them. One by one, he blew each bag open, placed a chunk of Chet into it, and tied it shut with a twisty tie. After filling two dozen small bags, he placed them into the same bowl that Chet had taken the Reese's from. The doorbell rang.

"Let the festivities begin..." the man said, as if he was about to host a party.

Molly was just far enough to the side that she could see the door, but the people on the other side could not see her. She didn't have her gag on so she knew she could scream for help. This was her chance! Hearing the door open, she started to scream.

"HELP! For god's sake, he killed my son! Help, please!" Over and over again she screamed. The man was obviously planning on this; he did have a blood-splattered apron on, after all. As the children asked for their treats, he cackled.

"Want to come in? Ha ha ha ha! You guys can be my next victims! Ha ha ha!" After laughing over and over, he dropped the goodie bags of Chet's still warm body parts into four different orange buckets held out before him. He even winked at the parents standing a few feet behind who were trying not to laugh at their scared children.

"Now don't open your treats until you get home! It would ruin the surprise! Besides, chunks of liver taste better with salt!" The man laughed again. Molly could hear the kids say *thank you*, and then he shut the door.

"That was fantastic! Now we only have to hope they actually don't open those bags until they get home. If all goes well, we'll have another two hours of this before I have to take off. Even if they do open a bag, they'll think it's a joke." Molly just stared at him, not believing what was going on. At first everything was real, her child was dead, but now she didn't know. It couldn't be real. Things like this didn't happen in life, and if they did, it was certainly not to her, let alone in her town or, hell, even in her state. She started to laugh.

"This isn't real! Ha! I can't believe this. I must have fallen asleep at work. Or maybe I got into an accident and I'm unconscious, but this isn't real!" Molly was laughing and crying. The man walked over to her, leaned over, reached between her legs and pinched the lips as hard as he could. Molly threw her head back and cackled even harder.

"You feel that, bitch? It's real alright! Hell, take a look at them." Spinning the chair around, she could see the other side of the room for the first time. An elderly couple sat on the couch next to each other, holding hands. Their chests were covered in blood. It took Molly a few seconds to realize that their heads were on the wrong bodies. The man had cut both of their heads off, then replaced the wrong ones back on the bodies. She laughed some more.

"Well, we'll see how much you laugh at this." Pissed she wasn't believing him, the man stomped over to Chet's body, dug around in a few drawers until he found a large cleaver, and slammed it down on the boy's neck. It took four solid whacks to remove the tiny head. Having already bled out all over the counter, the decapitated head bled very little as he carried it over to Molly. She wasn't laughing any more but the smile was still on her face. As the man held Chet's head right to her face, she leaned back from it a bit; her lip quivered, but she forced the smile on her face.

"Kiss your son! KISS HIM!"

"This is fucked up. This is one messed up hallucination. I want to… wake up now."

241

"There is no waking up. And if you're not going to kiss your own son's adorable face, I guess he'll have to go back to where he came from: your cunt." The man lowered Chet's head to Molly's bare thighs and rubbed the boy's cold lips against them, slowly teasing her into reality. She started to sob hard. Slowly but surely, the man edged the head closer to her crotch, then forcefully slammed it hard into her vagina. Molly could feel Chet's cold nose, the nose she just made him blow a few minutes before, force its way into her. She knew this was all too real.

Leaving Chet's head there, the man walked back to the headless body, whistling. Molly just stared straight at him: no longer crying, not smiling, not laughing. She wanted desperately to wiggle the head out of that place, to get it away from her, but at the same time it was... Chet. She couldn't let his head fall to the floor, to see his eyes stare up at her, asking, *why didn't you protect me?*

Over the next two hours, the man handed out sixty-eight bags filled with parts of Chet's body. All the while, Molly didn't move an inch, didn't say anything, and hardly blinked.

A few minutes before ten, the man grabbed a plastic shopping bag, walked over to Molly, and picked up Chet's head. He placed it in the bag, tied a knot with the handles, and leaned over to whisper in her ear.

"I'll make you a promise... I know you'll want nothing more than to kill yourself after tonight. After all, you did let your son die. But let me ask you this, how could you let your son be buried without his head? If you kill yourself, I'll personally piss on your son's head every

day for the rest of my life. But if you stay alive, I will give you his head back next year... on Halloween. Don't worry: I'll find you." With that, the man opened the front door and disappeared.

A year later, the crime was still unsolved. Molly refused all media interviews yet resumed her nursing job three months after the incident. She lost all contact with her family and friends. She merely showed up for work and left. She was never seen outside of her house other than those times. Slowly but surely, she became the strange lady that lived on the street. The woman whose house children would dare each other to ring the doorbell. Then, in August of the next year, she quit her nursing job. She was seen out the next day at several stores, but after that, no one saw her leave her house.

If she had told the police the last thing the man had told her, they would have had her house staked out that next Halloween. They didn't though, for she never told anyone his vow to come back. Only a few news media vans filmed a quick segment in front of her house to talk about the anniversary of the country's most gruesome Halloween murder. As the sun set that Halloween, the neighborhood kids avoided her house. But one Trick-or-Treater did not. Just as Molly expected, he had shown up.

Watching on the small black and white TV monitor in the kitchen, she saw a man at her door. He wore a hat and a heavy coat and carried a bag. She couldn't see his face, but she knew it was him.

For the past year, Molly had purposely not trimmed her bushes, leaving the front door invisible from the street. Grabbing a wire next to the door, she gave it a light tug. Instantly, an axe swung from the bushes and right into the back of the man's right leg, sending him toppling towards the door. She pulled it open just in time for him to fall flat on his face inside the house. Face down, the man tried to pull a gun out of his belt, Molly grabbed another axe from the counter and swung it down on the back of his head. The axe went half way through his skull, splitting the back of the baseball cap in two. The man twitched a few times then stopped moving; Molly pulled the axe back out and swung it back down into his back.

Satisfied he wasn't going to attack her, Molly dropped the axe and dove for the bag on the floor next to him. The small pool of blood that was spreading across the floor was already touching it. Molly fell to her knees and clasped the bag in her hands. She thought about Chet's funeral, the closed casket. His headless, organ-less body sitting in the ground forever. At least now he would be whole again, and then she could put an end to her misery with a lone bullet to her head. She felt relieved, happy almost for the first time since that day. Not wanting to see what time had done to her son's head, but needing to, she opened the bag. Inside was a homemade pie with note on top. *That bastard... cooked him?* She grabbed the note and flipped it open in rage and read it.

From the Detectives at District 12: We want you to know that our thoughts and prayers are with you tonight. And that we will not rest until this case is solved.

Molly dropped the card, turned to the body, and pushed it over. It only rolled halfway; the axe sticking in his back stopped him from making it all the way over. It wasn't the man. It was the lead detective on her son's case.

Four months later, Molly sat by the window in the hospital, the same hospital where she used to work, only now she was a patient and on a different floor, the one she never had security clearance to and still didn't. The meds and constant surveillance made it impossible for her to kill herself like she so desperately wanted to.

"You got a letter! A lovely man just dropped it off. Said he wanted to visit, but that it would be too hard to see you this way. I told him to come someday: you need visitors," the overly gay day nurse chirped behind her. At first, she didn't realize it was for her. She hadn't gotten any mail or visitors that weren't reporters since she had been deemed unfit. The nurse placed the letter on her lap and walked away, humming a familiar tune. The tune snapped her out of a daze. She turned around to ask he where she heard that song, but the nurse had already left the room. Instead, she turned her attention to the letter. It simply had her name on it. Flipping it over to open it up, she saw a Jack-O-Lantern sticker on the back. She started to tremble.

Pulling out the letter, she knew it was from him. It had to be. Trying not to scream, she read the few lines.

So sorry I missed you at Halloween. But when I arrived you were already being taken away. Pity, was that axe meant for me? Guess you now have blood on your hands too. It's a wonderful feeling, isn't it?

Anyway, just wanted to let you know that I have been taking good care of your son. He makes a great pencil holder. I keep him on my desk. I have enclosed a picture in case you miss him.

Always,
Your Trick or Treat friend!

PS- Get yourself better and I'll make sure to return him next year, as promised.

Ready to burst, Molly pulled out the picture, took one look at the pencils sticking out of her son's shriveled and rotting head and fell to the floor. In that same instance, she no longer wanted to kill herself-- *she couldn't just yet.* If she was deemed "sane," she could leave the facility, find this bastard, kill him, and get back Chet once and for all. As quietly as possible, Molly ripped up the letter and picture into as many pieces as possible, then tossed them into the trash along with a cup of water to make it even harder to put back together if one of the stupid nurses tried.

From that day forth, she made sure she was a model patient. Any time she wanted to blow up, to go nuts and

fight, kick and scream, she swallowed it back down and put on a smile. During this time, she ate the food she was given, put some weight on her frail frame and started to exercise. She was feeling good physically, but mentally, while she could think clearly, she knew she wasn't all there. Nothing, nothing at all mattered or got into her mind other than killing that man. No matter what was on the television, she would stare at it, but she couldn't tell you one thing she saw, for all she thought of were ways to torture him.

It took seven months and four panels turning her discharge down, but the fifth panel finally stated that she was sane enough to leave the hospital, though she would have to live in a half-way home for the first six months of her release to help her adjust to the outside world. This didn't sit well with her, for that meant she would be in a house with a bunch of other women on Halloween. It would be much harder to get away with, but it didn't matter: all she needed was the man dead and Chet's head back, and then she could end it all.

Living in the house was hell, worse than the hospital. She was living with convicts and drug addicts trying to make it back in the civilized world. They were bitches: out of hand, fighting, stealing, lying, and always trying to sleep with her. She forced a smile and ignored everything the best she could. The first few months in the home, she explored it, trying to figure out the best way to set up a traps for the man's visit. The house was three stories and large; it was an old Victorian mansion that had been bought out by the government when the city went

downhill and all the rich people left. Most of the other houses on the street were turned into two to five-family apartments that housed low income trash. The large size would help her if she had to run, but the creaking floors and echoing hallways would not conceal her too well.

Molly's worst fear was that the man wouldn't show up, but she knew, just knew deep down that the sicko wouldn't do that. He would show up-- he got off on messing with her. The question was, should she try to set up a trap inside the house or something outside in case he didn't attempt to come in? After a month of thinking, outside it was. She couldn't risk him not coming inside. She'd have back-up traps inside, but catching him outside was the way to go. There was a small front yard with a walkway right to the front porch. The porch itself wrapped around the entire front of the house and was mostly just used as the women's smoking area. Typically, Molly avoided it, not wanting to breathe in the fumes, but for four days solid, she sat on the porch, thinking and planning. Then one day, it finally hit her: a plan that couldn't fail.

Three days before Halloween, Molly didn't sleep more than five minutes at a time. She was excited, nervous, and more so, eager to finish everything. On the morning of the fateful day she had waited two years for, she got up, stretched, and went to the store to buy all the girls in the house some donuts. She might hate them, but the food was necessary for her plan. The rest of the day she sat looking at a picture of Chet that she kept next to her bed. Usually it hurt looking at him, but today, seeing his smile warmed her heart as she knew she would be

with him soon. As the sun started to set, she went down, sat on the porch, and waited.

There were a few shabby-looking pumpkins on the porch and the light was on, but no kids dared come up to the house. They were too smart; their parents told them to stay away from this house, as it was full of "bad women." In the two hours she sat alone, not one child or adult walked up. Then, a black sedan silently slid in front of the house just before eight. Molly tensed up as the driver's door opened up. A man got out and she instantly knew it was him, though last time she had thought that and had killed a cop. This time, however, she saw his face as he looked over the roof at her and smiled. Knowing it was him without any doubt, she let out a soft whistle from her mouth. It was hard to not get up and charge after the man, but she had to keep still, keep calm for the plan to work. When the passenger door opened up and another man she recognized got out, the panic set it. *What the fuck was he doing here?* It was the detective that worked the case, the partner of the man she killed last year. Molly's mind started to slam with questions, it wanted to burst open and explode with anger and confusion, yet she sat still.

The men approached with grim looks on their faces. When they reached the bottom of the stairs, the detective talked first.

"Molly. I know this isn't the best day for any of us to visit, but there has been a major break in your case. Agent Orlowski from the FBI here has some evidence he wants to show you." So that was *his* plan. He knew that

this year *she* would have a plan, so he came with protection, a cop. That way, he could rub in Chet's death and if she threw a fit and screamed he was the killer, they would think she was just having a breakdown-- it was the anniversary, after all. She couldn't help but smile. The sick bastard was smart.

"Do you mind if we come in?" The detective asked, motioning to the door, putting one foot on the steps. Molly put her hand up to stop him. Then she whistled, an odd, but direct tone. Within a minute, twelve tough and dirty-looking women surrounded the two men. Some came out from the bushes, others from the windows, a few from the street. A few held knives, two had guns, and the others had blunt objects ready to attack. The detective tried to pull out his gun, but one of the women yelled at him to not move. Knowing he was outnumbered, he did as he was told. Molly didn't move.

"Hey, Mol, this wasn't the deal. These are cops. What the fuck is going on?" the tough butch woman to Molly's right asked as she nervously aimed the gun at the detective.

"The bald one: that's him. He is pretending to be a FBI agent just so he can rub it into my face," Molly said, sitting forward a bit.

"Molly, call them off. This man is with the FBI, I checked it out. And none of you women want to do this; you'll all go back to prison," the detective yelled out. A few of the women backed off, but most stayed, confused and not sure what to do.

"You sure about this Mol? That is the man?"

Molly nodded. The next few minutes were nothing but chaos. The detective was subdued by three women and cuffed with his own handcuffs and brought inside. The man-- the killer, the girls were not as nice to. By the time they had him in the basement, he was bleeding heavily and hardly able to talk.

Molly ordered the women to bring the detective down to the basement to watch. She was more than pleased to see the man was tied to a table just like she asked the women to do. It might have cost her her life savings, she might have had to talk to each one of these woman a hundred times about how they would do this to someone if their own son had been murdered, but it worked; they helped her out and now they had her back. When the detective kept protesting, one of the women gagged him and made him watch.

The man, groggy with pain, started to laugh as he woke up. "You stupid bitch. I underestimated you."

Molly walked over to the table and stared at the man's face.

"I thought you would be harder to crack." Again, the man laughed at Molly.

"Why pretend I didn't do it? You will kill me anyway. I might as well get the credit for my amazing work!" This line set Molly off. She grabbed a knife, raised it above the man, then hesitated.

"Take him out of here, we got the confession: that is all he needs to hear. The rest of you... I suggest you leave too, you are not going to want to see this or be a part of it any more than you have been... I can't thank you all enough." The women grabbed the detective and

brought him upstairs. One by one, the women left her alone, most touching her shoulder in a show of support on the way out.

"So, what are you going to do with me, bitch? Torture me until I die? Ha ha. Tell you what. When I get to hell, I'll make sure I take care of your little boy." Molly again raised the knife, and this time she let out a scream...

A year later, on Halloween, Molly made two visits. The first one was to the graveyard to see Chet's grave, which was now complete with his head that was found in the trunk of the man's car after last Halloween. After telling Chet how much she loved him, she put some Reese's on the stone, whispered *Happy Halloween*, and walked away. As she walked away, she fought off the thoughts of suicide that she struggled with every day. She had to stay alive now; she didn't know why, but she knew it was necessary. The second visit she made that day was to the same hospital where she had been locked up not too long ago. After signing some papers and walking through security, she sat at a table and waited.

When she heard squeaking from an old wheelchair, she knew he was being brought to her. As the man was placed in front of her, the nurse whispered to him that he had a visitor.

"Who... who is there?"

"Happy Halloween."

The man's lip started to quiver at the sound of Molly's voice. She couldn't help but smile as she looked at the man who killed her son. For now he had no eyes,

no fingers, and two stumps where his feet used to be. "You fucking bitch! Why didn't you kill me?"

Molly stood up, walked over to the man, and leaned down.

"Because, how else would I visit you every Halloween?"

ACKNOWLEDGEMENTS

If I had my way, I wouldn't have any interaction with the living. However, this book could not be possible if it weren't for the few people who I have come across that have beating hearts, who support my sick and twisted mind.

Like always, thank you to Michael Aloisi, for starting me on this path and to Dark Ink and its employees for working so hard to get this book out.

A great thank you to Alicia C. Mattern for creating a brilliant cover that I can love and stare at forever. Thank you for being so easy to work with. Make sure to check out her great, creepy books for kids at www.ZombieSquirts.com.

Charles Carter, thank you for being my first and biggest fan (if I dare say I have them) and for reading the book before the rest of the world to give me your opinions.

Thank Rebecca Rowland for pushing me to put out another collection. I wasted six years and would have wasted six more if you hadn't forced me to sit, focus and get this book done. Thank you for reading, critiquing, helping shape some of the stories and for your brilliant editing. This book would still be on the first story if it wasn't for you. Now that you have gotten me back on track, the stories will not end, countless books will follow. Thank you.

The nurse who took care of me in maximum security during my… stay, I may never know your name, but your kindness, sympathetic eyes and grace with a needle showed me that maybe there can be hope for the living.

The man who caused that stay, Rupert Stillwater, thank you for being an evil, despicable human being. The rage and contempt I have for you and the desire to kill you slowly, fuels much of the stories within these pages. I pray one day I find your cold mangled corpse on my table.

ABOUT THE AUTHOR

Michael Gore was born in a small town in New England. His earliest memory is of his father standing above him with a bloody knife. Being that his father was a butcher, he was around blood and raw meat his entire childhood. It is probably why at a young age he was fascinated with dead animals and even ended up in therapy at the age of nine for "finding out what made them tick." After that, he learned to keep his curiosity to himself.

At sixteen, he was a horror film fanatic. Not only did he watch every slasher film he could get his hands on, he took it a step further and got a job at a local funeral home, even though he already worked sixteen hours a week cleaning the intestines his father used to make sausage. After several years of cleaning up the funeral home, they let him assist in the embalming practice. This only fed into his appetite for the macabre.

Though his father wanted him to take over the butcher shop, Michael decided to play with human flesh instead of animals. In 2000, he graduated from Mortuary School and secured employment as a mortician. Currently, he works at a small Massachusetts funeral home as the head mortician, full-time.

Now, in-between draining bodies of blood, Michael spends his time writing. When asked why he writes such

dark things, his only reply is, "to keep me from doing them in real life."

Michael is notoriously reclusive and has never, nor will ever, do book signings or appearances. While he shuns the outside world, from time to time he will do the occasional interview or respond to fans via email. You may contact Mr. Gore at Gore@AMInkPublishing.com or follow his advice column, *Ask a Sociopath*, at his website, AuthorMike.com

Keep an eye out for a third book in the *Tales from a Mortician* series as well as Michael's first novel, *Urge*!